CASTING PROS TO KNOW

REALITY TV EDITION

YOUR GUIDE TO GETTING CAST

CASTING PROS TO KNOW

REALITY TV EDITION

YOUR GUIDE TO GETTING CAST

ASJAI LOU

Casting Pros to Know: Reality TV – Your Guide to Getting Cast

This is a work of nonfiction.

Casting Pros to Know: Reality TV Edition Your Guide to Getting Cast

ISBN: 978-1-959811-64-0 (Paperback)
ISBN: 978-1-959811-65-7 (e-book)

Library of Congress Control Number: 2024919549

Cover Design: Melvyn Paulino
Interior Design: Melvyn Paulino
Author Photo: SHOTTI NYC
Editor: Majorie Winful

Pics for the forward
Credit: Laetitia Rumford

Published in the United States by Wordeee,
New York

1st Edition

Website: www.wordeee.com
X Formerly Twitter: wordeeeupdates
Facebook: facebook.com/wordeee/
e-mail: contact@wordeee.com
Website: AsjaiLouCasting.com
e-mail: Assistant@AsjaiLouCasting.com
Instagram: @AsjaiLouCasting
TikTok: @AsjaiLouCasting

TABLE *OF* CONTENTS

DEDICATION

To my Prayer Warriors—Mom, Gerri, Benji, Serina, the late Charles, and the late Mrs. Annette. Your prayers are my armor and my compass. Every day, I am strengthened, inspired, and encouraged because of the love you pour into my life. I am endlessly grateful for each one of you.

To my beloved Amanjah Anthony, my best friend and eternal muse. Though you are no longer here with me, your spirit, laughter, and boundless creativity live on in my heart. You showed me how to live authentically, and I carry your light forward, always grateful for the gift of you.

To my mother, Sharron Cannon. My heart and my best friend, the strongest woman I know. You gave so much of yourself so Kenny and I could have every opportunity, and for that, I am forever grateful. Your wisdom, tenacity, and boundless love are at the core of who I am. Growing up beside you taught me to embrace my dreams, work hard, and believe that anything is possible. Thank you for being my hero, my teacher, and my biggest fan. I am honored to be your daughter.

To my father, Kenneth Crutchfield. Thank you for the creativity and joy you brought into my life. I'm proud of the relationship we're building and grateful for the lightheartedness and humor you passed down to me. And to Teri, thank you for being such a wonderful partner to my dad. Your warmth and kindness mean so much to me; I'm lucky to have two mothers in my life.

To my brother, Kenny Allen: the one who never fails to make me laugh, my protector, creative genius, biggest supporter, and personal chef (lol). Your talent is boundless, and I couldn't be prouder of the person you're becoming. Remember, the world is ready for everything you have to offer—go after it with all you've got. I'll always be here, cheering you on every step of the way.

To my late great-grandmother Theola, my grandmother Vivian, my Poppa Lawrence, my Aunt Penny, Uncle Julius, Aunt Shirley, Uncle Robert, and Aunt Hazel. You were my foundation of love, forgiveness, and authenticity. Thank you for building a legacy that I carry with me every day. I miss those summers we shared, and I feel your presence with me always.

To my four-legged family members, both past and present—my nephew Rocky, my brothers Knoxford and Beanie, my cousins Angel, Ziggy, and Zuri, and my late daughter,

Little Momma. You brought such joy into my life. Thank you for the unconditional love, protection, compassion, and friendship you shared with me. My life was truly enriched by your presence. I love you all!

To my extended family in Port Tampa, my incredible family and friends who make it the most amazing place to call home. Aunt Clara, Auntie Sharnee, Uncle Ben and Aunt Nikki, MY J.J, Uncle Ike, cousins Tameeka, Tiffany, Iyesha, Katina, Fluffy, Jazz and her five Z's—my babies, Zion, Zoe, Zhane, Zhi, and Zackhi, Plook, Pie, Ulyssia, Daja, Brandon and Camdon, Lexi, Angel, Shannon, and my super star rapper cuz Mya. I love each of you deeply. Thank you for showing me that family means love, laughter, and endless support. Dream boldly, and go after all this world has to offer—you've got it in you.

To the Cannon, Crutchfield, Johnson, Betts, Evans, and Williams families—my heart is full of love for each and every one of you. We may not gather as often as we should, but you are always in my thoughts and prayers. Let's come together soon, celebrate our bond, and make new memories that honor the legacy we share. I am deeply grateful to be part of this beautiful lineage, surrounded by strength, love, and history. I carry you all with me, always. With all my love and gratitude. To my cousin Mookie, I hope we find our way back. Love to your family. Shout out to my WEST COAST cousins Shay, Nia, Porscha, and Dre. My friends James and Jaray, I love yall like family!

To my chosen family, my friends who hold me up in every season, thank you. To my POPS, aka Jim, I'll never forget how you welcomed me with open arms during one of the most difficult and sensitive times in my life. You offered me love, guidance, and the kind of support I didn't even know I needed. And to my sis, Nicole—thank you for sharing your dad with me. That gift meant more than words can express. Ariel Houston, my best friend for life—thank you for every late-night and early-morning therapy session, for being my person in all the ways that matter. Rae, my cousin and bestie, thank you for all our relaxing Miami days and life-planning sessions—I wouldn't trade them for anything, Enter Stef—the emotional rollercoaster Rae swears is my soulmate. Only time will tell, but either way, we're locked in. Be proud of how far you've come. You're doing WONDERFUL. Love will find its way. One day, you'll get it right. Get out of your head. Love you always! Malita, our friendship may be new, but I'm so grateful to have someone I can truly be myself with and rely on. I look forward to seeing our friendship grow. Lindsay, I'm so thankful we reconnected. Having you back in my life has been everything I didn't know I was missing. TK from BK—my forever fashionista, always ahead of the trends! Love you, girl. XOXO. Jeanine... or should I say **Judge** Jeanine! LOL. Love you, sis! I'll always put some RESPECT on your name. Thank you for blessing us with baby Bryson—he truly is the light of our lives. Sujotta—new friendship, but such a solid one. We're gonna do **all** the things! Can't wait to grow together and claim everything that's meant for us. Datwon—you already know the vibes. I tell you all the time, but it's worth repeating: I truly appreciate your time, mentorship, and support. You're a real one. Much love and respect always. To my PPAS family—I miss all of you! Praying life is treating you well wherever you are. Jamal, mom and I are still waiting on our dance lessons, when are you gonna take us seriously? lol. My Queen P, Porsha—the creative genius! Trust that your time is coming. Keep pushing, keep creating, and keep being you. You have everything it takes to reach your destination, and I'm so glad to call you my sister. To my dear Wendy,

I love you, girl! Thank you for getting me out of the house, reminding me to live life to the fullest, and sharing your family and friends with me. I love me some Isaam! To Darnell, Enjoli, Dawn, Belinda, Alycia, Keith, Trevor, Denise and Cindy, you will always have a space in my heart. I know life be lifing, but we all can do better with showing up for one another. Shout out to my Brooklyn family, PS11 day 1's, old school 90s Institutional of God and Christ Family. Janelle, you will always be my big sis, and Judy, you will always be my other momma! RIP to my sis Tiffany and my lil brother Justin. Can't ever forget my BK 169 fam—Chuck, April, CJ, Aunt Faye—some of the best years of my life. LOVE Y'ALL forever! To my Dix Hills, L.I. family—Doretta, Calib, Pops, Lauren, Lashawn, and my babies Geo and Chyna (you'll **always** be my babies)—I miss you deeply and carry you in my heart every day. And of course, I can't mention L.I. without showing love to my FTC crew—Five Towns College, y'all know who you are! Big love, always—especially to my birthday twin, Flash. We locked in for life. To my favorite photographer ever—Shotti, I'm so proud of everything you've accomplished. Your talent and drive are unmatched. Wishing you even more success ahead—this is just the beginning! Jasmine—I love me some Maestro... and you're pretty cool too! LOL. XOXO.

To my Double Phatt family, I MISS Y'ALL! What a time we had! When I think about all the things we used to do, I laugh and shake my head. We were doing THE MOST. I've never been around so much talent. I truly learned how to spot talent from all of you. We need a reunion! Life is too short—let's make it happen. Imajin (John, Olamide, Talib, and Jamal), y'all need to just get back together. The magic y'all had will never go away. The world still needs you! There's so much opportunity out there for you. Thank you, Bert, Shirley, LB, Miz, Johnny (aka Cupac lol), Lena, Sonya, Ryan, Ariel, Lindsay, Sunni, Corey, and Imajin—you all made such an impact on my life, and I will never forget the times we shared together. And to my heart, Rell—REST IN POWER, brother. You are missed.

To Lawrence aka Redy, No matter matter where life takes us, you will always have a friend in me.

To my godbrother Bazaar Royale and my sister Beverly Bond—I'm grateful to be more than friends, to be family. You both have shown me the strength of true partnership, and I love watching you thrive and grow together. Black love is truly powerful.

Bazaar, you are the coldest writer, producer, and rock star I know. Keep pushing out that fire—the world needs your music!

Beverly, seeing you build one of the most empowering and influential brands for Black women—a message we need every day—is inspiring beyond words. I admire your courage to stand strong, challenging the system and taking on every high and low with such grace. Keep representing and fighting for us. #BlackGirlsRock

To my casting sisters, Telon, Thea, and Diona—look at what your little big sis just accomplished! We absolutely have to celebrate, and yes, Telon, if we're in the club, you're in the club too! The friendship I share with each of you is truly one of a kind. You each bring something so unique and essential into my life, and I love you like family. Knowing you're in my corner, supporting every vision, means the world to me. Your minds, your hearts, your brilliance—this world has so much to gain from all you create. Here's to all the amazing work we'll do together!

To my spiritual supporters and counselors, Bishop Noel Jones and Pastor Kirk Lyons—thank you for taking my late-night calls with questions. I know you never have to, but you always show up for me. I appreciate you!

Last but certainly not least, to my right hand and the person who ensures I execute with precision—my assistant, Emmelyn Carta. Thank you for standing by my side, keeping me organized and prepared to face the world. You have been an incredible blessing in my life.

From Emmelyn to her family:

Para sa aking pamilya, salamat sa inyong pagmamahal, suporta, at lakas. Ang lahat ng tagumpay na ito ay para sa inyo.

ADVANCE PRAISE

Casting Pro QUOTES:

"*Casting Pros To Know: Reality TV Edition. is* essential for aspiring Reality TV talent because it grants access to the industry's top casting professionals and their insider secrets that can enhance aspiring talent's knowledge for a chance to land a spot on a show."

—Telon Weathington
Big Brother, Ready to Love, Married at First Sight
Casting Producer, Casting Associate, Editor, Recruiter

"The release of *Casting Pros To Know: Reality TV Edition* is going to shake up the industry by peaking behind the curtain, swinging the pendulum, and for once empowering Reality TV stars. Many reality stars learn on the job and unfortunately too many times it's just too late. Asjai's expertise and dedication in the casting industry are unparalleled, and it shows in the way she has transformed lives, including my own. If this book encapsulates even a portion of the guidance and insight she provides, it will be an invaluable resource for aspiring Reality TV talent and the industry as a whole."

—Thea Washington
Great Christmas Light Fight, Ready To Love, Bachelorette
Casting Director, Casting Producer, Casting Associate, Recruiter

"As a seasoned Casting Director and owner of a reality casting company, I can't think of a better resource for talent than *Casting Pros To Know: Reality TV Edition*. The landscape of reality television has changed immensely over the years, and the tips and information in *Casting Pro to Know: Reality TV Edition, are game changers*! This book should be the go-to resource for connecting with casting directors and learning how to book the job successfully."

—Diona Vaughan Mankowitz
Real Housewives of Atlanta, Summer House, and Survivor
Divergent Content

"This is a must-have guide for aspiring reality TV stars. It demystifies the casting process with insider tips and strategies, ensuring you're fully prepared to make a memorable impression and secure your spot on your desired show.""

—Costas Nicolas
Building Off The Grid, Wizards Of Baking, Top Chef
Casting Producer

"This book is vital for aspiring talent because it unlocks the keys to the castle when it comes to getting selected for an unscripted talent or challenge-like show. There have been many books on scripted auditions featuring tips and tricks on auditioning in general, but when it comes to unscripted casting little has been said about what casting producers, such as Asjai Lou, are looking for. In this book, she breaks down how to be authentic, have a brand, and the art of getting discovered on your social media platforms. Reality Television has leveled up, and former scripted stars now have crossed over, so make this your cheat sheet into how to break into the business!"

—Josh Randall
American Idol, The Floor, Building The Band
Casting Producer and Host

"As a Casting Director, I want every aspiring reality talent to understand the audition process so they can get their chance to shine on TV! You can achieve your dreams—and this book can offer you insights into how to make that dream a reality!"

—Kristen Moss, CSA
ABC's The Great Christmas Light Fight, MasterChef, To Tell the Truth
Casting Director

"At Major Media & Casting, we believe connection is the cornerstone of opportunity in the entertainment industry. This directory is an invaluable resource for individuals seeking to break into unscripted television, providing direct access to the casting directors who shape the stories that entertain and inspire audiences worldwide. This book celebrates unscripted casting directors and their vital role in bringing real stories to life because there is no programming without talent."

—Evan Majors
Rhythm + Flow
Owner, Major Media & Casting

FOREWORD

There are few things more important than the art of curation. Whether it's a mouth-watering food menu for a holiday bash, the perfect Soul Train line inducing playlist for a grand gala, or the curated fashion selections laid out for a discerning fashionista, someone must create the vibe for events, projects, and life's celebrations.

Thankfully, we're blessed by those whose taste surpasses the average, pointing us toward quality, presence, and assured value. It takes more than a preference for a specific individual or item to make a curator act. Many factors lead them to say, "Yes, this will work." It could be the way they tilt their head when the visual matches the vision or the way they catch a faint sound that can make all the difference, leading someone toward fame and fortune.

In the entertainment and lifestyle world, many unsung heroes have transformed the projects and creations we know and love, yet they are seldom in the spotlight. In music, it could be a funky drummer suggesting a tempo change or the unseen engineer who adjusts the sound on your favorite track. In fashion, it's the tailors who bring top designers' sketches to life; without them, couture wouldn't fit or flow with style. But the most lucrative sector—reality TV—is where some of the industry's most influential yet unknown tastemakers reside, consistently producing hidden star-makers within the genre. This book is about to change that. For the first time ever, you'll have access to a reality TV casting pro directory, giving you insight into those who believe in today's rising stars and make tomorrow's superstars.

Listing the greatest reality shows (and even the less memorable ones) would take as long as the industry's lifespan itself. Yet we rarely give credit to those who find the talented gems behind these epic presentations. Those people are reality TV casting directors, casting producers, casting associates, casting assistants, and recruiters. They're the ones shaping productions of all scales, creating entertainment that captivates everyone from energetic kids to the homebound elderly, to fast-living adults.

One exceptional casting director and producer, and the author of this incredible book, is Asjai Lou. This Los Angeles native has a vision to bring acknowledgment to the behind-the-scenes star-makers like herself. Countless talents, including Jay Copeland, Nutsa Buzaladze, Gabby Samone and Alyssa Wray, got their start on *American Idol* through her efforts. For Lou, believing in talent doesn't stop at simply finding it—casting pros like her often have to fight for the unproven. After a series of "nos" Claire Rehfuss was finally selected for the CBS hit *Big Brother*, thanks to Lou's persistence. That persistence paid off as audiences and CBS fell in love with Rehfuss, leading to her appearance on another hit show, *The Amazing Race*, where she won one million dollars! This proves that expertise and a keen eye can be invaluable, especially when talent thrives across shows and even shapes an entire season.

Another example of Lou's impact is Jasmine Monroe. Although Monroe didn't make it onto *Big Brother* the first time Lou pitched her, Lou's influence endured. When Monroe joined a later season—one Lou wasn't casting—the impact of Lou's original pitch was still felt. Monroe's casting was ultimately due to Lou's vision from a previous season. The influence of visionary casting professionals is profound, and this book will help you learn to recognize it.

Asjai Lou has cast hundreds of commercials for major brands we all know—McDonald's, Volkswagen, Target, Ford, Heineken, Burger King, Amex, and more. A two-time Artios Award nominee, she was recognized for her work on *Amazon's Making The Cut* season 3, where she cast the million-dollar winner Yannik Zamboni, and ABC's *The Great Christmas Light Fight season 11*. Lou's true passion lies in discovering hidden talent, dedicating herself to quality and authenticity in every project.

Now, as a visionary casting professional, Asjai Lou offers a comprehensive guide for aspiring reality TV participants. This guide reveals the ins and outs of the casting process, introduces the key players, details what casting pros seek, and includes a "who casts what" breakdown for targeted outreach. With this insider knowledge, you'll gain a competitive edge in achieving your reality TV dreams.

Let's face it, breaking into the entertainment industry isn't easy. It often requires connections and resources. However, this book, written by an industry veteran with decades of experience, gives you an insider track. You'll learn secrets to getting noticed by reality TV casting pros, from how to apply and interview to standing out as a genuine, compelling individual. Trust Lou's expertise to guide you on your path to reality TV success. Even I have seen her magic touch over the years, watching her cast music videos early in her career for artists like Kanye West, Kelis, Mariah Carey, Dipset, The White Stripes, Black Eyed Peas, Mary J. Blige and Fabolous, among many others. She impressed me further when, in a pinch, she secured jewelry by Melody Ehsani for our Regan Gomez shoot for *KING magazine*.

The mind of a casting director is a kaleidoscope of personalities, a bustling marketplace of human potential. They recall the witty banter of a quick-thinking problem-solver, perfect for *Survivor*, alongside the compassion of a natural caregiver, fitting for *The Great British Baking Show*. The energy of a born entertainer, destined for *RuPaul's Drag Race*, dances alongside the determination of a DIY enthusiast ready to tackle any *Home Town* renovation. Each unique personality is a puzzle piece, waiting to be placed in the perfect reality TV show.

When filming wraps, casting doesn't stop. The quest for talent continues in every corner—social media, bars, YouTube, voicemails, emails, and leads from friends and colleagues—all to find the perfect fit. It takes more than a hefty contact list to create the magic we see on screens. The meticulous searching, pruning, and unwavering belief in the unseen demand casting professionals' utmost dedication. When you cheer for a beloved reality star or revel in the portrayal of a compelling character, remember to tip your hat to the casting pros. They make it all happen.

Now, dive into this book to discover the jewels of becoming a reality TV star. If you've read this far, you're already invested in your journey. Embrace it—you were destined for this! Enjoy.

Dayton

Datwon Thomas

Journalist. Producer. Creative.

WHO IS ASJAI LOU?

Asjai Lou:
Hollywood Native,
Reality TV Matchmaker,
Your Next Obsession

→

Asjai Lou might be an LA native, but her showbiz soul was forged on the bustling streets of New York City. Her father, Kenneth Crutchfield, was a renowned jazz musician on Broadway; her mother, Sharron Cannon, was an executive powerhouse in television and film; and her godfather, Jim Brubaker, was the former head of Universal Pictures. Talk about being born for the spotlight!

Growing up on film sets like *I Like It Like That*, *Above the Rim*, *GIA*, and *The Devil's Advocate*, her playground wasn't a sandbox—it was a world of cameras, stars, and backstage drama. Her hustle? Charging adults for curse words (hey, a girl's gotta get paid!). Instead of playing with dolls, Asjai dissected headshots, already honing her eye for the next big thing.

Her first casting gig? Assisting the legendary Tracy Moore on *New York Undercover*—no pressure, right? Tracy tasked her with finding those "straight from jail" headshots, and Asjai nailed it.

Fast-forward to her senior year of high school and college days: Asjai lands an internship with NYC music video queen Mellicent Dyane. Think epic videos like Kelis's "Milkshake" and Juelz Santana's, "There it Go" (the whistle Song)—Asjai had a hand in casting those, along with countless others featuring stars like Jay-Z, Mariah Carey, The Strokes, Lil' Kim, The White Stripes, Kanye West, and Mary J. Blige. She was spotting superstars before they even knew it, even landing some of her college friends in those early videos!

After graduating, Hollywood beckoned her back to work with commercial comedy queen Alyson Horn and iconic director Paul Hunter, alongside her dear friend and mentor Melissa Feliciano. It was during this time that she connected with her BFF Cindy Estada, who later founded the powerhouse Good People Casting with Lyle Dohl. Here, Asjai found her tribe; they taught her the ins and outs of finding gems within the world of everyday people (what we call "real people casting"). After working on thousands of commercials and music videos, she became unstoppable.

Ever screamed at *American Idol* contestants? That's Asjai. Riveted by *Big Brother* drama? That's her playbook. Obsessed with the juicy moments on *Real Housewives*? You can thank her for that too. And those heartwarming scenes on *Ready to Love*? She's got an eye for those gems. Asjai Lou is the queen of finding the personalities that keep you glued to the screen. Think of her as the ultimate matchmaker, pairing those undiscovered stars with the shows that make them shine.

Currently, Asjai works with powerhouse networks like FOX, Bravo, ABC, CBS, VH1, and Lifetime, to name a few. She collaborates with top casting companies, including Divergent Content, owned by her casting big sis Diona Markewitz, and she's part of the Fremantle team that brings *American Idol* to your screens yearly. She's still creating magic in commercials alongside her BFF Cindy Estada of Cindy Estada Casting. But her true passion lies in casting projects under her own company, Asjai Lou Casting, where she works alongside her casting family—Queen P, Telon

Weathington, Andre Savage, Khrissy, and Thea Washington.

Her most cherished project to date was the first under her own banner, casting for the Black Eyed Peas' iconic music video "I Gotta Feeling."

From Hollywood kid to reality TV royalty, Asjai's journey proves that with a sharp eye for talent, a sprinkle of magic, and a whole lot of hustle, you can conquer the unscripted world. So, are you ready?

A MESSAGE *FROM* ASJAI

BUILDING A MOVEMENT: CELEBRATING & EMPOWERING CASTING PROS

Photo Credit:
Asjai Lou, CSA
www.AsjaiLouCasting.com
IG: @AsjaiLouCasting

In pic:
Asjai Lou, CSA
www.AsjaiLouCasting.com
IG: @AsjaiLouCasting

Rebecca Snavely
Vital Casting

Alissa Haight Carlton, CSA
Vital Casting

Christian Estrada
IG: @ChrisEcasting

Building a Movement: Celebrating and Empowering Casting Pros

This book marks the start of something far bigger than myself. It's not just a guide or a resource—it's the foundation of a movement. A movement to celebrate casting pros, amplify our voices, and showcase the art and heart of what we do. As casting pros, we are the unseen architects of reality TV, shaping the stories and personalities that resonate with audiences across the globe. Now, more than ever, it's time we step into the spotlight and honor the incredible impact we have.

Casting is so much more than finding the right people for the screen. It's about recognizing stories, shaping narratives, and creating moments that deeply connect with audiences. As casting pros, we are the curators of those stories. Yet, too often, our contributions remain hidden behind the curtain. That's why this book exists—to change that narrative, to celebrate the brilliance of what we do, and to ensure our work gets the recognition it deserves.

But this book isn't just about shining a light on the past—it's also about preserving our legacy for the future. By documenting our contributions, we're creating something timeless—a tribute to the artistry, dedication, and creativity that casting pros pour into their work. This is our chance to leave a mark, inspire future generations, and lead our own legacy in an industry that thrives on storytelling.

This movement is also about empowerment. It's about equipping us to thrive in an industry that often demands more than it gives. By expanding our reach, strengthening our networks, and creating new income streams, we can build the stability and growth that we, as freelancers, deserve. We can create a future where we not only care for ourselves and our families but also pave the way for those who follow in our footsteps.

Together, we are more than casting pros. We are storytellers, visionaries, and changemakers. We are shaping stories that define culture, create connection, and leave a lasting impact.

This is just the beginning. Together, we can build something extraordinary—a community where every casting pro feels valued, celebrated, and empowered to lead their own legacy.

Let's make history, together.

A Mission for Us All

The mission of this book—and the movement it represents—is clear and impactful. First, it's about empowering everyday people with the tools, insights, and guidance they need to navigate the reality TV casting process. Second, it's a platform for casting pros to memorialize their contributions, share their stories, celebrate their achievements, and expand their outreach and networks. It's also a resource for freelancers to create new income streams, ensuring greater stability and growth in a constantly evolving industry.

Each annual edition of this book will highlight the story and journey of a different casting pro, capturing the collective wisdom, challenges, and triumphs of those who shape this field. This is not about one person's perspective; it's about honoring the voices of many. By coming together, we can build a legacy that recognizes our work, uplifts our community, and inspires future generations to understand casting as an essential part of storytelling and culture.

This is more than a book—it's a mission to celebrate our craft and ensure our impact is never forgotten.

An Invitation to Join the Movement

Every industry has room to grow—room for more understanding, compassion, and better communication. Casting is no different. It's time for us to confront the challenges we face, not with rants or division, but with honest, solution-driven conversations. Yes, these discussions may be uncomfortable at times, but they are necessary if we're going to move forward. Together, we can tackle these issues with open minds and a shared commitment to making our field stronger.

This isn't about egos or pride—it's about the future. The world is changing rapidly, and so is our industry. Technology and shifting landscapes mean we must adapt, innovate, and work together to preserve and elevate the art of casting. I believe in us. I believe we have the passion, creativity, and resilience to overcome these challenges and emerge even stronger.

To all casting pros: This is your invitation. Join me in this mission to elevate our field, celebrate our wins, and share the lessons we've learned along the way. Each of us brings a unique story and perspective to the table, and together, we can amplify our voices, expand our reach, and ensure our contributions are recognized and celebrated.

If you have a story to share or want to be featured in a future edition, I want to hear from you. Your voice matters. Your experiences matter. Together, we can build something that uplifts our craft, strengthens our networks, and provides us all with the tools to thrive—professionally, creatively, and personally.

This book isn't just a resource. It's the start of a movement to honor our work, build a community of support and respect, and secure our legacy in the ever-evolving world of storytelling.

Let's make it unforgettable—together.

Photo Credit:
Isaac Alvarez
www.isaacalvarez.com
IG: @isaacealvarez

In Pic:
Thea Washington, CSA
Www.TheaWashingtonCasting.com
IG: @theawashingtoncasting

Diona Vaughan Mankowitz
https://www.divergentcontent.com/
IG: @divergent.content

Asjai Lou, CSA
www.AsjaiLouCasting.com
IG: @AsjaiLouCasting

Telon Weathington, CSA

LaGrande Powe

YOUR **REALITY** TV DREAM STARTS *HERE*!

Photo Credit:
Asjai Lou, CSA
www.AsjaiLouCasting.com
IG: @AsjaiLouCasting

Ever binge-watched *Big Brother* or *Real Housewives* and thought, "I could totally be on those shows?" Well, guess what? You probably can. I'm Asjai Lou, and I've helped make those shows happen! Now, I'm sharing all my insider secrets to get YOU on screen.

Why This Book is Your Golden Ticket

Whether you're talent, a network, a studio, or a production company, this book is your ultimate resource. From discovering top casting pros to navigating the reality TV casting process, everything you need is right here.

This book is:

➔ **A Scam-Free Zone**: No shady business here! Every casting professional featured in this book is the real deal—personally vetted and guaranteed.

➔ **Your Backstage Pass to Casting Pros**: Meet the behind-the-scenes talent scouts who bring unforgettable personalities to your favorite shows. This book is your exclusive access to the visionaries shaping reality TV.

➔ **Get Ahead of the Competition**: In the fast-paced world of reality TV, this book connects you with casting pros who are always searching for fresh faces, helping you stay one step ahead.

➔ **Insider Secrets to Stand Out**: Skip the guesswork! I'm sharing pro tips and insider insights that can set you apart and help you catch the eye of reality TV casting pros.

➔ **Calling All Networks, Studios, and Production Companies**: Looking for the ideal casting partner for your next reality TV sensation? This book is a treasure trove of talent waiting to be discovered.

➔ **And a Shout-Out to the Real MVPs**: Let's celebrate the casting pros who bring drama and excitement to life! It's time to recognize their hard work and the magic they create behind the scenes.

What You'll Find Inside This Book:

A jam-packed list of top-tier reality TV casting pros (think directors, producers, associates, recruiters—the whole crew!) and everything you need to know to get their attention.

To Get the Most Out of This Book:

1. Follow, Follow, Follow: Hit that follow button with every pro listed. More connections = more opportunities.
2. Notifications Are Key: Turn them ON so you know the second a hot new project pops up.
3. Play Favorites: Love a specific show? Make a list of the casting pros behind it. They're your best bet for landing a similar gig. Add them to your list of favorites on Instagram.
4. Sign Up for Everything: Newsletters, emails, smoke signals—whatever they're sending out, get on it!

So, if you're ready for your reality TV close-up, *Casting Pros To Know: Reality TV Edition* is more than a book. It's the key to unlocking your dream. Let's make some TV magic happen!

FROM CANDID CAMERAS TO CASTAWAYS—A WILD RIDE THROUGH REALITY TV HISTORY

Photo Credit:
Asjai Lou, CSA
www.AsjaiLouCasting.com
IG: @AsjaiLouCasting

Can you imagine a world before The Kardashians and dance battles with celebrities? Believe it or not, there was a time when TV wasn't all about "unscripted drama" (wink-wink). But fear not reality TV fanatics, because reality TV history is just as dramatic, surprising, and full of twists as your favorite show. So, grab some popcorn and settle in for a wild ride through the evolution of reality TV!

Early Days: Pranks, Pageants, and the Power of Ordinary People

Way back in the 1940s and 50s, television was a wide-eyed newcomer. Shows like *Queen for a Day* were among the first to peek into the real world, where women were awarded extravagant prizes based on their "hard-luck stories." Talk about emotional roller coasters! Then came *Candid Camera*, the OG prank show, using hidden cameras to capture people's hilarious (and sometimes embarrassing) reactions to staged situations. It turns out that watching people get tricked never gets old!

Other early players were talent programs like *Ted Mack and the Original Amateur Hour*, which showcased everyday folks with extraordinary skills, proving that stardom wasn't limited to Hollywood.

The 70s: When Documentaries Got Real (Literally)

The 1970s saw a shift toward a more documentary-style approach with shows like PBS's *An American Family*, which broke new ground by following a real California family for a year. Capturing their everyday lives, arguments, and even a shocking coming-out story was pure gold. This show sparked controversy for its unfiltered portrayal of a real family, paving the way for a new era of unscripted television.

The 80s: Cops and Contests Take Center Stage

The 80s brought a new wave of reality with a focus on professions. Shows like *Cops* offered a thrilling glimpse into the world of law enforcement, while *The Dating Game* (complete with some seriously questionable fashion choices) showed the awkward and hilarious world of finding love on TV.

The 2000s and Beyond: Reality Gets Even More Real (or Does It?)

The new millennium saw a boom in reality subgenres. We got cooking shows (*Hell's Kitchen*), dating shows with even more outrageous twists (*The Bachelor*), and renovation shows that made us all want to rip out our drywall (*Fixer Upper*). Reality TV became a pop culture juggernaut, influencing fashion, music, and even our vocabulary ("fetch" anyone?).

The 90s: The Golden Age of Reality TV Arrives!

The 90s were when reality TV truly exploded. MTV's *The Real World* threw strangers together in a house (think *Friends* without the script) and documented the inevitable drama. This show, along with competition beasts like *Survivor* and *Big Brother*, introduced us to the concept of reality stars and the drama-filled competition format that continues to dominate today.

The Future: What's Next for Reality TV?

Reality TV continues to evolve. Today, there are shows about everything from tiny houses to *Tiger Kings* (seriously). With the rise of social media, the line between contestants and influencers is blurring. Will we see more audience participation or entirely virtual reality shows? One thing's for sure: the future of reality TV is as unpredictable as a dramatic elimination ceremony.

WHAT IS REALITY TV? WHY WE LOVE IT, *AND* HOW IT CAN CHANGE YOUR LIFE

Photo Credit:
Asjai Lou, CSA
www.AsjaiLouCasting.com
IG: @AsjaiLouCasting

Let's break down the dazzling, chaotic, sometimes glamorous, and always entertaining world of reality TV.

So, What Is Reality TV?

Reality TV is like a slice of life caught on camera, with a generous dose of drama and a sprinkle of the unexpected. Imagine this: a bunch of strangers competing for love (or like, a hefty cash prize), a family facing the hilarious ups and downs of a massive home renovation, or a team of dancers vying for the ultimate stardom. It's real people, real situations, and a whole lot of unscripted moments.

Subgenres: It's a Reality Buffet!

The world of Reality TV is as vast as it is fascinating. Each subgenre offers a unique flavor of entertainment, drawing us in with captivating personalities, unexpected twists, and a voyeuristic glimpse into worlds both familiar and extraordinary.

Here's a taste:

- ➔ **Competition:** Think **Survivor, The Amazing Race,** or **Top Chef**. Adrenaline-pumping challenges, intense rivalries, and the thrill of seeing someone crowned the ultimate winner.
- ➔ **Dating: The Bachelor, Love is Blind**, and similar shows bring all that awkward yet addictive drama of finding love (or failing spectacularly!) under the spotlight.
- ➔ **Renovation: Flip or Flop, Fixer Upper**... we secretly all want to demolish a wall and turn a wreck into a dream home.
- ➔ **Celebrities Unfiltered:** Remember **The Osbournes**? That was some wild stuff! Celebrity-focused Reality TV pulls back the curtain on the lives of the rich and famous.
- ➔ **Docu-drama:** Shows like the **Real Housewives, Basketball Wives,** and **Love and Hip-Hop** franchises, immerse us in the lavish lifestyles, interpersonal dramas, and over-the-top antics of socialites, celebrities, and their entourages.
- ➔ **Talent Showcases:** From singers and dancers to magicians and daredevils, shows like **American Idol, America's Got Talent,** and **The Voice** celebrate the raw talent and inspiring stories of everyday people chasing their dreams.
- ➔ **And So Much More!** There are cooking competitions, game shows, hidden camera pranks, shows about everyday folks in extraordinary jobs... the list goes on!

Why We Love It: The Secret Sauce

Reality TV has an undeniable hold on pop culture. But what is it that makes us crave it like comfort food on a rainy day?

- ➔ **Relatability:** Even amidst the drama, there's something relatable about seeing "regular" people become the stars of their own shows.
- ➔ **Escape:** Life can be mundane. Reality TV lets us dive into over-the-top situations we'd never encounter otherwise. It's a juicy distraction.
- ➔ **The Unexpected:** You can script a drama, but you can't script reality. Expect those "Did that really just happen?!" moments.
- ➔ **Community:** Reality TV creates fandoms with a passion! Discussing the latest twists or rooting for your favorite contestant forges new online connections.

The Reality TV Advantage: Changing Your Life

Okay, hear me out. Yes, Reality TV is entertainment. But getting your 15 minutes of fame can go a lot further. It can offer:

- ➔ **A Platform:** Maybe you're launching a business, promoting a cause, or sharing

your talents. Reality TV is like having a giant megaphone pointed at you.

- **Unexpected Opportunities:** Suddenly, doors are open—book deals, brand sponsorships, maybe even a spin-off show. It's not guaranteed, but it happens!
- **Self-Discovery:** Being put under pressure in front of the world might not sound fun, but it can lead to crazy personal growth.
- **Memories:** Even if you don't win, it's a once-in-a-lifetime adventure that you'll tell stories about for years!

So, should you quit your job and dedicate your life to becoming a reality TV star? Probably not. But if the idea excites you, if you see a little bit of yourself in the personalities who light up your screen—go for it! Reality TV thrives on real lives, real stories, and real people. It's about who you are, what you do, and how you navigate the world around you.

Don't hesitate to throw your hat in the ring. You never know what a casting pro might be looking for, and your everyday life could be exactly what they need. Keep living your life to the fullest, because your unique experiences and personality are your greatest assets in this all too real world. Reality TV is full of surprises, and who knows, your next adventure might be just a casting call away. The choice is yours—will you take the leap?

Photo Credit: Nappy

DITCH THE SCRIPT, *EMBRACE* YOUR STORY: REALITY TV CASTING WANTS YOU!

Photo Credit: Erika Reyes

Forget the scripted world of Hollywood where polished actors deliver lines on cue. Reality TV is a whole different ball game, one where the ordinary becomes extraordinary and *you* have the power to shine! This isn't about perfect resumes or years of acting training; it's about celebrating real people with real stories that captivate audiences.

What is Real People Casting?

Unlike traditional casting, where professionals step into fictional roles, real people casting seeks out genuine individuals with compelling narratives. Reality TV Casting Pros embark on nationwide and even global quests searching for people whose everyday lives are filled with the unscripted magic that makes for great television. They're not looking for actors, they're looking for you: someone with a captivating life story, a vibrant personality, and the ability to navigate the unique challenges of Reality TV.

What Makes you a "real person" in Reality TV Casting

In reality TV casting, **a "real person" is someone with no professional entertainment experience.** This means they have not built a career in acting, hosting, or other forms of on-camera performance. Every network and show has its own guidelines, but generally, a **real person** is:

1. **Not a professional actor** (has never had a principal role in a scripted TV show or film).
2. **Has not been a co-star, guest star, or lead in scripted content** (background work is okay).
3. **Has not had a speaking role in commercials** (featured non-speaking appearances may be fine).
4. **Not a professional TV host or media-trained personality.**
5. **Not a past reality TV cast member in a major role.**
6. **May have background acting experience but hasn't pursued a full-time career in entertainment.**
7. **Not currently represented by an acting or hosting agent or manager.**

These criteria are based on what has worked on various shows, so keep them in mind as you prepare to apply.

When the Rule May Be Flexible

While many shows prioritize casting **completely new faces,** some may allow:

- ➔ Individuals who appeared on TV as a child but have not been active in entertainment as an adult.
- ➔ Those who have done extra/background work but never had speaking roles.
- ➔ Non-working actors who haven't booked significant roles or actively pursued the industry in years.
- ➔ Public figures or social media personalities if their story or presence aligns with the show's vision.

Why This Matters in Casting

Reality TV is about **authenticity and relatability.** Casting pros look for people whose stories, personalities, and lifestyles come across as naturally engaging—not as if they're performing. While some shows have more flexible guidelines, understanding these basics helps ensure the right fit for each project.

Why Real People Are Perfect for Reality TV Casting

- ➔ **Your Story is Your Superpower:** Have you overcome obstacles, pursued a dream with unwavering passion, or developed a unique talent? Your experiences, no matter how ordinary they may seem to you, are what set you apart. Your journey is what will resonate with viewers and make you a compelling cast member.
- ➔ **Be Yourself, Shine Brightly:** Leave the pretense at the door. Casting pros can spot inauthenticity a mile away. Be genuine, embrace your quirks, and let your natural charisma shine through. Your true self is your greatest asset.

- **Your Life is Your Resume:** Forget about fancy credentials or industry experience. Reality TV casting thrives on fresh faces and new perspectives. Your experiences as a teacher, mechanic, stay-at-home parent, artist, or whatever you are could be the perfect blend of skills and personality for a show.
- **Adaptability is Key:** Reality TV is unpredictable by nature. Are you comfortable stepping outside your comfort zone and embracing the unexpected? Your ability to adapt to new situations is crucial for not just surviving but thriving on a reality show.
- **Vulnerability is Your Strength:** Reality TV resonates with viewers because it's real. Sharing your story, your struggles, and your triumphs with the world creates a genuine connection that draws people in. Your willingness to be vulnerable and show your true self is what makes you relatable and inspiring.

Actors vs. Real People: Who Does Reality TV Want?

Reality TV has always set itself apart by seeking everyday people with little to no experience in entertainment, focusing on real personalities over trained actors. Unlike traditional television, which relies on actors for scripted roles, reality TV is built on capturing raw, unscripted stories from people who bring authenticity and unpredictability to the screen. This emphasis on relatable, unfiltered experiences allows viewers to connect more deeply with the cast, seeing real emotions and genuine reactions. By spotlighting real people, reality TV has even influenced other genres, showcasing the power of unscripted moments. Ultimately, reality TV is all about finding memorable personalities with unique stories—people who resonate with viewers and make the experience feel accessible, drawing audiences into the unpredictable world of real-life drama.

Should Actors Apply to Reality TV?

The answer to this question really comes down to **what an actor wants for themselves.** Reality TV can be a massive platform, but for those who dream of **scripted roles, major commercials, and blockbuster films,** there's a lot to think about before stepping into the unscripted world.

As much as we, as people, never want to be labeled, **labels exist in entertainment**—and they can be hard to shake.

The Reality TV Label & Its Impact on Acting Careers

Once an actor becomes a **major player in a reality TV series,** they are often seen as a **"reality TV personality"** first, regardless of their original career goals. And while some casting pros and producers might not openly say it, the reality TV label can make it **harder to break into scripted TV and film.**

Why? Because:

- **Reality stars are seen as "themselves" rather than transformative performers.** Scripted casting pros may struggle to separate the real-life persona from the character an actor is trying to play.
- **It's rare for major reality TV stars to land blockbuster films and scripted roles.** While exceptions exist (*Jamie Chung, Analeigh Tipton*), it's not the norm. Many actors find that once they're known for reality TV, opportunities in traditional acting spaces become limited.
- **Hollywood often keeps reality TV and scripted entertainment separate.** The industry sees them as different lanes, and crossing over isn't easy. A casting pro for a prestige drama or action film may hesitate

to cast someone who built their career in unscripted television.

The Flip Side: When Reality TV Works for an Actor

That said, not every actor has the same goal. Some may be new to the industry, open to different opportunities, and genuinely love reality TV—whether as a side hustle, a way to get exposure, or simply because they enjoy the experience.

In this case, reality TV can:

- ➔ **Give you visibility** – If you're looking to build a following, reality TV can put you in front of millions of people overnight.
- ➔ **Help with personality**-driven opportunities – Hosting gigs, influencer deals, and brand collaborations can come from reality exposure.
- ➔ **Be fun and fulfilling on its own** – Some actors find that they enjoy reality TV and decide to stay in it, whether it's through multiple shows or growing their brand in unscripted entertainment.

The key difference? If you're an actor who dreams of a traditional film and TV career, reality TV may not be the best move. If you're someone who enjoys reality TV for what it is, isn't attached to scripted success, and is open to different types of entertainment, it can work.

A Word of Caution: Casting Pros Can Spot Wrong Intentions

Reality TV can open doors, but if your sole reason for applying is to get famous, book acting jobs, or chase clout, casting pros will sniff it out **a mile away**. They are looking for **authentic people** with real stories, personalities, and motivations—not someone who is just using reality TV as a stepping stone to something else.

Can reality TV **help** you gain exposure, make connections, and lead to opportunities? Absolutely. But if that's the **only reason** you're doing it, it will show—on camera, in interviews, and throughout the casting process. Be mindful of what reality TV can do for you, but remember: **genuine interest, engagement, and personality always come first.**

Scripted vs. Unscripted: Two Different Worlds

The reality and scripted TV worlds operate differently, and it's difficult to juggle both. **Very few people can successfully transition from one to the other.** Most actors will have to choose a lane—or accept that reality TV could redefine their career path.

At the end of the day, **it all comes down to what you want for yourself.**

If your goal is to be a serious actor in films and scripted TV, think carefully before applying to reality shows.

If you enjoy reality TV and are open to wherever it takes you, go for it.

The entertainment industry is full of possibilities, but knowing how you want to be seen—and where you want to go—will help you make the best choice for your career.

The Rewards of Reality TV

Reality TV is more than just a chance to be in the spotlight—it's an opportunity to experience personal growth, professional advancement, and once-in-a-lifetime moments. While every participant's journey is unique, the rewards of stepping into the world of reality TV can be profound, both on and off the screen.

1. The Fame Factor

For many, the most immediate and noticeable reward of reality TV is the fame it brings. Whether you're on a hit dating show, a cooking competition, or a lifestyle docu-series, being broadcast to millions of viewers catapults you into public recognition. People know your name, follow your story, and engage with you on social media.

This newfound visibility can open countless doors. Suddenly, opportunities for partnerships, endorsements, and collaborations arise. The exposure alone has helped contestants launch careers in acting, hosting, music, fashion, and beyond.

2. A Platform to Share Your Story

Reality TV allows participants to share their unique stories, passions, and struggles with the world. Whether you're advocating for a cause, breaking stereotypes, or showcasing a unique skill, the platform gives you the opportunity to connect with audiences on a deeper level.

This storytelling power has led to participants becoming spokespeople for movements, launching nonprofits, or even inspiring viewers to make changes in their own lives. It's a chance to leave a mark far beyond the duration of the show.

3. Networking and Industry Access

The people you meet during the production of a reality TV show can be just as rewarding as the show itself. From producers and casting directors to fellow contestants and industry professionals, the connections you make can help shape your future.

Many contestants stay in touch with castmates and crew long after the cameras stop rolling, collaborating on projects or supporting one another in their careers. For example, musicians from talent shows often go on to collaborate with other performers, while entrepreneurs on shows like *Shark Tank* gain mentorship and financial backing.

4. Personal Growth and Self-Discovery

Participating in reality TV is not just a test of talent but also a test of character. The intense environment—challenges, high-pressure situations, and being away from home—often pushes contestants to their limits.

Many participants discover new strengths, develop resilience, and gain confidence. They learn to navigate criticism, embrace vulnerability, and adapt to unexpected situations. These lessons extend beyond the show, enriching your personal and professional life.

5. Financial Benefits

For some reality TV shows, there's a tangible financial reward. Competition shows often offer cash prizes or career-launching packages. But even if there's no direct payout, the exposure can lead to lucrative opportunities post-show.

Contestants often monetize their fame through brand partnerships, merchandise, public appearances, and speaking engagements. Influencers from shows with strong fan bases can earn income from sponsorships and affiliate marketing, turning their social media followings into steady revenue streams.

6. Travel and Unique Experiences

One of the most exciting rewards of reality TV is the chance to experience things you might never have encountered otherwise. Shows often involve exotic locations, access to exclusive events, and the opportunity to work with top-tier professionals.

Imagine competing on a cooking show with world-class chefs or performing on a stage in front of millions of viewers. These unforgettable experiences often become cherished memories and career highlights.

7. A Foot in the Door

For aspiring entertainers, reality TV is often a stepping stone to larger opportunities. Many Hollywood careers began with a stint on reality TV. Stars like Jennifer Hudson (*American Idol*), Cardi B (*Love & Hip Hop*), and Emma Stone (*In Search of the Partridge Family*) used their TV appearances as launchpads for greater success.

Even for those not in the entertainment industry, the exposure can help build a personal brand. Entrepreneurs, chefs, fitness coaches, and others have turned their time on reality TV into booming businesses.

8. Building a Loyal Community

Reality TV allows contestants to build a connection with viewers. Fans see you at your most vulnerable, cheering for your wins and empathizing with your struggles. This relatability often creates a loyal following.

Contestants with strong social media presences can use this connection to grow communities, launch initiatives, or simply stay engaged with supporters long after the show ends.

9. Breaking Stereotypes and Inspiring Others

Reality TV often shines a light on stories and perspectives that don't always get mainstream attention. For participants from underrepresented groups, the platform is a chance to challenge stereotypes and bring visibility to diverse experiences.

Your time on reality TV can inspire others to follow in your footsteps or to see possibilities they never considered before. Many participants have shared how viewers reached out to thank them for representation or encouragement.

10. Memories That Last a Lifetime

Beyond the fame, opportunities, and lessons, reality TV offers something intangible but deeply rewarding: memories. The bonds you form, the challenges you face, and the moments you create become stories you'll carry with you forever.

For some, the most valuable reward is the experience itself—a chance to live boldly, try something new, and make their mark on the world in an unforgettable way.

Why the Rewards Are Worth It

The rewards of reality TV are as varied as the participants themselves. While not everyone leaves with a career-changing opportunity or widespread fame, the experience can offer personal growth, connections, and a platform to share your story.

Taking the leap into reality TV isn't just about the destination—it's about the journey, the lessons you learn, and the opportunities you create along the way. For those willing to embrace the adventure, the rewards can be truly life-changing.

The Afterlife of Reality TV

When the cameras stop rolling and the spotlight dims, what happens next? For those who step into the world of reality TV, life after the show can vary dramatically. Some ride the wave of newfound fame to launch lucrative careers, while others quietly return to their everyday lives. The afterlife of reality TV is as unpredictable as the shows themselves, shaped by the type of program, the persona you portrayed, and the strategy you employ after your final episode airs.

The Different Paths of Reality TV Alumni

The afterlife of reality TV isn't one-size-fits-all. For some, the exposure leads to exciting opportunities. Contestants from competition shows often land endorsement deals, speaking engagements, or professional gigs in their areas of expertise. Personalities from dating shows may become influencers, capitalizing on their newfound followers to build brands. Meanwhile, participants in docuseries or lifestyle-based shows might use their time on TV as a platform for activism, business ventures, or artistic pursuits.

However, not all stories follow this trajectory. For every breakout star, there are dozens whose time in the spotlight fades quickly. This disparity often comes down to two factors: the type of show and the individual's approach to leveraging the experience.

The Role of the Show

The type of reality show you're on plays a significant role in shaping your afterlife. Competition-based shows like *American Idol*, *Survivor*, or *Making the Cut* tend to offer participants tangible stepping stones, whether it's prize money, industry recognition, or access to influential networks. Lifestyle or docu-series shows, on the other hand, rely heavily on the relatability and charisma of the cast to determine their post-show success.

Similarly, dating shows and social experiment formats often provide a built-in audience for contestants to engage with afterward. Shows that create strong fan communities, like *Big Brother* or *Love Island*, can help cast members amass loyal followings, leading to opportunities in content creation, product endorsements, or even public speaking.

Strategy is Key

Success after reality TV isn't just about being on the right show; it's about what you do with the platform once the show ends. Some participants treat their reality TV stint as a business opportunity, using it to network, market their skills, or build a personal brand. Social media plays a critical role here. Staying active, engaging with fans, and creating compelling content can help sustain interest and turn fleeting fame into long-term opportunities.

A clear strategy matters. Did you position yourself as a professional in a specific field? As a relatable everyman? As the show's breakout star? Understanding how you're perceived by the audience allows you to build on that persona in meaningful ways.

The Dark Side of Reality TV Fame

While there's potential for incredible highs, the afterlife of reality TV can also be challenging. Public scrutiny can be intense, and editing may leave participants feeling misrepresented. Social media, while an essential tool, can also become a space for criticism or trolling.

Some participants struggle with the loss of the spotlight or the return to a quieter, less glamorous reality. Without a clear plan or support system, it's easy to feel adrift. Mental health challenges are common, highlighting the importance of taking care of yourself during and after your reality TV journey.

Why It's Still Worth the Leap

Despite its unpredictability, stepping into the world of reality TV is often worth the gamble. It's a platform to share your story, connect with others, and, in many cases, transform your life. It costs nothing but your time and energy to apply, and the potential payoff—whether personal growth, new opportunities, or simply an unforgettable experience—can far outweigh the risks.

For many, the afterlife of reality TV is what they make of it. By understanding the industry, crafting a strategy, and staying true to yourself, you can turn your time in the spotlight into something lasting and meaningful.

Whether you're the next big star or someone who simply enjoyed the ride, remember this: the end of the show is only the beginning of your story.

Ready to Take the Leap?

So, are you ready to step out of the ordinary and into the spotlight? Dust off that application, let your true self shine and show the world what you're made of. Reality TV casting is searching for its next star—and it could be you! They're not looking for Hollywood perfection; they're looking for real people with real stories. And that's exactly who you are. This could be the start of an incredible journey that changes your life forever.

Photo Credit:
Markcos Gonçalves

THE UNSUNG HEROES: WHO ARE REALITY TV CASTING PROS *AND* WHAT DO THEY DO?

Photo Credit:
Isaac Alvarez
www.isaacalvarez.com
IG: @isaacealvarez

In Pic:
Jeffrey Marx
IG: @jeffmarxthespot

Torriel C. Simon Martin
IG: @torricasting @nolanyce

Think of reality TV casting as assembling a championship-winning sports team. The casting director is the seasoned general manager, who strategically selects and assembles a diverse group of players to create a winning and dynamic team on the field (or in reality TV's case, the screen), but there are a host of others who help to make a team a true winner.

Meet the Crew: Building the Reality TV Casting Dream Team

➔ **Casting Director: The General Manager (GM):** The GM is responsible for the overall vision and success of the team. They work closely with the networks and production companies to define the perfect roster for a given show, making key decisions about who to draft and how to cultivate their talent.

➔ **Casting Producer: The Head Coach:** The casting producer is like the head coach, taking the GM's vision and transforming it into a winning game plan. They actively scout for talent, conduct tryouts (interviews), and develop strategies to bring out each potential cast member's best qualities. Casting producers have a unique talent for uncovering the story that will be the perfect fit for the project, drawing out the most compelling personalities from candidates. They are the true MVPs behind the scenes, skillfully piecing together casting tapes to shape a dynamic cast that brings the project to life.

➔ **Casting Associate: The Assistant Coach:** Assistant coaches provide essential support to the head coach. They help evaluate talent, organize training sessions (auditions), and manage the day-to-day operations of the team.

➔ **Casting Assistant: The Team Manager:** Like a team manager, casting assistants handle the logistics and behind-the-scenes details. They ensure everything runs smoothly, from paperwork to travel arrangements, allowing the coaches to focus on developing the team.

➔ **Recruiter: The Scout:** Scouts are the talent hunters, constantly searching for promising prospects. They attend games (events), watch highlight reels (social media), and network with other scouts (industry professionals) to identify potential stars for their team.

The Casting Director: Calls the Plays

As the GM, the Casting Director (CD) has the final say on who makes the team. Their responsibilities include:

➔ **Building the Coaching Staff:** Casting Directors carefully select the producers, associates, and recruiters who will work with them, and best complement their leadership style. CDs share their vision with the support team who will execute and implement the vision in practical, tactical, and strategic ways.

➔ **Drafting and Developing Talent:** CDs conduct tryouts (interviews), review game footage (audition tapes), and work with the coaching staff to create highlight reels that showcase the strengths of potential players (cast members) to the network.

➔ **Communication with Ownership:** They act as the liaison between the coaching staff, the production company (team ownership), and the network, ensuring everyone is aligned and working towards a common goal.

➔ **Making the Final Cut:** Ultimately, the casting director decides who makes the final lineup. They present their top picks to the production and network executives (team owners), who then make the final decision on which players will represent the team on game day (the premiere of the show).

The World Behind the Screen

On game day everything looks perfectly choreographed and the team is in sync. To present such harmony requires a host of people and actions behind the scenes. The casting process as it is, is a complex and dynamic operation, much like the inner workings of a professional sports team. It requires a dedicated team of professionals, each with their unique role, working together to create a winning combination of talent, personality, diversity and chemistry. So, the next time you tune into your favorite reality show, remember that behind every captivating moment, there's a team of casting professionals who have meticulously crafted the perfect ensemble cast. They're the unsung heroes who make the magic happen, turning ordinary people into reality TV stars.

Breaking into Reality TV Casting: Insights and Essentials

Who Hires a Reality TV Casting Director?

Behind every unforgettable reality TV moment is a casting director who helped find the perfect mix of real people to bring the show to life. But who actually hires them?

1. Production Companies

Most casting directors are hired by the production company responsible for creating the show. These companies are the ones developing and pitching reality concepts to networks or streamers, and once a show is greenlit, they bring on casting professionals to start building the cast. In some cases, casting begins even before the show is fully sold to help sell the concept with talent.

2. Networks and Streaming Platforms

In certain cases—especially for big franchises or network-owned formats—the network itself might hire the casting director directly. This is more common when the network has specific casting standards, brand requirements, or is deeply involved in creative decisions.

3. Executive Producers and Show Creators

For passion projects, independent concepts, or shows still in development, the show's creator or executive producer may hire a casting director early in the process to help shape the cast and overall direction. Sometimes, these casting directors work closely with talent to create sizzle reels or casting presentations that help sell the show to buyers.

4. Branded Content & Advertisers

Reality-based content isn't limited to television. Brands creating digital series, branded docuseries, or unscripted content for marketing campaigns may also hire reality casting directors. These roles often involve finding compelling real people who align with the brand's messaging.

Who Hires the Casting Team?

Casting a reality show is never a one-person job. While the casting director leads the charge, they need a strong team behind them to handle the massive amount of outreach, interviews, submissions, and coordination that reality casting demands. But who builds that team—and how?

1. The Lead Casting Director

In most cases, the lead casting director is responsible for building their own team. Depending on the budget, timeline, and size of the show, they'll hire trusted collaborators to fill specific roles—such as casting producers, associate producers, casting assistants, researchers, editors, and social media scouts.

The casting director chooses team members based on:

➔ Their experience in specific genres (dating, competition, docu-follow, etc.)

➔ Their ability to connect with real people and find great talent

➔ Strong interviewing and storytelling instincts

➔ Reliability, hustle, and chemistry—because casting is fast-paced and collaborative

2. The Production Company (Occasionally)

Sometimes, the production company may recommend or provide team members—especially for long-running shows or internal projects. Even then, the lead casting director typically has input on the final team and can request additional hires if needed.

Getting Hired: Why Casting Is a Niche Industry

Reality casting is a small, tight-knit world. Most jobs are booked through **word of mouth**, referrals, or someone vouching for your work ethic and vibe. There isn't a traditional job board for most opportunities—one call, text, or recommendation can land you your next gig.

That means getting your foot in the door can feel tough—but it's absolutely possible. Here's what helps:

➔ **Reputation matters.** Show up, be prepared, work hard, and stay humble.

➔ **Network like it's your job.** Stay in touch with casting professionals you admire, and don't be afraid to let people know you're available.

➔ **Take entry-level roles seriously.** Many top casting directors started as assistants or researchers and worked their way up by being reliable and bringing great people to the table.

➔ **Keep learning.** Watch casting reels, learn what makes a great story, and understand how different types of shows work.

Once you're in, and you're good—**you're in**. This is an industry where people remember how you made them feel and how well you delivered under pressure.

Who Makes the Final Casting Decisions?

Even with a brilliant casting team and hundreds (sometimes thousands) of applicants, the final decision on who makes it onto a show doesn't sit with the casting director alone. Reality casting is a **collaborative process**, and depending on the project, several key players have a say in who gets cast.

1. The Network or Streaming Platform

Ultimately, the network or platform airing the show has the final approval. Their executives need to sign off on the cast to ensure it aligns with their audience, brand, and legal standards. They often give feedback at every stage, especially during final rounds.

2. Executive Producers & Showrunners

The executive producers—both from the production company and the network—are heavily involved in casting. They shape the show's tone and story arcs and work closely with the casting team to balance personalities, relationships, and storylines. Their creative vision plays a major role in final decisions.

3. The Production Company

If the production company developed the show, they usually have strong influence over casting. They may run internal approval rounds before presenting a final cast to the network.

4. The Casting Director

While casting directors don't always make the final call, their influence is massive. They're the ones who scout, interview, and develop talent, and they usually present a **final shortlist** of cast options for approval. In many cases, their opinion is trusted and respected because they've spent the most time with the applicants.

It's a Team Decision — But the Right Story Wins

Final casting isn't just about who's the loudest or most dramatic—it's about **who fits the story the show is trying to tell**. Sometimes incredible people don't make it because there isn't room for their story in that particular season. That's why casting directors often say: "**A no now doesn't mean a no forever.**"

What Aspiring Casting Pros Should Know

If you're considering a career in reality TV casting, here are some things to keep in mind. Not every show lists a casting director; sometimes, you'll only see titles like "casting producer." This is because casting producers often perform similar roles, managing talent searches, interviews, and working with production to bring the cast to life. But ask a group of casting professionals to define their roles, and you'll likely hear a range of answers! Each casting pro's approach is unique, and because our work world is as dynamic and unpredictable as the shows we cast, our specific duties can vary from project to project.

This is also a niche community where, generally, you'll need to start from the ground up. Many pros begin as recruiters, working their way up as they gain experience and build their skill set. Of course, there are exceptions to this rule; if you have deep connections in the industry, a significant social media following, or a large mailing list, those assets can fast-track your career. One piece of advice I wish I had known when starting out is the importance of building a personal database. Casting is all about getting the word out as widely and quickly as possible, and having your own database can give you a powerful edge.

Finding a Mentor in Casting

Finding a casting mentor is invaluable in this industry. Because reality TV casting is a niche field, learning the ropes from an experienced pro can give you a huge advantage. A mentor can guide you through the complexities of casting, introduce you to key contacts, and help you develop the nuanced skills required to succeed. Start building your network by using this book as your starting point. Take note of the professionals listed who have worked on the types of shows you're interested in, and don't hesitate to reach out to them. Let them know you're seeking mentorship and are eager to learn. Networking doesn't stop there—attend casting industry events and keep an eye on what the Casting Society (CSA) has to offer. They frequently host events and courses that provide invaluable insights into the world of casting.

Be sure to join the CSA's mailing list and job board to stay updated on opportunities and industry news. Remember, mentorship is a two-way street focused on learning and growth. Approach it with an open mind and be ready to take on any role, no matter how small, that helps you build a strong foundation for your career.

Tips for Building Essential Skills

To thrive in casting, you'll need to develop a versatile skill set. Here are some key areas to focus on as you get started:

- **Interviewing and Storytelling:** Take courses or workshops that teach interviewing techniques and narrative building. These skills are essential for uncovering compelling stories in potential cast members. Reading my Find Your Story Workbook will be a valuable investment, as it provides guidance on the questions you need to ask to draw out someone's story. You'll also gain an understanding of the key components of a person's life that can contribute to creating a strong narrative. You can find it here: https://www.asjailoucasting.com/store.
- **Build Your Social Media:** Building a strong social media following is a valuable skill for anyone interested in casting reality TV. Social media platforms are a gold mine for discovering untapped talent, spotting trends, and connecting with diverse communities. A strong presence not only boosts your credibility but also allows you to engage directly with potential cast members, understand what resonates with audiences, and promote casting calls effectively. In the fast-paced world of reality TV, being social media savvy helps you stay ahead, expand your network, and ensure you're casting people who align with the ever-changing interests of viewers.
- **Editing and Graphic Design:** Basic editing and graphic design skills are increasingly valuable for creating casting materials and promoting casting opportunities. Many jobs now require some editing abilities, so having these skills can give you an edge. With graphic design knowledge, you'll be able to create eye-catching social media flyers and content that capture the attention of potential candidates.
- **Administrative Skills:** Organization, scheduling, and time management are all crucial for keeping projects on track.
- **Build Your Personal Database:** Creating a personal database of friends, family, co-workers, organizations, businesses, and unique individuals you encounter can be an invaluable resource for casting reality TV. Often, the best talent comes from everyday connections—people with compelling personalities, interesting stories, or standout traits that make them perfect for the screen. By maintaining an organized record of these potential cast members, you'll always have a go-to network to draw from when filling roles. This proactive approach ensures you're never scrambling to find fresh faces and keeps you ahead in the competitive world of casting.
- **Stay Up-to-Date with Technology and AI:** Keeping up with the latest technology and AI can revolutionize how you connect with talent and manage your casting process. From social media algorithms that help you reach the right audiences to digital organization tools that streamline your workflow, technology can make your business more efficient and effective. AI-powered tools can help you track industry trends, automate repetitive tasks, and organize candidate data, freeing up more time to focus on what really matters—finding the perfect talent. Embracing these advancements not only keeps you competitive but also ensures that your operations run smoothly and professionally. Staying tech-savvy is essential for thriving in today's casting industry, helping you adapt to new challenges and stay one step ahead.

- **Stay Approachable and Respectful of All Perspectives:** In the casting industry, staying approachable and open-minded is crucial. Respecting diverse perspectives and understanding the cultures of all people allows you to connect genuinely with candidates from various backgrounds. Being approachable fosters trust and encourages individuals to show their authentic selves, which is essential for finding the right fit for each project. Respecting different viewpoints and celebrating diversity in your work not only enriches the stories you bring forward but also creates an inclusive environment that candidates feel comfortable in. Embracing this mindset ensures that your casting process is fair, welcoming, and reflective of the world's vast array of experiences and voices.
- **Celebrate Your Own Wins and Keep Seeking:** In casting, you're only as great as your latest find, so the search for exceptional talent never stops. Remember, this is a field where self-celebration is essential—you'll rarely get a "thank you" from a past candidate you coached and pitched for a show, and it's uncommon to hear a "great job" from your boss, even if you've found the star of the season. There's no bonus for discovering the winner or a breakout personality, but the sense of accomplishment is priceless. Take pride in your work, and always uplift yourself; don't wait for validation from others. Your contribution matters, and every successful match you make leaves a lasting impact on the story and the industry.

Challenges and How to Overcome Them

Casting can be a high-pressure environment with unique challenges. Here are some common obstacles and strategies to overcome them:

- **Tight Deadlines**: Stay organized and develop a system for managing your time effectively.
- **Finding the Right Talent for a Specific Role:** Keep an open mind and stay persistent in your search—often, it takes extra effort to find that perfect fit. Don't be afraid to throw in a wild card now and then. When I say "wild card," think of it as coloring a little outside the lines. It still fits the show but is packaged differently. These unexpected choices often lead to new beginnings and firsts. Networks and productions don't always know what they want until they see it. Personally, I always aim to include at least one option in every delivered batch that they didn't specifically ask for but would be great for the show—something fresh and completely different from the original request.
- **Being the Only Diverse Voice:** Being the sole representative of diversity in a room can feel isolating and challenging, but it's also a powerful opportunity to make an impact. Embrace your unique perspective as a strength, and don't shy away from advocating for inclusion and authenticity. While it may require courage to challenge the status quo or educate others, your voice is essential in ensuring representation that resonates with broader audiences. Remember, your presence in that room can open doors for others who may follow.
- **Managing Burnout:** Casting can be demanding, so it's essential to set boundaries and prioritize self-care to avoid creative burnout.
- **Professional Boundaries:** While casting requires empathy, it's important to maintain professional boundaries to

manage your relationships with potential talent and casting teams.

The Role of Social Media and Digital Tools in Casting

Social media and digital tools have transformed casting. Platforms like Instagram, TikTok, and YouTube provide casting pros with a vast pool of potential talent and allow for rapid outreach. Make the most of these tools by learning how to spot talent online, create engaging social media posts, and manage digital submissions efficiently. A strong online presence can also help you connect with others in the industry, build a following, and expand your reach.

The Power of Diverse Casting Teams

For networks, production executives, and casting professionals responsible for building teams, diversity should be at the top of the list. A successful cast reflects a blend of personalities, backgrounds, and cultures, and a diverse casting team is essential to achieving this. When casting teams are diverse in race, age, sexuality, religion, and more, they bring a variety of perspectives and experiences that resonate with a broader range of potential talent and viewers. Each team member can connect with different individuals, offering insights that appeal to various audiences and helping to create a cast that feels authentic and relatable.

To make great TV that reflects real life, it's crucial to create teams that embrace diversity, ensuring that the stories and characters we see on screen are vibrant, dynamic, and truly representative of the world around us.

A Final Encouragement to Aspiring Casting Pros

Casting is an exciting yet unpredictable career that calls for creativity, resilience, and adaptability. If you're thinking about pursuing a career in casting, embrace the unknown and stay curious. Be open to learning new skills, connecting with a wide range of people, and adapting to each project's unique demands. Every casting call is a new adventure, and every perfect match brings a story to life. The journey has its challenges, but the impact is incredibly rewarding. Lead with integrity, and stay true to your personal boundaries—people may test them in all directions. As long as you remain grounded within yourself, you'll be equipped to navigate any situation with confidence and grace.

Photo Credit:
Isaac Alvarez
www.isaacalvarez.com
IG: @isaacealvarez

In Pic:
Joy G. Herrera
IG: @castingwithjoy

Thea Washington, CSA
Www.TheaWashingtonCasting.com
IG: @theawashingtoncasting

Erin Tomasello, CSA
https://erin.live-website.com/
IG: @castingerin

UNVEILING THE CASTING PROCESS

Photo Credit:
Isaac Alvarez
www.isaacalvarez.com
IG @isaacealvarez

In Pic:
Kristen Moss, CSA
KMossCasting.com
IG: @Reality_TV_CastingCalls

Melissa Kellner, CSA
IG: @MelKel_MelissaKellner

Secrets of Reality TV Casting: Spill the Tea

Ever watched your favorite reality show and thought? "I could totally do that."

Guess what? You absolutely can! Reality TV is *the* platform for everyday people who have extraordinary stories, passions, and personalities. So, let's uncover the path from your living room couch to the reality TV spotlight!

The Casting Call: Your Invitation to Shine

Reality TV casting calls aren't exclusive VIP events—they're open to anyone with the courage to step up and stand out. These calls pop up everywhere: Network and production company websites, in your social media feed, at virtual events, in-person open calls, and even on the bulletin board at your local coffee shop. You might even find yourself face-to-face with a casting pro on a random Tuesday afternoon!

Casting calls are less about finding the "perfect" candidate and more about discovering real people with captivating stories. While the show's name is often kept under wraps, casting calls usually offer hints about the type of personality they're seeking. Think of it as a treasure hunt to reveal your unique self!

Here's a pro tip: Follow all the casting pros featured in this book on social media. They often post casting calls there first, giving you a head start on your Reality TV journey.

So, keep your eyes peeled—your unexpected invitation to shine could be just around the corner, waiting in a social media post!

Your Audition Starts Here: Nailing the Reality TV Application

You've found a casting call—now it's time to *apply*! The first step in your journey is completing the application. Remember, this isn't just paperwork; it's your first audition and a chance to show casting pros who you truly are. While the application will gather some basic information, the real focus is on telling your story through the prompts provided.

Casting pros aren't just looking for facts—they're searching for a captivating narrative that brings your personality to life. Think of each prompt as an opportunity to share experiences, qualities, and unique details that make you unforgettable. Write like you talk; this shouldn't feel like a job application. Keep it conversational, authentic, and true to you. Your story is the heart of your journey, and how you convey it can be the difference between blending in and standing out.

Approach your application knowing that storytelling is key. Let your personality, experiences, and unique perspective shine, and answer each question as if you're already speaking to your future audience. This is your chance to make an impression—make it count!

PRO TIP: It might sound simple, but be sure to follow all instructions, answer every question, and complete the requested videos. Never give one-word answers—share stories! Don't just tell us who you are, show us through your experiences.

Unpacking Your Story: The Key to Your Reality TV Application

While many applicants might share similar narratives—lifelong hobbies or early passions. What truly captures casting pros are unique, personal details that bring your story to life. Audiences connect with authenticity, so go beyond the basics and reveal what sets you apart. Give casting pros a genuine look into the experiences, values, and quirks that make you who you are.

Here are some ideas to dig even deeper:

- **Family Dynamics and Upbringing:** Share details about your family background and dynamics. Are there unique aspects of your upbringing that have shaped who you are today? Is your family supportive of your goals, or has it been a challenging journey? The influence of your family can add an authentic and relatable layer to your story.
- **Educational Background:** Are you studying or have you studied something unique or unexpected? Maybe your academic pursuits contrast with your journey in a way that adds intrigue and depth to your story. Educational experiences can reveal interesting dimensions of who you are and show unexpected sides of your personality.
- **Biggest Life-Changing Moment**: Think of a moment or event that transformed you or gave you a new perspective. This could be a challenge you overcame, a choice that defined you, or a significant experience that shaped who you are today.
- **Hidden Passions:** Is there something you're passionate about that most people wouldn't expect? Maybe it's a cause you're dedicated to, a personal project, or a hobby that adds a new layer to your personality.
- **Cultural or Community Background:** Does your culture, heritage, or community shape your perspective in a way that brings a fresh viewpoint? Consider family traditions, unique customs, or values that have influenced your journey.
- **Unique Talents or Tricks:** Have a quirky skill or hidden talent that always surprises people? This could add an unexpected twist to your story and show a different side of you.
- **Unusual Hobbies:** Are you into something uncommon or unexpected? This might be a unique interest, collection, or hobby that shows you in a new light.
- **Little-Known Facts:** Is there something surprising or interesting about you that most people wouldn't guess? These little-known details can add intrigue and make your story memorable.
- **Sports or Special Skills:** Do you have an athletic background or a skill that would surprise others? This might be a unique edge that sets you apart from other applicants.
- **Interesting Connections:** Are you related to a public figure or connected to someone well-known? Unique connections or relationships can add an extra layer to your story.
- **Intriguing Job or Background:** Does your family dynamic, job, or background have an unexpected twist, like growing up in a distinctive subculture, an unusual family business, or an adventurous lifestyle?
- **Defining Relationships:** Who has impacted your life most profoundly? Sharing a story about a key relationship—whether it's family, a mentor, or a close friend—can reveal a lot about your values and character.
- **Celebrity Adjacent Stories:** Have you had a surprising or interesting encounter with a celebrity? Whether it's funny, shocking, or unexpected, these stories can make you stand out and showcase your unique experiences.
- **A Personal Motto or Mantra:** Do you live by a specific phrase, quote, or saying?

Explaining why this mantra resonates with you can give casting pros insight into your mindset and motivation.

➔ **Your "Why":** Dig into why you want to be on reality TV beyond fame or exposure. Is it to share a meaningful story, represent something you're passionate about, or inspire others? Being clear about your purpose can make your application stand out and resonate with casting pros.

➔ **Embarrassing Moments:** Everyone has had an embarrassing moment that sticks with them. Sharing yours can reveal your sense of humor, relatability, and ability to laugh at yourself—all qualities casting pros love.

➔ **Unexpected Challenges:** Has there been a challenge in your life that shaped you in ways others might not know? Sometimes, opening up about these experiences can create a relatable and impactful connection.

Uncovering these aspects can add richness and make your story unforgettable. If you're finding it challenging to bring out these layers, try my *Find Your Story Workbook* at https://www.asjaloucasting.com/store, filled with exercises to help you shape a powerful narrative that makes casting pros (and audiences) sit up and take notice.

Your Story is Your Power

A well-crafted story is one of your most powerful tools in the casting process, so don't hesitate to reveal the real you. This is your moment to connect with casting pros on a personal level and stand out in a meaningful way. Embrace every part of your journey, and let the world see what makes you unique. Don't try to guess what you think casting wants to know about you—just be authentic. Show that you have storylines and things to talk about. Demonstrate that you can tell great stories and aren't afraid to speak up.

Follow these golden rules to set yourself up for application success:

Golden Rule #1: Follow the Yellow Brick Road (aka the instructions). Imagine showing up to a costume party dressed as a hot dog when everyone else is channeling their inner superhero. Awkward, right? The same goes for your application. Submitting the wrong file type, missing questions, sending it in late, or not following video instructions (like uploading a random video instead of the one requested) is a fast track to the "NO" pile. So, read those instructions like they're the map to your Reality TV gold—and follow them closely!

Golden Rule #2: Spill the Beans (and the photos) Don't just say you're a thrill-seeker—tell them about the time you bungee-jumped off a bridge with your grandma! Stories are your secret sauce; make them juicy but real. Add photos or videos as the cherry on top. Remember, if there are no pics or videos, casting pros might assume it didn't happen. And if your social media doesn't match who you say you are, it could make them question your authenticity.

Golden Rule #3: Let's be real—"normal" is overrated. Casting pros are searching for the quirky, passionate, one-of-a-kind *you* that makes the world more interesting. So, embrace your inner weirdo, show off those hidden talents, and share your unique perspective. Write like you talk, and let your personality leap off the page!

Golden Rule #4: Don't Hit Snooze. If you see a casting call that speaks to your soul, don't wait for tomorrow! *Carpe Diem!* Opportunities can disappear faster than pizza on a Friday night. Be thorough but be swift. While you're napping, the early applicant might just snag the golden ticket to reality TV stardom.

Remember, this opportunity is your chance to introduce yourself to the world—not as a list of qualifications, but as a vibrant, multi-faceted person. Share your dreams, your passions, and your wildest adventures. Be yourself, be bold, and let your story open the door to reality TV magic. Authenticity is your VIP pass!

You Got a Call! Woot Woot! You're One Step Closer to Reality TV!

Your application dazzled the casting team, and now a casting pro is calling you—congrats! This is a huge milestone, as casting pros sift through hundreds, sometimes thousands, of applications. Getting that call means we see something special in you, so let this be the beginning of your journey. And don't stop applying!

First up is the phone interview. This isn't a casual chat with your bestie—it's your chance to spill the most hilarious, dramatic, and heartwarming details of your life story. Think of it as a confessional (minus the dramatic music, for now). The casting producer, associate, or sometimes even the casting director will be all ears, ready to soak up your unique tales. Bring your A game, let your personality shine, and show them why you're the perfect fit for their show!

Next Step: The VIP Virtual Interview!

Congratulations! You've made it past the application and phone interview, and now you're onto the next major step: the virtual interview, most likely on Zoom. This is the holy grail of the reality TV casting process—a huge milestone that only a select few reach. Take a moment to celebrate; this means you're meeting many of the show's key requirements. But remember, while this is a significant achievement, it doesn't mean you've booked the show just yet.

The virtual journey typically begins with a one-on-one recorded interview with a casting director or casting producer. If they're captivated by your personality and story, you may be invited back for additional rounds, possibly with other casting professionals or executives joining in. This part of the process is all about showing who you truly are, and it's where your unique storytelling skills become essential.

How to Prep for Your Virtual Interview

Your virtual interview setup is essential for making a memorable impression. Casting pros will typically send detailed information on how they want you to set up your virtual interview, so always read their emails thoroughly. They can be lengthy, but every detail is there to help you succeed—so please read carefully! Below are some basic tips to know, but if your casting pro provides specific instructions, always follow those.

Follow these steps to create a polished, professional environment that allows casting pros to see you at your best:

➔ Choose an Outfit that Pops

Wear something that stands out on camera and reflects your style. Avoid colors that might wash you out, and choose shades that complement your skin tone and contrast well with your background.

➔ Create a Background that Reflects You

Avoid plain white walls, bland backgrounds, or any type of actor blue/green screen backdrops. Instead, choose a real spot in your home or office that feels natural and well-lit. Try to avoid having your bed in the shot to maintain a more polished and professional look. Set up in a space that reflects your personality without distracting from your presence. A few added touches—like a plant, artwork, or well-placed items—can create a professional yet inviting look. Never do a virtual interview in a restaurant, cafe or car; a home or office setup is always best.

➔ **Perfect Your Framing and Eye Contact**

Position yourself in the center of the screen with the camera at eye level. Your frame should capture everything from just below your waist to a few inches above your head, allowing casting pros to see your face clearly and making space for natural hand gestures. Look directly into the camera to make eye contact, and if needed, stack a few books under your device to ensure it's at the right height. For an even better setup, consider using a computer or cell phone stand or a tripod to achieve the perfect angle. Check out options here: https://icumusthaves.com/.

➔ **Master Your Lighting**

Good lighting is essential. Avoid placing windows to your side or behind you, as they can create shadows or glare. If possible, position yourself so natural light is in front of you, illuminating your face evenly. If lighting is limited, experiment with lamps or consider investing in a **ring light** for a professional look. Find recommended lighting options here: **https://icumusthaves.com/**.

➔ **Ensure a Quiet, Private Space**

Choose a quiet, private room where you won't be interrupted. Background noise or nearby distractions can affect your focus. Also, check that your internet connection is strong and reliable to avoid interruptions during the interview.

➔ **Do a Test Run**

Before your interview, do a test run on the same platform the casting pros will use. Ask a friend or family member to join a video call to check your lighting, audio, and internet connection. This practice session ensures everything works smoothly and gives you time to make any last-minute adjustments.

With these setup tips, you'll be ready to present yourself in the best possible light—both literally and figuratively. A well-prepared setup allows casting pros to focus on you and helps you leave a memorable impression.

Don't feel discouraged, let your personality dim, or get anxious if a casting pro asks you to make changes to your setup. They know what's needed and what works for this production and network. Be open to their feedback—they want you to succeed! Trust that following these instructions will give them a great starting point. They'll appreciate your effort, so don't worry or feel like you've done anything wrong.

Deepening Your Story for Your Virtual Interview

As you prepare for your virtual interview, take time to reflect on the highlights of your story shared in your application or phone interview. Revisit the moments that resonated, and think about how you can add new depth. Casting pros want to see an evolving, layered story, so consider sharing unique aspects you haven't discussed yet or new experiences that add to your personality.

Here are some storylines casting pros often find compelling:

➔ **The Hero/Heroine**: You're the underdog, the one everyone roots for. Showcase your determination, resilience, and fighting spirit to bring this part of your journey to life. Think about a time you overcame a major obstacle or persevered through challenges—specific examples add richness to your story.

- **The Drama Magnet**: You're no stranger to chaos—whether you attract it or create it! Embrace the entertaining side of drama, but stay relatable and engaging without crossing into "trainwreck" territory. Reflect on a few lighthearted or outrageous situations that reveal how you handle chaos with humor or honesty.
- **The Quirky Enigma**: You march to the beat of your own drum, and it's AMAZING. Own your eccentricity; casting pros are drawn to unique personalities that stand out from the crowd. What's an unexpected habit or interest that's truly "you"? Don't be afraid to lean into your quirks and showcase how they make you different.
- **The Transformation**: Are you undergoing a major life change or personal reinvention? Casting pros love stories of growth and transformation, like weight loss journeys, career changes, or lifestyle shifts. Share a turning point or a specific challenge you're tackling right now—these moments make your journey memorable and relatable.

These are examples to help you brainstorm, but remember—your story doesn't need to fit into any single category, and it shouldn't. Focus on being authentic, passionate, and true to yourself. Look for fresh stories or experiences that highlight different sides of you. And remember: the best stories are often in the details. Think about how to let your personality shine, allowing casting pros to see who you are beyond the basics.

This is your moment to make a lasting impression, so don't hold back. Embrace your unique qualities, dig deep, and show casting pros exactly why your story deserves to be heard!

Preparing Your Photo and Video Drive

Once you make it to the virtual auditions, a casting producer or casting associate will likely ask you to upload visuals to a shared drive. Being prepared in advance can make a huge difference. Set up a drive with folders dedicated to different types of photos and videos. This way, you'll always be ready and won't have to scramble to gather materials. Remember to keep it personal—try to avoid including random people in your photos. If others do appear, they should be either part of your story (such as family or friends you mention) or directly related to your narrative.

Here are some key types of photos and videos to include in your drive:

- **Background Photos**: Pictures from your childhood, family gatherings, college days, etc., to give a sense of where you come from.
- **Personality Photos**: Images that show off your unique personality—these can include snapshots of you being silly, adventurous, or simply being yourself.
- **Close-Up Photos**: A clear, everyday close-up of your face (no actor headshots—just natural shots).
- **Full-Body Photos**: Full-length shots to give a complete view of your look and presence.
- **Photos with Friends**: Fun, casual shots with friends that highlight your social side.
- **Professional Photos**: Shots of you in action at work, or doing activities related to your career or interests.
- **Hobby/Passion Photos or Videos**: Images or short clips of you engaging in hobbies or passions, especially ones you've mentioned in your application.

- **Story-Backed Photos**: These are must-have images that support the personal stories or traits you've shared—proof of your experiences. If you don't have photos or videos to back up a great story, that doesn't mean you shouldn't share it. **STILL SHARE THE STORY**. Let the casting pro decide what to use and what not to use.

These basics will give casting a well-rounded view of who you are, and having them ready in advance ensures you can focus on your interview with confidence. Keep in mind that some shows may require more specific images or videos, so stay open to additional requests and always follow your casting pro's instructions. This setup is an excellent start and will come in handy throughout the casting process.

Collaborating with the Casting Pro

The connection you create with the casting pro is key; they know exactly what the network wants and can guide you toward success. Here's how to make the most of this collaboration:

- **Embrace the Collaboration:** Reality TV thrives on the unexpected, so be open to exploring different angles of your story. The casting pro might see a side of you that you didn't even know existed.
- **Be Honest, Be Real:** Faking it won't get you far. Casting pros can sense inauthenticity a mile away. Your real quirks, vulnerabilities, and genuine excitement are what will shine through.
- **Own Your Narrative:** Don't be afraid to pitch your own story ideas. Did you get lost on a trek through the Amazon and make friends with apes? Casting pros **love** a unique backstory.

Remember: This is Your Time to Shine!

The virtual audition is your moment to be confident, engaging, and completely yourself. Tell your story with passion and authenticity, and let the casting pros see the star within. When you shine, they shine too—and who knows? You just might be the breakout star of the next hit reality sensation!

What Happens After Your Virtual Interview

After your virtual interview, the casting director, casting producer, and sometimes the entire casting team will come together to decide if you're a good fit for the show. If they give you the thumbs up, your virtual interview recording is sent to an editor, who will create your official casting tape. Most casting tapes are 3–10 minutes long, depending on the type of show. These tapes highlight the best moments from your interview and include any photos or materials you've shared, creating a compelling presentation for the network and production to see what you'd bring to the screen.

Once your casting tape is ready, it goes through the first round of consideration with the production team, which decides which candidates will be presented to the network. The second phase of consideration is the network presentation—this is when the network reviews the top picks from production. The final selection is a collaborative effort involving the network, production team, and input from casting. Ultimately, it's the network and production team who decide which individuals are the best fit for the show.

The Real Deal (In-Person Auditions)

While not all shows conduct in-person callback auditions, if yours does and you've made it to this stage, congratulations! You've earned your golden ticket to the big leagues. Get ready to impress a panel of network executives and producers in person. This is your chance to showcase your confidence, charm, and unforgettable stories—your opportunity to prove you're the next Reality TV sensation! Remember, it's all about presenting the authentic you: your vibrant personality, your undeniable spark. So be confident, be engaging, and most importantly, be yourself.

Patience is a Virtue (Ugh!)

Hold your horses, eager beaver! Casting is a marathon, not a sprint. We're talking weeks, sometimes even months, of waiting, wondering, and maybe biting a few nails. Why does it take so long? Casting teams are juggling a circus of personalities and details to find the perfect mix for each show. Sometimes, they may put you "on ice"—meaning you're a fantastic candidate, just not quite right for the current project. Don't despair! This isn't a rejection; it's simply a delay.

In the meantime, keep applying to shows that interest you. Don't take it personally if you don't hear back right away—every "no" only brings you closer to a "yes." Stay positive, keep your energy high, and celebrate each milestone, even if it's just landing the virtual interview. You never know when the stars will align, and your moment will come. Patience may not be the most thrilling virtue, but trust us, it's worth the wait!

The Big Moment (Finally!)

"You're Cast!" (Maybe...): Getting that call is thrilling, but don't start packing your bags just yet. It's usually a conditional "yes." There are still background checks, psych evaluations, and other hoops to jump through before the final yes. Reality TV isn't child's play, after all! But hey, even a conditional yes is a HUGE victory!

Alternate: Sometimes, you might be the casting team's plan B. Don't fret! Life happens, people drop out, and you could be the next person up. Stay positive and keep that phone close—your Reality TV dreams could still come true!

Important Stuff to Remember

- **Interviews, Interviews, and More Interviews:** Big shows mean big stakes, and that often means a series of interviews. Be ready to share it all—your life, your loves, your dreams, and yes, even your most embarrassing moments!
- **Secret Squirrel Mode:** Keep it under wraps! Talking about the show before the official announcement could cost you your spot. Remember, loose lips sink ships (and Reality TV careers).
- **The Final Verdict:** While the casting director plays a crucial role in the process and shares their input, they aren't the ultimate decision-makers. The final call lies with the network and production executives, so keep your fingers crossed and hope you're the perfect fit for their vision.
- **Hearing Back from Casting:** If the casting team is interested in you for the current project, they will reach out. Due to high volumes of applicants and tight deadlines, they might not respond to everyone, so if you don't hear back within

a few months, consider it a "no" for that show. But don't be discouraged! It's not necessarily a "no" forever with this casting team or professional, as most casting pros often reach out to individuals who may not have been the right fit for one show but could be perfect for another.. Reality TV casting is a wild ride, full of ups and downs. Expect to hear many "no's" before that magical "YES!" Embrace the journey, keep applying to shows that fit your vibe, and be unapologetically yourself. Who knows? Your next audition could be the one that changes everything!

Trust the Process

If casting is interested, they will reach out—just make sure to follow all instructions carefully. The best thing you can do is apply, give it your all, and then let it go. Trust the universe to work its magic. Release any attachment to the outcome and focus on creating new experiences, connections, memories, and skills that will make your story even stronger for the next opportunity. Don't get caught up obsessing over your application or interviews. If you're the right fit, casting will contact you. Trust the process and keep growing.

Stay Top-of-Mind: The Art of Being Unforgettable

The casting process can be a L-O-N-G journey. Here's how to stay memorable without overdoing it:

➔ **Follow Up (Once, and Make It Count):** After a virtual interview, a single, polite follow-up email is enough to show interest without coming across as pushy. Express your enthusiasm, thank the casting team, and let them know you're excited about the opportunity—but keep it brief and to the point. Find that sweet spot of showing interest without being overbearing!

➔ **Social Media Smarts:** If casting pros are following you on social media, use it to your advantage. Share glimpses of your life that match the vibe of the show—whether that's travel, adventure, family, or hobbies. Your online presence is an extension of your personality, so keep it authentic, positive, and relevant.

➔ **Showcase Your Talents:** If the show requires specific skills like cooking, dancing, or fitness, keep practicing and post about it. Demonstrating improvement not only ups your value but also shows dedication to your craft.

➔ **Stay Ready:** Be open and enthusiastic about any last-minute requests from the casting team. Flexibility and a positive attitude can go a long way, so be ready to jump in if they need additional information, updates, or a quick follow-up. Showing you're willing and excited for every step speaks volumes about your commitment!

Casting is a marathon, so stay patient and focused. Your goal is to keep yourself on the casting team's radar, showing that you're dedicated, adaptable, and ready for your moment.

Photo Credit: RUN 4 FFWPU

BEYOND THE REJECTION NOTICE — HANDLING REJECTION, UNDERSTANDING CASTING DECISIONS, AND GETTING READY FOR FUTURE *OPPORTUNITIES*

Photo Credit: Firshad Muhmmad

Rejection—an unavoidable part of the reality TV casting journey. One minute, you're picturing yourself as the next breakout star; the next, you're staring at a "Thank you, but no thanks" email. It stings, but don't let it define you. Learning to handle rejection is a vital skill in this industry, so let's turn that disappointment into momentum!

Rejection: It's Not Always About You

Casting is like putting together a complex puzzle, and sometimes you're a great piece but just don't fit this particular picture. Here's why a "no" doesn't mean you're not good enough:

- **The Vision**: Maybe they already have someone in the cast with a personality or backstory similar to yours, and they need a contrasting type.
- **Show Needs**: Casting can change direction mid-process, meaning your profile may no longer match the vibe or story they want to tell.

- **The Competition**: With hundreds of applicants for each spot, sometimes it's a matter of pure timing and luck. Remember, it's not all about talent!

Handling the Sting: Be Kind to Yourself

- **Feel It, Don't Dwell**: Disappointment is natural, so give yourself a moment to feel it. But don't let it drag you down—self-doubt won't help your journey.
- **Hold On to the Positive**: Did you get even a little positive feedback? Take that "We liked your energy" and use it to fuel your confidence.
- **Self-Care Is Key**: Step away, do something you enjoy, and remind yourself of your worth outside the casting world.

Digging Deeper: Seeking Feedback

Sometimes, you can respectfully ask why it wasn't a fit. Be polite and understanding—casting teams aren't obligated to respond, but if they do, any insights they offer could be golden for your next opportunity.

The Growth Zone: Turn Rejection into Your Power Source

Rejection can be a valuable opportunity for growth. Take the time to examine your application, interview materials, and social media presence to see where you can improve. Here's how to use rejection to build a stronger, more compelling presence:

Assess Your Application

Start by reviewing your application closely. Were your videos and materials the best representation of you? Did you carefully follow every instruction exactly as outlined? Reflect on the clarity and authenticity of your answers and how well they showcased your personality. This is your first impression, so look for ways to refine and elevate how you present yourself for the next opportunity.

Enhance Your Storytelling and Visuals

Reality TV casting thrives on captivating stories and strong visuals. Take a look at your photos and videos—are they current and a true reflection of who you are right now? How well did you convey your story? Consider if any details need tweaking or if you could benefit from more practice in storytelling. Did you include photos or videos that highlight the main points of your story? Catching a casting pro's interest with your story is the first step, but keeping them engaged with updated, authentic visuals is what really makes an impact.

Emphasize Your Unique Factor

Did you clearly communicate what makes you unforgettable? Did you share any unique qualities, unusual hobbies, or bold life experiences that set you apart? Take time to dig deep and identify what makes you distinct. Casting pros look for standout personalities, so make sure you're showcasing the qualities that make you one-of-a-kind.

Perform a Social Media Audit

View your social media profiles as if you're seeing them for the first time. Does your online presence match the person you described in your application? Consistency is crucial, as casting pros may check your profiles to confirm your story. Ensure your social media reflects your true personality, highlighting the traits and stories that make you unique. Think of your profiles as an extension of your application, reinforcing your authenticity and strengthening your overall presence.

Stay Open to New Opportunities

Remember, rejection is often just a redirection. New shows and casting calls are constantly emerging, so keep your eyes open and stay ready for the next opportunity. By refining your approach and staying open, you'll be prepared to apply with renewed confidence when the right role comes along.

Turning rejection into a growth opportunity will only make you stronger and more resilient in your journey. Keep sharpening your skills, and remember that every "no" brings you closer to the right "yes."

One "No" Isn't the End

Most reality stars you see on screen heard "no" before that life-changing "yes." Resilience is everything! Persistence, self-belief, and a drive to learn from each experience are your most powerful tools for navigating the competitive reality TV world. Keep your spark alive—remember, you've got to be in it to win it! Apply to shows that feel right, and who knows? That "yes" might be closer than you think.

Affirmations to Transform Rejection into Growth

Affirmations can be a powerful way to turn rejection from a setback into a source of strength and resilience. By repeating affirmations, you remind yourself of your worth, focus on personal growth, and open your mind to new possibilities. To get the most out of affirmations, say them with intention—try speaking them aloud, writing them down, or placing them somewhere you'll see them regularly, like on your phone or workspace.

Why are affirmations so impactful? They build self-confidence and help you embrace the journey, even in difficult moments. Rather than seeing rejection as a failure, affirmations let you view it as a step forward on the path to your goals. With each affirmation, you strengthen your resilience, reinforce your self-worth, and deepen your commitment to your journey, helping you stay motivated and open to what's next.

Empowering Affirmations

1. I am unstoppable, and every setback is a setup for a stronger comeback.
2. Rejection is a stepping stone toward the right opportunity, guiding me to what's truly meant for me.
3. I am enough just as I am; my worth is not defined by any single outcome.
4. Every "no" leads me closer to the perfect "yes" that aligns with my purpose.
5. I trust the journey and embrace each experience as part of my growth.
6. My courage in pursuing my dreams is a victory in itself—I am proud of my progress.
7. I am open to learning from every experience, and I emerge stronger each time.
8. I let go of doubt and focus on the limitless potential within me.
9. I embrace each challenge as an opportunity to discover new strengths within myself.
10. The right opportunity will find me, and I am preparing myself to be ready when it does.

Use these affirmations to keep moving forward with confidence, knowing that each step—whether a "yes" or a "no"—is leading you toward your best self and your goals.

BONUS SECTION: YOUR REALITY TV CASTING *SURVIVAL GUIDE*

This section is your ultimate guide to mastering the reality TV casting process with confidence. Packed with expert tips, it will help you stand out and make a lasting impression on casting pros. You'll also learn the best strategies for following up, including when and how to reach out to maximize your chances of success.

DIG FOR GOLD— FIND THE STORY THAT MAKES YOU SHINE

Photo Credit: Jeff Denlea

We all know that story is everything in reality TV. Casting Pros aren't just looking for someone with a pulse—they want the special sauce that sets you apart. But where do you even start to find your IT factor? Let's go treasure hunting!

Your Life: The Ultimate Reality Show

Think of your life as one long, unscripted show. You're the star, and you've already got episodes full of drama, comedy, and those unpredictable twists. Here's how to find those golden moments:

- **The Highlight Reel:** Jot down the most EPIC moments of your life. The time you survived a crazy storm, when you faced a major challenge, or that hilarious travel mishap that still makes you laugh years later.
- **The Supporting Cast:** Who are the key players in your life story? Crazy family members? A lifelong bestie? Even your rivals can add spice!
- **Hidden Plot Twists:** Dig deeper. What are your secret dreams? Fears? Skills you never show the world? Those unexpected layers make you intriguing.

Beyond the Basics

Your story isn't just about WHAT happened, it's about HOW it shaped you:

- **Triumph over Adversity:** Did you overcome a big obstacle? Casting pros LOVE a fighter who has an inspiring journey.
- **Transformations in Progress:** Are you on a quest for change (weight loss, new career, reinvention)? That growth creates a storyline they can build on.
- **Contradictions = Fascination:** Are you a shy person with a wild hidden talent? A tough exterior with a soft heart? Paradoxes make you memorable.

The "Why Should I Care?" Test

Put on your casting pro hat. Ask yourself, "Why would a total stranger be glued to MY story?"

- **Relatable Yet Rare:** Is there something everyone can connect with (fear, love, dreams), but with YOUR unique spin?
- **The Emotional Hook:** Will your story make them laugh, cry, or feel inspired? Emotions are what keep viewers coming back.
- **Uniquely You:** Can someone else EASILY step into your shoes? If so, it's time to uncover what makes you different!

Pro Tip: Practice Makes Perfect

- **Storytelling Workshop:** Can't tell your story in two minutes or less? Practice! Ask friends for feedback and keep refining it until it's punchy and powerful.
- **Video Vixen:** Even if a video isn't required, record yourself telling your story. You might discover angles you never considered.

Need Some Help Digging?

Sometimes, uncovering our own story can be tricky. Moments that feel significant to us may not easily translate on paper. That's where my *Find Your Story Workbook* comes in! I've designed it with specific exercises and questions to guide you through the process, helping you uncover those hidden gems and shape a compelling narrative that will make reality TV casting pros sit up and take notice. Your story isn't something you create out of thin air—it's already within you, just waiting to be unearthed. Be honest, be brave, and don't be afraid to show that vulnerable, messy, human side that will make viewers love (or love to hate) you! You can find the workbook at **https://www.asjailoucasting.com/store**.

SOCIAL MEDIA AS YOUR SPOTLIGHT: *WHERE YOUR TRUE SELF SHINES*

Photo Credit: Ahsheai Media

In the world of reality TV, authenticity is gold. Casting pros aren't looking for polished or manufactured personas—they're seeking the real, raw, and undeniably captivating. Your social media can be your secret weapon, giving casting pros a taste of who you truly are. A quick note: don't worry about your follower count. Casting pros are far more interested in what you bring to the table than in how many followers you have!

Building Your Social Media Foundation

Before diving into posts, make sure your social media basics are casting-ready:

- ➔ **Public Profile**: How can casting pros get to know you if your profile is private? If you're applying, make sure your social media profiles are set to public. Casting pros often review profiles to learn more about potential applicants, and if yours is private, they're likely to move on to the next candidate.
- ➔ **Informative Bio**: Think of your bio as your elevator pitch. Include your full name, age, location, job, and maybe even a hint of your unique side (e.g., "NYC accountant, aspiring goat yoga master"). Make sure to include an email address you check regularly, and if you're comfortable, a phone number too—casting pros may reach out through these channels if they want to connect with you quickly.
- ➔ **Relationship Status**: If you're applying for a dating show, make sure your profile shows you're single! Casting pros look for the details that align with each show's needs.
- ➔ **Ditch the Filters**: Overly edited photos can read as inauthentic. Casting pros want to see the real you—natural photos, genuine smiles, and your authentic self are what stand out.

Show, Don't Just Tell

Your social media should feel like your own mini-documentary:

- ➔ **Align Your Story**: Mentioning an epic jungle trek in your application? Share those moments with pics, videos, and anecdotes on your profile to keep it consistent.
- ➔ **Highlight Hobbies & Passions**: Love rock climbing, cooking, or ballroom dancing? Don't hide it! Casting pros seek people who live their passions, and showing it can make you unforgettable.
- ➔ **The Everyday is Interesting**: Your life doesn't have to be extravagant. Showing unique angles on your daily grind displays that special talent of finding fun in the ordinary.

Pro Tips for Standing Out

- ➔ **Hashtags**: Use relevant hashtags that match your interests and favorite shows (#adventuretravel, #foodie, #survivorfan). Casting pros often search these to find unique personalities.
- ➔ **Be Real, Be Active**: Don't force your posts. Regular, genuine updates from your life are far more compelling than staged content.
- ➔ **Showcase Your Talents**: Got a skill? Share it! Whether it's singing, stunts, or cooking, short videos grab attention and show casting pros what you've got.

Aligning Social Media with Your Application

Think of social media as visual proof of your application. If you say you're hilarious, your feed should have some side-splitting content. Adventurous? Let them see you on those hikes or daredevil slopes. Consistency between your application and social media builds trust with casting pros.

Important Note: Online History Matters

Casting pros dig deep, so be mindful of your digital footprint. Scrub anything offensive or inappropriate, and focus on showcasing your best self—the one they'll want to put in front of millions. Authenticity is key. Let your true personality, passions, and unique experiences radiate through your posts. That's how you become unforgettable to casting pros—and maybe just the breakout star everyone will be talking about!

If This is Reality TV, Why Do I Need to Do All These Things? Aren't I Enough?

Great question! Yes, casting pros want the real *you*—but they also need someone who can tell their story in a way that captivates. Think of it like this: Reality TV isn't about acting or putting on a show; it's about finding people who genuinely know themselves, are unfiltered, can express what makes them unique, and aren't afraid to share their perspectives and emotions openly. Casting pros are on tight deadlines, so they're looking for people who are ready to go, able to communicate who they are confidently and clearly, and can reveal what sets them apart from others. It's not about creating fabricated stories or "performing" a character. It's about being authentically *you* and being able to stay true to that, even under the pressures that reality TV brings. So, take the time to know yourself and practice sharing your story—not as an act, but as the most engaging, unapologetic version of *you*. That's what makes unforgettable Reality TV.

Photo Credit:
Centre for Ageing Better

WHEN IS IT OKAY TO CONTACT CASTING PROS? *HERE'S THE RIGHT APPROACH*

Let's set some expectations: randomly reaching out to casting pros and asking them to "keep you in mind" is generally not the way to go. While, yes, we do outreach and sometimes find potential fits through social media, expecting us to remember you with no prior interaction is asking a lot. Casting pros meet hundreds, sometimes thousands, of people per project and simply can't keep everyone in mind. We're not agents—our job is to cast for specific projects, not to find work for individual applicants.

The best time to reach out to a casting pro is when you see a current casting notice that interests you. Make sure you've applied first, and if you still want to follow up, keep your message short and focused. Following casting pros on social media or signing up for their newsletters can also keep you in the loop for new projects, but it's ultimately up to you to watch for open calls and apply.

How to Reach Out Effectively

Only contact a casting pro when they're actively casting. If you've already applied and want to increase your chances, you can send a brief DM or email with these essentials:

➔ **Greeting and Introduction**: Share your full name, age, height, weight, location, and occupation.

➔ **What Makes You Unique**: Briefly describe any qualities, experiences, or interests that set you apart and fit the show's vibe.

➔ **Specific Details from the Casting Notice**: Address any specific requirements listed in the casting notice (e.g., single for a dating show). If you're a fan of the show, highlight qualities the show typically looks for that you have. Mention what you'd bring to the show that hasn't been seen before.

➔ **Attach a Clear Picture**: Include a recent, unfiltered photo of just you—no group shots or professional actor headshots; casting pros want to see the real you.

Remember, keep it simple and to the point—bullet points are best for casting outreach. You're not telling a story with each bullet point; just write the answer. This approach makes it easy for casting pros to quickly assess if you're a fit, and if they're interested, they'll be more likely to locate your application. Send the message in two parts: 1) the text message, and 2) the photo. That's it. Each platform has different character limits, so tailor your message accordingly.

Note: This streamlined format is just for your initial outreach. When it comes to the application, be detailed! Write as you talk, make it engaging, and keep us wanting more.

Example Message

Hi [Casting Pro's Name], I would love to be considered for [Show Name]. I have already submitted my application. Here's a little about me:

➔ **Name**: [Your Full Name]

➔ **Age**: [Your Age]

➔ **Height**: [Your Height]

➔ **Weight**: [Your Weight]

➔ **Location**: [City, State]

➔ **Occupation**: [Your Job]

- **Unique Qualities**: [A few key traits, like "outgoing personality and fearless spirit"]
- **Specific Qualities for the Show**: [Briefly mention qualities that align with the show, like "competitive, passionate, loyal"]
- **What I Bring That's Never Been Seen Before**: [One unique trait or experience that makes you unforgettable]
- **Relationship Status**: Single (if relevant for a dating show)

Looking forward to the opportunity and hoping to connect! Thank you so much for considering my application.

Attach photo after the message.

When to Follow Up After a Phone Call or Virtual Interview

Once you've had an initial phone call with a casting team, if you aren't scheduled to meet with a casting director or producer within two weeks, it's likely that things may not be moving forward right now. However, Reality TV is unpredictable—networks and production companies often change their needs and sometimes revisit past candidates. The best approach? Let your application, phone interview, or virtual interview go out to the universe, and focus on living your life and making new memories for future applications. Casting is constantly evolving, and there's always a chance the team may circle back.

Avoid repeatedly reaching out for updates. Most of the time, casting pros won't have an answer to give right away, and if we've spoken with you, you're already on our radar. Casting teams work to present networks with multiple strong options, and we need you as much as you need us. If you're a match for what the show needs, trust that casting will reach out.

If you feel the need to follow up, it's best to wait until after your virtual interview and only reach out if you haven't received an update after 3-4 weeks. Keep in mind that casting pros are often managing many candidates, so responses can take time. Following up after a phone interview isn't typically recommended, but if you feel it's necessary, wait 3-4 weeks and keep your message brief.

Here's an example:

"Hi [Casting Pro's Name], this is [Your Full Name]. I had a [phone/virtual] interview on [Date]. Thank you again for the opportunity! If there are any updates you can share, I would greatly appreciate it."

Remember: Short and sweet is the way to go! Most casting teams will send a blanket email to thank everyone for their submissions once a show is fully cast.

Photo Credit:
ALLAN FRANCA CARMO

YOUR VOICE, YOUR STAGE: *A CRASH COURSE ON MUSIC COMPETITION SHOWS*

Gabby Samone
IG: @gabbysamonemusic

Imagine yourself singing in front of millions, with industry icons evaluating every note. Music competition shows could be your golden ticket to stardom. Don't think of them as a last resort; these shows offer serious exposure, powerful industry connections, and invaluable opportunities for growth as an artist. But here's the thing: knowing who you are as an artist is essential—but so is showing versatility.

There's a fine line between staying true to your style and demonstrating range. After six years of casting for *American Idol*, I've seen firsthand that most contestants show up with song choices only from their favorite genre. But versatility is what takes a singer from good to unforgettable. Being able to sing across genres not only prepares you for these competitions but expands your fan base and elevates your artistry.

The key to excelling in music competitions is being able to take any song, in any genre, and make it uniquely *yours*. When you can bring your signature sound to a variety of styles, it shows casting pros that you're adaptable, creative, and truly ready for the spotlight. Trust me, this approach will get casting pros excited about you and boost your chances of standing out. So, keep your unique style, but don't shy away from expanding your repertoire—casting pros love to see that you're ready for anything!

Why Music Competitions Are Your Secret Weapon

A music competition show is a crash course on the music industry, offering a whirlwind of real-world experiences that can launch your career in ways traditional paths might not. Here's why these shows are the ultimate platform for aspiring artists:

- ➔ **Exposure**: Imagine millions of viewers tuning in each week—this kind of visibility is nearly impossible to achieve independently. A high level of exposure like this can instantly boost your career, getting your name and voice out to potential fans, collaborators, and industry pros.
- ➔ **Mentorship**: You'll receive guidance from top professionals, including Grammy-winning artists, producers, and vocal coaches, who can offer invaluable insights on everything from technique to navigating the business side of music. Their advice and feedback will help you better understand what it takes to succeed in the industry.
- ➔ **Networking**: You'll have the chance to connect with industry insiders, including music execs, producers, and even former contestants who can offer advice and encouragement. Building these relationships can open doors to new opportunities, collaborations, and future projects.
- ➔ **Fan Base**: Music competition shows are perfect for building a loyal following, regardless of whether you win. By sharing your voice, story, and personality with millions, you can gain fans who will support your journey long after the show ends.
- ➔ **Personal Growth**: Each week brings challenges, critiques, and immense pressure, which push you to grow as a performer and hone your artistry. This process helps sharpen your skills, test your resilience, and strengthen your ability to handle high-stakes situations.
- ➔ **Real-World Experience**: Beyond the music itself, competition shows offer hands-on experience in the broader aspects of the music industry. From working with a production team and handling media interviews to performing on-demand and in front of live audiences, you'll be learning on the job. This real-world practice prepares you for the realities of the music industry.

Music competition shows offer you a unique blend of experience, exposure, and industry knowledge—a combination that's hard to find anywhere else. Embrace the process and let it prepare you not only to compete but to thrive in the music world.

Music Competition Casting Process

The casting process for music competition shows is a multi-step journey designed to discover exceptional talent with star potential. While every music competition has its own unique approach to casting, most follow a similar structure. Typically, the process begins with either virtual open calls or applications where contestants submit videos showcasing their vocal skills and stage presence. From there, casting teams review submissions, looking for standout qualities such as vocal ability, unique artistry, and a compelling backstory. Selected applicants may be invited to attend in-person or virtual callbacks, where they perform live for producers and casting directors. Personality interviews are often included to assess charisma and relatability, as these traits are crucial for audience connection. The final stages involve input from executive producers and network decision-makers, narrowing down contestants who not only have extraordinary talent but also fit the show's overall vision and narrative. The process is rigorous but provides an incredible platform for those ready to shine.

Pro Tips for Navigating the Music Competition Casting Process

Here are some tips to keep in mind, no matter where you are in the music competition casting process.

Pro Tip: Review the credits and take note of the casting professionals mentioned in this book who specialize in music competition shows. Reaching out to them with a short, thoughtful message and a video showcasing your talent can make a strong impression. If they're interested, they'll reach out to you.

Getting Competition-Ready: Building Your Song Choice Arsenal

One of the most challenging yet crucial parts of preparing for a music competition is choosing the right songs. Song choice can make or break a performance—it's not just about finding songs you enjoy but selecting ones that showcase your vocal range, stage presence, and artistic personality. Many contestants stumble here, but if you follow this plan for building a song arsenal, you'll be well-prepared and miles ahead of the game.

Build Your Song Choice Arsenal

Most shows require multiple song options, so it's smart to have a well-rounded selection. Here's a lineup to ensure you're ready for any scenario:

- ➔ **(3) Current Up-tempo Pop Hits (2024 or later)**: Choose high-energy songs that showcase your vocal abilities, stage presence, and unique flair. Pick crowd-pleasers that will make judges and audiences sit up and pay attention.
- ➔ **(3) Current Ballads (2024 or later)**: These selections should highlight your emotional depth and control. A strong ballad can create a powerful connection with the audience, letting them experience the soul of your voice.
- ➔ **(3) Up-tempo Pop Hits (pre-2024)**: Opt for songs that have stood the test of time, which gives you a chance to show off a familiar classic with your own twist. Pick an energetic song that highlights your range and shows you can bring a timeless hit to life.
- ➔ **(3) Ballads (pre-2024)**: Timeless ballads are great for showing off your vocal control and creating an emotional experience.

Choose songs that allow you to slow things down and make a lasting impression.

- **(3) Songs in Your Genre of Choice:** Prepare three songs in your genre: an original (if you have one), an up-tempo hit, and a ballad.
- **(3) Wild Cards**: These are your secret weapons! Choose an original song or something outside your typical genre to surprise the judges. Wild cards give you a chance to show versatility and stand out with a performance they'll remember.

Song Choice Tips

- **Make it Your Own**: Don't just imitate the original artist. Bring your unique style and personality to every song. Imagine this is **your** song, and you're recording it as if it were a release under your name. The judges and audience have already heard the original—now, they want to hear **your** take on it.
- **Make Every Note Count**: With limited time, each note is essential. Use every second to demonstrate why you deserve a spot on the show. Select songs and arrangements that you can perform consistently well. Avoid flat or missed notes—they will count against you. Know your vocal range and pick a piece that highlights your strongest abilities.
- **Think Outside the Box**: Get creative with your song choices and arrangements. Try experimenting with different genres and styles to show your versatility. Most music competition shows will have you performing various genres, so embrace a wide musical palette. Open up your playlist to incorporate all types of music and show that you're adaptable and unique.
- **Record Yourself During Practice:** Always make it a habit to record yourself when practicing. Watching and listening to your recordings allows you to see your performance from an audience's perspective and evaluate your vocal technique. It gives you insight into how you move, express emotions, and handle challenging notes. You'll be able to identify strengths to emphasize and areas to improve, like pitch, breath control, or timing. Recording yourself regularly also tracks your progress, showing how you're growing over time. Treat each recording as a valuable tool for refining your performance and making sure you're delivering your best.

Formatting Your Songs for Maximum Impact

- **60-90 Second Clips**: Each song should be a 60-90 second snippet that includes a **verse, chorus, and bridge.** This allows you to introduce the song, build momentum, and leave the judges wanting more.
- **Build to a Climax**: Choose the part of the song that showcases your vocal range and control, leading up to a powerful, memorable moment. Aim for a high note, a long belt, or a climactic point that becomes the highlight of your performance, showing off your full vocal potential.

Video Submission Tips

Casting pros want to see the real you, unfiltered and unpolished. Here's how to make your video submissions stand out:

- **Live Vocals ONLY**: This is essential. Lip-syncing or using pre-recorded tracks is a no-go. Casting pros are looking for raw talent, so show your voice as it really sounds—no music videos, big stage performances, or fancy effects.
- **Keep it Simple**: Unless a casting pro specifically requests a capella, always include some type of music accompaniment—whether it's a YouTube

instrumental, a karaoke track, or even a friend, teacher, or family member playing alongside you. From my experience with **American Idol,** a simple backing track or live accompaniment helps highlight your vocals and gives a fuller sense of your performance style without overpowering your voice.

➔ **Sing and Play (If You Can)**: If you play an instrument, consider showcasing that skill as well. However, only do so if you can perform both effortlessly—otherwise, it's better to focus on one at a time.

Building a song choice arsenal is about more than picking tunes you like; it's about understanding how each selection plays a role in your strategy. With the right preparation, you'll be able to show casting pros that you're versatile, unique, and ready for anything the competition throws at you.

Perfecting Your Virtual Audition for a Music Competition

Your virtual audition is your chance to showcase not only your talent but also your unique story. While many applicants might lead with "I've been singing since I was five" or "This is all I know how to do," those statements alone don't make you memorable. They're a part of your journey, but they don't tell the full story that captivates casting pros and audiences. A standout audition combines a powerful vocal performance with a compelling and relatable narrative.

Crafting a Compelling Story

Start by watching past music competition shows and analyzing how contestants tell their stories. You'll find that crafting your story for a music competition is much like preparing for any reality TV show—just with a few minor adjustments. Notice how each contestant's story goes beyond their love for music, often focusing on personal and impactful moments that help audiences connect on a deeper level. To create a memorable narrative, think beyond "music is my dream" and consider the experiences, relationships, and qualities that make you unique. Here are some elements that can help bring depth to your story:

➔ **Biggest Life-Changing Moment**: Reflect on an event or challenge that gave you a new perspective on life. What shaped you into who you are today?

➔ **Hidden Passions**: Is there something you're passionate about that people wouldn't expect? Whether it's a hobby, cause, or talent, sharing these details adds depth.

➔ **Cultural or Community Background**: Does your heritage or community influence your artistry? Highlight family traditions, values, or unique customs that shaped your journey.

➔ **Family Dynamics and Upbringing**: Describe your family background—does it add to your story in a way that shows resilience or support? How does your family feel about your dreams?

➔ **Educational Background**: Are you studying something unusual or unexpected? Sometimes academic pursuits that contrast with your music journey can add an intriguing layer.

➔ **Unique Talents or Tricks**: Do you have a quirky skill or talent that surprises people? This unexpected twist could make you memorable.

➔ **Unusual Hobbies**: Are you into something unique or unexpected? This can show another side of you that people won't expect.

➔ **Defining Relationships**: Who inspired your love for music? A family member, friend, or mentor who shaped your journey can reveal your values and passions.

- **Your "Why" for Singing**: Go beyond "this is my dream" and dig deeper. Do you want to inspire others or represent a cause? Being clear about your purpose can resonate with casting pros and audiences.
- **Unexpected Challenges**: Has there been a unique challenge in your life that shaped who you are? Sharing this adds relatability and depth.
- **Celebrity Adjacent Stories:** Have you crossed paths with a celebrity in a way that left a lasting impression or created a great story? Sharing this can make you stand out and showcase your unique experiences.

Your story is unique to you. Take the time to outline these elements and find the moments that will make you stand out. A well-crafted story can create a strong connection with the audience and turn a good audition into a memorable one.

How to Shine in Your Video or Virtual Audition

Once your story is polished, shift your attention to the technical setup and delivery of your video submission or virtual audition. Use these tips to ensure your environment, presentation, and performance showcase you at your very best.

1. Wear an Outfit That Stands Out

Choose an outfit that reflects your personality and makes you pop on camera. Opt for colors that flatter your skin tone and steer clear of anything too plain or muted. Your wardrobe is a powerful tool to make a memorable impression, so don't be afraid to be bold and showcase your style!

2. Choose a Background that Reflects Your Personality

Your backdrop should subtly highlight your personality while keeping the focus on you. Avoid plain, generic spaces, and do not use any actor backdrops, as they can feel impersonal and staged. Instead, choose a setting that gives casting pros insight into who you are, like a thoughtfully arranged area in your home. A personal, intentional background creates an authentic vibe that stands out. Never attend a virtual audition from a car or cafe—your setup should convey professionalism and effort, leaving a lasting impression.

3. Perfect Your Framing and Eye Contact

Position yourself with the camera at eye level, framing yourself from slightly below your waist to a few inches above your head. Looking directly into the camera will simulate eye contact, helping create a connection with casting pros. Consider using a computer stand, cell phone stand, or tripod to get the perfect angle. Explore options here: **https://icumusthaves.com/**

4. Optimize Lighting

Good lighting is crucial. Position a light source in front of you, like natural light from a window or a soft light lamp, to avoid shadows. If you need extra lighting, consider a ring light. **https://icumusthaves.com/**

5. Ensure a Quiet, Private Space

Choose a quiet, private room where you won't be interrupted. Background noise can be distracting, so make sure the space allows you to focus fully. Confirm your internet connection is stable for a smooth, uninterrupted experience.

6. Do a Test Run (Virtual Audition)

Before your virtual audition, practice using the same platform to ensure everything runs smoothly. Invite a friend or family member to join the call and give feedback on your audio, video quality, and lighting. Perform your full audition during the test, and if possible, record it to review and make any necessary adjustments before the big day.

Delivering a Winning Performance

1. **Engage with Your Audience**

   Treat the camera as your audience. Look directly into it to convey confidence and connection, using facial expressions and gestures to make the performance feel natural and engaging.

2. **Give It Your All—Don't Hold Back**

   Approach your audition as if you're performing on a big stage. Show casting pros you're ready for the spotlight by bringing energy and passion to every note or gesture. Treat it as if this is your moment at Madison Square Garden, fully embracing the performance. If you have any special skills or hobbies, find ways to weave them in—this is your time to stand out.

3. **Connect Emotionally with Your Song**

   Whether you're singing or telling your story, connect deeply with the emotions behind it. Understand and feel the story you're sharing; when you're emotionally invested, it resonates powerfully with your audience.

4. **Warm Up and Hydrate**

   Always warm up thoroughly before your audition or video recording. Run through vocal exercises to prepare, and stay hydrated for vocal clarity. Keeping water nearby is also helpful.

5. **Dress Like the Star You Are**

   Rock an outfit that makes you feel like the artist you envision! This is your moment, so bring your unique style and personality. Choose something bold that shows you're serious about your craft but aren't afraid to stand out. Imagine stepping onto the stage—dress like the star you know you are!

6. **Manage Nerves**

   Nerves are natural, so embrace them. Practice breathing exercises or perform in front of friends to ease anxiety. Nerves are a sign that you care about your performance, so channel that energy positively.

Final Checklist for Virtual Auditions and Video Recordings

- ➔ **Background with Personality**: Avoid plain blue or gray backgrounds—choose a space that reflects you.
- ➔ **No Need for a Microphone**: Casting pros want to hear your natural voice, so avoid mics or headphones.
- ➔ **Perfect Lighting**: Place lighting in front of you for clear, vibrant visuals.
- ➔ **Check Your Internet Connection**: Make sure your internet is reliable for smooth streaming.
- ➔ **Test with a Friend**: Do a run-through with a friend or family member to catch any issues.
- ➔ **Record Yourself**: Rehearse, record, and watch it back to catch areas for improvement.

With these steps, your virtual audition can be impactful and memorable, showcasing your true talent and personality. A well-prepared setup and a powerful, authentic performance will help you stand out and make a lasting impression. Good luck!

MASTERING YOUR REALITY TV APPLICATION: *TAILORED TIPS FOR EVERY GENRE*

Photo Credit:
RDNE Stock project

General: Applicable To All Genres

Capitalize on Exposure, but Keep it Genuine

While it's smart to think about how reality TV exposure might benefit you down the line, promoting your talent or business shouldn't be your only reason for applying. Casting pros can sense when someone's there only for self-promotion. Instead, view reality TV as a chance to grow, connect, and impact viewers genuinely. Strategize to make the most of it but don't make it your primary focus.

Handle Sensitive Topics with Care

If your story includes challenging experiences (such as trauma or abuse), think carefully about how you present them. While these moments may have shaped who you are, they may feel too intense for certain shows. Frame your experiences around resilience and growth, choosing details that align with the show's tone and that demonstrate your strength.

Understand the Show's Tone and Purpose

Each reality show has its own vibe and mission. Before applying, watch recent episodes to get a sense of the show's tone. This will help you tailor your story and responses to match the show's energy, whether it's fun and lighthearted or deeply introspective. This understanding makes your application feel more authentic and aligned with what casting pros are looking for.

Practice Telling Your Story Clearly and Concisely

Reality TV casting often requires video applications or interviews, where you'll have limited time to share your story. Practice summarizing who you are and what makes you unique in under two minutes to ensure your story lands with impact. This skill will help you stand out during interviews.

Know How to Answer "Why This Show?"

Casting pros appreciate applicants who know why they're drawn to a specific show. Prepare a short, genuine answer that expresses your passion for the show and connects your interests with its format or mission.

Stay Engaged and Responsive Throughout the Casting Process

In reality TV, schedules can change rapidly. Show casting pros that you're reliable, adaptable, and easy to work with by being responsive and prepared. Make sure to read and follow all instructions carefully, as casting pros often include small details that help you stand out.

Competition Shows

Make Votes Count: Develop a Social Media Strategy for Fan-Based Shows

If public voting is part of the show, a well-planned social media strategy from day one can make a huge difference. Here's how to keep fans engaged and voting, even if you're not managing it yourself:

1. **Get Your Team Ready**

   Select a trusted group of friends or family members to manage your social media presence while you're on the show. They should be reliable, creative, and fully supportive of your journey.

2. **Create a Fan Base Name**

   Choose a fanbase name that captures your personality and builds a sense of community. It makes it easier for fans to rally behind you and creates a memorable identity.

3. **Set Up a Mailing List**

   Establish a mailing list where fans can sign up for updates, exclusive content, or voting reminders. This allows you to keep fans engaged both during and after the show.

4. **Assign Regular Content Posters**

   Designate a lively, engaging friend or family member to post updates, share voting reminders, and interact with fans. If possible, have them go live during episodes to connect with viewers and add fun commentary.

5. **Encourage Fan Interactions**

   Use hashtags, graphics, and fan challenges to boost excitement. Creating a community through interactions makes fans feel actively involved in your journey.

Show Your Competitive Edge

Casting pros love seeing contestants with a strong, unique strategy. If the show involves strategy, describe how you'll approach the competition—whether it's through teamwork, alliances, or personal strengths like resilience or quick thinking.

Show Your Readiness for Physical and Mental Challenges

If the show involves high-stress environments, explain how you've handled similar situations before. Mention any past experiences that show you can handle pressure, as competition shows often test both physical and mental stamina.

Dating Shows

Approach with Genuine Intentions

If you're applying to a dating show, be ready to build a real connection. Viewers and casting pros can tell if someone isn't genuine, so show them you're genuinely invested in the experience and open to finding love.

Ensure You're Fully Single

Make sure your relationship status is unambiguous—whether single, divorced, or unattached. Ambiguity can raise concerns during casting, so be completely transparent.

Optimize Your Social Media for Consistency

Make your social media profile align with your dating show application. Include details like your age, location, height, occupation, and single status. Casting pros often check profiles to ensure they're consistent with your application.

Emphasize What You're Looking for in a Partner

Mention specific qualities you seek in a partner to help casting pros understand your personality and compatibility. Describe what makes a relationship meaningful to you.

Show Willingness to Be Vulnerable

Successful dating show contestants are often open about their emotions. Casting pros want to see that you're ready to share your journey and connect with someone deeply, so don't be afraid to show your more vulnerable side.

Be Playful and Open to New Experiences

Dating shows often feature fun and quirky activities. Show that you're open to trying new things, stepping out of your comfort zone, and embracing the adventure.

Ensemble Shows

Be Ready for Friendships—and Feuds

Ensemble shows thrive on diverse personalities and interactions. Show casting pros that you're comfortable in group settings and can handle both friendships and rivalries in an entertaining way.

Have Engaging Stories on Hand

Prepare personal anecdotes about friendships, funny memories, or unique life experiences. These relatable stories help casting pros see your personality and imagine you in group dynamics.

Illustrate Your Adaptability in Group Settings

Ensemble shows often involve navigating diverse personalities and conflicts. Share examples of how you've adapted to different group dynamics or resolved conflicts, showing that you can handle both harmony and drama.

Embrace Your Role in Friend Groups

Are you the leader, peacekeeper, or the life of the party? Mention your natural role in friend groups to help casting pros visualize how you'll fit into the ensemble.

Be Open About Flaws and Strengths Alike

Casting pros for ensemble shows appreciate well-rounded personalities, including both strengths and quirks. Don't hesitate to mention imperfections that add depth to your personality—this can make you more relatable to viewers.

Skill-Based Shows

Showcase Your Skills on Social Media

Casting pros for skill-based shows want to see your dedication to your craft. Post videos, tutorials, or examples of your work to demonstrate your talent and growth in your field.

Keep Improving and Learning

Skill-based shows are about growth as much as talent. Show that you're committed to learning and expanding your skill set, whether it's by taking classes, learning new techniques, or collaborating with others.

Describe Your Skill Development Journey

Explain how you started, the challenges you've faced, and key milestones in your craft. This adds depth to your application and shows that you're on a meaningful journey.

Highlight Unusual Techniques or Specializations

If you have a unique approach to your skill, mention it! Casting pros appreciate contestants who bring something distinct to the table, which can help you stand out.

Discuss Your Creative Process

Share a bit about how you approach projects or find inspiration. Casting pros love hearing how contestants think and create, as it adds richness to your skill set.

Show Consistent Commitment to Improvement

Casting pros value contestants who are continuously honing their craft. Share examples of workshops, classes, or projects you've done to keep improving. This dedication will reflect well on your passion for growth.

Share Your Future Goals and Aspirations in Your Craft

Mentioning your larger goals and aspirations demonstrates that you see the show as part of a bigger journey. Casting pros appreciate applicants who view the show as a stepping stone toward achieving their dreams.

These additions bring out the depth of your personality, skills, and intentions, showing casting pros that you're not only suited for their show but also bring a unique and authentic perspective. Tailor your approach to the specific genre and let your individuality shine.

Photo Credit: Parker Knigh

CASTING PROS SPILL: *WHAT NOT TO DO!*

Photo Credit:
Asjai Lou, CSA
www.AsjaiLouCasting.com
IG: @AsjaiLouCasting

Get ready for some straight talk from reality TV casting pros! This chapter dives into their biggest pet peeves—some points may come up more than once, which only emphasizes how crucial they are. These tips are gathered directly from a questionnaire sent to the casting pros featured in this book. Take each to heart, and make sure to avoid anything on this list. Think of it as your "Avoid at All Costs" guide for standing out the right way!

- ➔ Never burn bridges.
- ➔ Never try to be funny, like not taking the application seriously.
- ➔ Never ghost a casting team! If you are not able to make a scheduled interview or need to drop out of casting consideration for any reason, clearly communicate these changes to all parties immediately!
- ➔ When people lie to us during the casting process, if we don't think that you're lying immediately, Twitter will alert us.
- ➔ If you include your Instagram link, make sure you have a public profile!
- ➔ I've come across so many applicants who fail to fill out the complete application.
- ➔ I've seen people use catchphrases in audition videos that are very generic and explain nothing about who they are.
- ➔ Read the submission guidelines carefully. People apply for stuff they know they will not be available for or try to be unrealistic in their demands.
- ➔ Using filters on photos? We love to see just you!
- ➔ Never bug casting producers. If they like you, they will contact you.
- ➔ When you don't have a story or an example to back up your claim.
- ➔ Say "I know what you're looking for. I can be like this." Never tell the producer you are acting. Let the producer do the producing.
- ➔ Be late or a no-show!
- ➔ Our show ratings won't go up because of you, so find another selling point.
- ➔ Not being authentic.
- ➔ I would not flood anyone's inbox with a million messages asking for updates. If you get the show, they will reach out to you.
- ➔ The past tense of "cast" is still "cast." You have been CAST for a show, not CASTED.
- ➔ Give your Zoom interviews the time and attention you would give to a job interview: dress up, put on makeup, and do not do it from your car. If work kept you late or traffic was bad, reschedule! It is better to have you reschedule than to give a bad first impression.
- ➔ Constantly messaging/texting asking for updates on the role they were interviewed for or sending updated materials for them to be cast in future projects that are irrelevant to the casting call is annoying.
- ➔ Direct call or email a casting director's personal phone or email.
- ➔ Submit for something you are not right for per the guideline breakdown.
- ➔ Never leave one-word answers in an application. Always fill out the application fully. We want to hear your story!
- ➔ Submitting to too many shows or submitting multiple applications to the same show.
- ➔ If being asked for photos, make sure you submit photos that complement you and make you look like a star!
- ➔ Avoid applying to castings that don't pertain to you! Instead, follow our socials for updates on new projects.
- ➔ Submit a video with no energy, in the dark. That doesn't tell us anything.
- ➔ Make sure your smoke detector's battery is fresh so it doesn't beep during your interview.
- ➔ People faking who they are to fit a mold they feel we want. My biggest pet peeve is when applicants say they're "editing" themselves in interviews. Don't say what you think we want to hear. Just be you. We want to know who YOU are.
- ➔ People who don't understand timelines and never get their applications in on time or respond to messages quickly. Fill out

your application if applicable sooner rather than later!

- Entitled people
- I CANNOT stand it when applicants think it's acceptable to have a recorded Zoom call in their car or at a loud cafe.
- In a Zoom interview, Casting wants to be impressed by your personality first and foremost, not by your resume. The less perfect and more human your interview is, the more dynamic your ultimate casting pitch will be.
- People who MISS AUDITIONS, no call, no show any step of the way!
- Calling every single day to check on casting status incessantly. This is why it is important not to get applicants' hopes up too high.
- Trying to "play it cool." Stop it! It just comes off as boring! Get excited!
- "I have a bubbly personality." Show us. Don't tell us.
- You should never lie, the truth always comes out.
- Being monotoned and unenthusiastic, not acting excited to be there
- Giving short answers.
- Sending photos that are old, blurry, or with sunglasses on.
- Ooh, there's so many! Constantly nagging, being rude, and not following directions are huge pet peeves!
- Send multiple applications without filling in ALL required questions!
- My biggest pet peeves are when someone flat out says they want to be on a show to become famous or when someone shows up to their interview looking like they just rolled out of bed.
- Excuses. Period!
- Saying, "You need me, I'll make great ratings."-That's almost a guarantee not to make a show. We want authenticity.
- Flakiness. Tardiness. Entitlement. Being unprepared for a producer's session.
- Never submit an application without a working or correct phone number or email address.
- Bad lighting!
- Please look like your pictures, no cat fishing!
- People don't want to watch boring people on TV...show your personality!
- Sunglasses are A NON-STARTER IN CASTING ZOOMS!
- Applicant who doesn't follow instructions.
- Please be ON TIME for scheduled calls or zooms! If you're unable to make it, just send a message to let us know BEFORE the scheduled time and we will be happy to accommodate. Just don't leave us hanging.
- Please answer your phone. We want to get to know your personality and a text just doesn't cut it.
- Anyone who wants to participate in a show to "amplify their brand."
- Most shows do not care about your social media following. Lead with who you are and not what you portray yourself to be!
- No need to tag casting producers over and over again. We saw it for the first time!
- When potentials who look perfect on paper don't have an amazing personality when you speak to them on the phone or Zoom.
- When people are given the opportunity to record a video on their application to show how great they would be on TV. Instead, they upload a random video of them spitting in the sink or picking lint off their sweater or some such thing. Or they record their video in one take when they just woke up in bed expecting us to know

how they would look and act with full hair and makeup when they are awake and in full energy.

- Applicants calling or texting at all hours of the night
- Not reading Zoom instructions.
- Getting ghosted on Zoom interviews! Ghosting. It's so disappointing when someone amazing (who says they're excited to be a part of the show) stops returning calls or emails. Are you busy? Are you out? We'll stop reaching out if you let us know!
- People who apply to anything without ever reading the casting call and submission instructions.
- Not providing what is requested in the post.
- Vertical Video.
- Friend requests from actors.
- When talent shows up to a casting interview not camera-ready.
- When candidates only want to know about the money.
- Asking to send self-tapes in late when I've already written on the directions that the deadline is nonnegotiable
- Not reading the directions for a self-tape and emailing with questions that could be answered by reading the directions!
- People who don't read confirmation emails.
- When a show is done casting people still reach out asking if I'm still casting that show.
- Smoke detectors beeping during interviews —COME ON PEOPLE!
- Agents and actors submitting knowing they are not available.
- I hate when people don't bring fun exciting energy to a casting interview.
- When individuals submit their application and they start to message the entire casting team even after they put a certain casting producer's name on the application.

Photo Credit: Christina Morillo

TAKEAWAYS YOU *DON'T WANT* TO FORGET.

Photo Credit:
Asjai Lou, CSA
www.AsjaiLouCasting.com
IG: @AsjaiLouCasting

This checklist is your go-to guide for making a memorable impression in the reality TV casting process. Think of it as *you, amplified*—bringing the best, most vibrant version of yourself to the spotlight. Whether applying to a show or preparing for interviews, use this checklist to ensure you're putting your best foot forward. Remember: *You have to be in it to win it,* so apply to the shows that interest you and bring your whole, unique self!

General Tips

- **Be Authentic, Not Promotional:** Casting pros can spot insincerity a mile away. They want real people excited to share their stories—not people focused solely on promoting a business or talent.
- **Be the Biggest Version of Yourself:** Amplify your personality, quirks, and charm. Show casting pros what makes you stand out from the crowd.
- **Help Us Help You:** Don't hold back in showing who you are. Be open, vocal, and ready to stand out.
- **Genuine Interest in the Show's Themes:** If you're applying to a show with a specific focus (like cooking, travel, dating, or survival), show genuine enthusiasm for those themes.
- **Strong Emotional Intelligence:** Shows often test emotional resilience, so casting pros look for contestants who can read social cues, balance empathy with assertiveness, and handle intense situations.
- **Unfiltered and Open with Perspective:** Casting pros are drawn to people who aren't afraid to speak their mind and share honest opinions. If you're open, direct, and comfortable being yourself, you'll bring refreshing energy to the show.
- **Don't Just Apply to Everything — Apply With Intention:** Only submit to shows that **truly** fit you and that you've actually watched. Casting pros can tell when someone's just throwing their name at every opportunity. That "any show will do" energy doesn't work here. Know the tone, style, and purpose of the show — and only apply if it makes sense for **you**. Everyone isn't for everything, and that's okay.

Get Huntin'! Where to Find Casting Calls

- **Explore Network and Production Company Websites:** Go directly to the source. Start by checking the credits on your favorite shows to find out which production companies and networks create them. Keep a Google Sheet to track each company's website, social media profiles, and the names of key casting team members. Many networks and production companies regularly post casting calls on their websites and social media, so following them can keep you updated on new opportunities.
- **Social Media:** Follow the casting pros listed in this book, as they regularly share what they're casting on their social media, websites, or newsletters. Staying connected with casting pros is one of the best ways to stay in the loop on current

casting opportunities. Often, networks and production companies don't pass along applicants from their websites to casting pros until later in the process—following them directly keeps you ahead of the game.

- **Join the Casting Pros to Know App Waitlist:** An app is currently in development to showcase all casting opportunities specifically for everyday, real-people castings. Get on the waitlist to stay updated and be among the first to access it! **https://www.asjailoucasting.com/join-the-mailing-list**
- **Word of Mouth:** Got connections in the entertainment world? Let them know you're reality TV-ready. Personal recommendations can be gold.

Application Tips

- **Know the Show:** Watch episodes of the shows you're applying to so you understand the vibe, format, and type of contestants they tend to cast. Knowing the show inside and out can help you tailor your application to better fit their style.
- **Craft Your Story:** Showcase what makes you memorable. Think about life experiences, talents, or quirks that make you unique. Always have a story or example to back up anything you say.
- **Physical Stamina (for Physically Demanding Shows):** If you're applying to a show like **Ninja Warrior** or **Eco-Challenge**, physical fitness and endurance are key. If you're active and thrive under tough conditions, make sure to showcase that strength in your application.
- **Competitive Spirit:** Reality TV is all about high-stakes moments, and casting pros look for people who are genuinely competitive, passionate about achieving their goals, and not afraid to take a risk.
- **Creative Problem Solving:** Many shows throw twists and turns your way, so if you're quick on your feet and can think strategically under pressure, showcase this in your application.
- **Photos That Tell Your Story:** Use images that reflect your true self and life. Authenticity matters—so skip the filters and overly posed photos.
- **Social Media Presence:**
  - **Public Profile:** Keep your profile public, and make sure to include contact information, like an email or phone number, so casting can easily reach out.
  - **Informative Bio:** Use your bio to showcase what makes you unique and memorable.
  - **Highlight Your Interests:** Whether it's rock climbing, cooking, or any other hobby, share what you're passionate about to give casting pros a better sense of who you are.
  - **Be Real:** Let your social media reflect your true self. Avoid over-curating and let your posts showcase your genuine personality.
  - **Consistency with Application:** Ensure your social media presence aligns with what you share in your application. Include photos and videos that highlight the stories and personality traits you mention, creating a cohesive and authentic picture for casting pros.

Phone Interview Tips

- **Short, Impactful Answers:** Speak confidently and to the point without rushing. Think of each response as a "mini story."
- **Highlight What Sets You Apart:** Be ready to explain what makes you different from others, and let your personality shine.
- **Stay Upbeat:** A positive, energetic tone makes you stand out and leaves a lasting impression.

Virtual Interview Tips

- **Lighting and Sound:** Make sure the light source is in front of you to avoid shadows, and keep your sound quality clear.
- **Practice Makes Perfect:** Do a complete run-through on the platform your casting pro will be using (e.g., Zoom) with a friend or family member. Ask for feedback on your setup, lighting, and sound quality to ensure you're camera-ready.
- **Engaging Background:** Choose a background that reflects your personality. Avoid plain or overly staged backgrounds.
- **Look Into the Camera:** Keep eye contact to show confidence and connect with casting pros on the other side of the screen. If you're looking for lighting or framing accessories to enhance your virtual interview setup, check out this curated list of options: **https://icumusthaves.com/**

Music Competition Tips
Build Your Song Arsenal:

- Prepare a mix of current and classic songs to show off your range and versatility:
  - (3) Current Up-tempo Pop Hits (2024 or later)
  - (3) Current Ballads (2024 or later)
  - (3) Up-tempo Pop Hits (pre-2024)
  - (3) Ballads (pre-2024)
  - (3) Songs in Your Genre of Choice
  - (3) Wild Card songs to surprise and demonstrate versatility.
- **Format for Impact:** Each song should be a 60-90 second clip, structured with a verse, chorus, and bridge. Make sure to include a powerful climax that highlights your vocal range and leaves a lasting impression.
- **Make It Yours:** Don't mimic the original artist—bring your style to each song.
- **Showcase Versatility:** Experiment with different genres to demonstrate adaptability and range.

Video Submission Tips:

- **Live Vocals Only:** Casting pros want to hear your real voice—so no lip-syncing or pre-recorded tracks.
- **Keep It Simple:** Use a basic backing track, have a friend accompany you, or, if you can effortlessly play and sing on your own, go for it. This enhances your performance.

Performance Tips:

- **Dress the Part:** Treat every performance as if you're onstage. Dress intentionally, showing you're prepared for the spotlight.
- **Engage with Your Audience:** Treat the camera as your audience; make eye contact and use natural expressions to stay engaging.
- **Give It Your All:** Perform with full energy, as if you're on a big stage. Show off any unique skills to stand out.
- **Connect Emotionally:** Feel the emotions in your song or story—authenticity resonates with your audience.

Take Action, Be Patient, and Repeat

- **Don't Give Up:** Rejection is part of the journey. Use it to refine your story, build resilience, and sharpen your pitch.

- **Stay Positive:** The Reality TV world can be tough. Surround yourself with supportive people and celebrate every small win.
- **Keep Growing:** Embrace life fully each day—explore new hobbies, build your skills, and seek new experiences. Create memories that could become great stories; you never know what casting pros will find intriguing about you!

Dealing with Rejection

- **Accept Rejection Gracefully:** Rejections happen in casting. Remember, it's not personal—casting is about finding the right fit.
- **Celebrate Every Step:** Each callback, phone interview, and virtual interview is a milestone worth celebrating.
- **Stay Positive and Persistent:** If this opportunity doesn't work out, the next one might be right around the corner. Keep applying, keep showing up, and keep the momentum going.

With this checklist in hand, you're ready to dive into the Reality TV casting process with confidence, authenticity, and excitement. Amplify who you are, stay true to yourself, and always remember—casting pros are looking for you, just amplified!

Photo Credit: Mayim Luna

ADVICE FROM REALITY TV CASTING PROS:

Photo Credit:
Isaac Alvarez
www.isaacalvarez.com
IG: @isaacealvarez

In Pic:
Asjai Lou, CSA
www.AsjaiLouCasting.com
IG: @AsjaiLouCasting

Telon Weathington, CSA

We've gone over casting pros' biggest pet peeves—now let's dive into the advice they shared specifically for reality TV hopefuls. These insights, gathered from their responses to our questionnaire, are invaluable for anyone aiming to make an impact. Some advice may feel familiar, but that only reinforces its importance.

➔ There are so many places to find opportunities for free such as Instagram accounts, Facebook groups, and TikTok-use them! Also, make sure you have the best setup for interviews that you can. I promise the interviews aren't as scary as they sound—they're my favorite part of the job!

➔ If you apply for a show, make your profile public, list your location in your bio, include your email address, and keep an eye on that inbox.

➔ If you're applying for dating shows, you should have all of your social media pages public and more than three photos.

➔ "Be Yourself." Keep it 100% real. Be authentic and genuine. Show up as your authentic self and don't hold back! Authenticity is **the** key! We aren't looking for the next "Kim K." We are looking for the next YOU! Be yourself and share your stories...and spill the tea/ This is not a "role," we want to know about you! We love stories and examples, so for every answer we want to hear, "Like this one time..." or "For example..."It may seem silly, but there's only one of you in the world, and being yourself is what is going to set you apart from everyone else! Whether they love you or hate you, people will have to respect the realness. So go on, smile, have good energy, and be real! No one can beat you at being you! Throw out any ideas of who you think we want you to be. YOU are enough! Know that I am rooting for you as soon as I hop on the phone/zoom with you or you come into the room with me.

➔ If one thing is asked within castings, it would be that applicants need to be amplified (yet authentic) versions of themselves. When interviewing, just be yourself! Bring your sass, pizzazz, and a whole lot of jazz!

➔ Know who you are! Know what you're looking to gain from a show and make sure it is something you are truly interested in. Then the passion will come through in your audition. Make sure you never lose sight of the goals you have for your life and make sure you're doing it for the right reasons. If selected for a callback or an interview, be yourself and SHOW YOUR PERSONALITY!

➔ Getting cast is a huge opportunity to make your dreams come true, please respond to our communications ASAP. Otherwise, you might miss your shot!

➔ I've been on the other side of the camera and it can be brutal. Don't sign up for a show for the sake of "fame." Make sure you have the support of a community behind you before going out for a reality show. And if it doesn't work out, it's just showbiz. It's never a reflection of your quality as a person.

➔ Don't answer questions the way you THINK we want. We always want big, exciting talent, so don't be afraid to be yourself. Just be authentic.

➔ Be prepared and nice to your casting team. Get all required materials in when requested.

➔ Be professional. Also, please be on time and be prepared to talk about yourself, your interests, and why you want to be a cast member for that particular show.

- Have great lighting! LOOK YOUR BEST IF YOU GET SELECTED FOR A FACE-TO-FACE INTERVIEW!
- Use your nerves to give you energy. Use your hands when you talk.
- Bring your A game and shine bright like a diamond! We love to laugh and get to know the people we talk to who sparkle.
- Always ask more questions during the casting process to see if the opportunity really is right for you.
- Always be honest with yourself and others. Under no circumstances should you lie. Chances are, we will find out the lie so please be honest with yourself & your casting team throughout the process. We simply want to get to know the real YOU!
- Have thick skin and always be polite. First, find a show that speaks to you. Don't just apply to everything. In this business, there are way more Nos than Yeses but keep going. Not every show is meant for you, but you'll increase your chances of being selected if you fill up on life! Do things, learn things, and practice how to authentically share your excitement, frustrations, and true feelings. Just because you interview for one show and it may not work out doesn't mean that its the end of the road for all Reality TV castings. Keep exploring different options and going outside of your comfort zone. Keep in touch with the producers whom you meet along the way. Those who are truly passionate about this industry are passionate because we love to help people and see them succeed. Life begins at the end of your comfort zone.
- Don't hold any cards close to your chest when writing to or speaking to casting! Be unapologetically yourself! When filling out written applications for shows (typically the first step in a casting process) always write how you speak! NOT formally! We need to feel a sense of your candid personality and voice, even from your written answers! In unscripted, your personality is your talent!
- If you feel strongly about a show, even if you don't think you'd be a perfect fit, apply! You may end up being selected for another opportunity. Just Jump in. Just apply and see what happens! Don't put off applying for things that interest you, and the earlier you can apply the better! Always, always give it a shot!
- Don't treat interviews like you're applying for a job. We want to see your personality! Most importantly, have fun!
- Think about what might make you stand out and stories to back it up are always great! Everyone has a story, it's up to you to unravel the layers.
- These are the traits we look for as Casting Directors: You are the best at what you do. You wear your emotions on your sleeve and you run unfiltered.
- Talent and personality are a dime a dozen, so what makes you SPECIAL? Show us what makes you DIFFERENT and UNIQUE.
- Be open-minded and willing to talk with anyone
- Our best advice is to apply to shows as early as possible and if casting asks for anything, try to get it back to them as soon as possible.
- Don't let fear keep you from reaching out. You never know what you'll find. Applying for shows that actually fit your lifestyle is the way to go. Don't apply randomly to things that don't fit you. Keep applying for what you love. Sometimes it's all about timing! Odds are you will eventually

get chosen if you have the enthusiasm and passion.

- Enjoy the process and have fun.
- Work hard, stay optimistic! Have faith in yourself and hone your skill sets!
- When it comes to casting, we want to find the people who are most relatable, bold, or have a distinguishable characteristic/ aspect to their personality that makes us and the audience want to get to know them better.
- Be professional, authentic, and prepared. Be confident and true to who you are! Always bring high levels of energy to interviews and focus on what makes you unique! Don't wait to show it, bring your energy from the jump, and have fun with it. Being who you are is already unique enough on its own. :) Be the biggest version of yourself and people will mirror your energy!
- Watch a lot of Reality TV! Networks just want to recreate already successful formulas, so knowing these formulas goes a long way. Study the shows you love and understand the game!
- Post great content on your social media platforms, show off your lifestyle and big personality.
- Have no expectations. Value the experience.
- Be patient.
- Be kind!
- Be disarming.
- Stay in it.
- Don't give up!
- Always keep your mind open to new opportunities!
- Remain creative in the process.
- Casting teams are on YOUR SIDE! We want you to succeed and are working hard to make you look good. Help us help you. Don't hold back. Be you to the fullest! Be open to the entire process from the casting to the development to the actual show itself. Just be open. It's a marathon, not a sprint.
- Don't get too in your head for your auditions! Be prepared and bring good energy! Jump in, meet me, and let's take a shot at it. No wrong answers, just bring your energy, and let's DO THIS!
- Stay positive & keep trying for what you want! Be passionate, be open, be brave about what you want, and go get it!
- Buckle up! Also, don't burn bridges. It's a very small community.
- Keep knocking on the door. Someone will answer.

QUIZ: "WHAT *KIND OF* REALITY TV STAR ARE YOU?"

Before diving into the directory, let's have some fun! Picture this: the lights are on, the cameras are rolling, and millions are tuned in to watch your every move. What kind of reality TV sensation are you destined to become? Take this quiz to find out where you truly shine!

Instructions: For each question, choose the answer that best describes you. Keep track of your choices!

1. **Your ideal weekend involves:**
   - **A.** A 5-star spa retreat with my besties.
   - **B.** Backpacking solo through uncharted territory.
   - **C.** Throwing the most epic party the neighborhood has ever seen.
   - **D.** Renovating my entire kitchen... myself.
2. **People would describe you as:**
   - **A.** Glamorous, with a flair for the dramatic.
   - **B.** Fearless and always up for a challenge.
   - **C.** The life of the party, with a contagious laugh.
   - **D.** Determined, with a knack for problem-solving.
3. **Your dream job is:**
   - **A.** Fashion designer or high-profile influencer.
   - **B.** Stunt performer or professional adventurer.
   - **C.** Talk show host or stand-up comedian.
   - **D.** CEO of my own construction company.
4. **You're most likely to get into a debate about:**
   - **A.** The latest celebrity gossip.
   - **B.** The best survival strategies in extreme conditions.
   - **C.** Who has the funniest viral meme?
   - **D.** The most efficient way to build something.
5. **When facing a setback, you:**
   - **A.** Cry a little, then strategize my comeback.
   - **B.** Dust yourself off and keep pushing forward.
   - **C.** Find the humor in it and turn it into a great story.
   - **D.** Analyze what went wrong and come up with a better plan.
6. **How do you handle drama or a challenging situation?**
   - **A.** Take a breath, but I'm ready with a clever comeback if needed.
   - **B.** Stay calm and tackle it head-on without letting it shake me.
   - **C.** Try to find the humor in it—sometimes you just have to laugh!
   - **D.** Step back, assess the situation, and make a plan to resolve it.

Time to Tally Your Results!

Mostly As: The Drama Queen/King

You thrive on high-stakes situations, bold fashion choices, and a healthy dose of shade. Audiences are drawn to your glamorous style and sharp comebacks.

Perfect for: *Real Housewives* style shows and dating competitions.

Strengths: You're bold, memorable, and radiate confidence.

Weaknesses: Your directness can sometimes spark extra drama!

Star Tip: Embrace the spotlight but stay grounded—audiences love a relatable Queen or King!

Your Ideal Show: You're made for glamorous reality TV shows where you can rule the screen with confidence and style.

Mostly Bs: The Adventurer

You're always ready for the next thrill, whether it's scaling mountains or taking on wild challenges. You're fearless, brave, and perfect for shows that push limits.

Perfect for: *Survivor, The Amazing Race,* or any extreme challenge show.

Strengths: Fearless, determined, and thrive under pressure.

Weaknesses: You may be so focused on the next thrill that quieter moments don't excite you as much.

Adventure Advice: Keep that bravery shining, but remember to share the quieter moments, too. Audiences love depth!

Your Ideal Show: You belong on extreme adventure shows where every day is a new thrill, and pushing limits is the name of the game.

Mostly Cs: The Class Clown

Your infectious energy and quick wit keep everyone laughing. You bring humor to any situation, and fans can't get enough of your entertaining antics.

Perfect for: Comedy challenges, *Big Brother* style social experiment shows.

Strengths: Your humor is magnetic, keeping energy high and audiences entertained.

Weaknesses: Sometimes, it's hard for people to take you seriously.

Spotlight Tip: Keep the laughs coming, but don't be afraid to show your serious side—it makes you even more dynamic!

Your Ideal Show: Comedy or ensemble reality shows are perfect for you—anywhere you can bring the fun and connect with others.

Mostly Ds: The Mastermind

With ambition, skill, and determination, you're ready to tackle anything head-on. People admire your problem-solving skills and hands-on approach.

Perfect for: Renovation shows, business competitions, or any show that requires creativity and strategy.

Strengths: You're strategic, focused, and know how to bring ideas to life.

Weaknesses: Spontaneity or letting loose may feel challenging.

Winning Advice: Show your journey! Audiences love seeing what drives your motivation and focus.

Your Ideal Show: You'd excel on a reality show that tests your creativity, strategic skills, or talents—where your persistence and talent will shine.

Final Thought: Remember, this quiz is just for fun! Reality TV loves a mix of personalities, so don't feel boxed in by your type. Now that you know a little more about your Reality TV style, jump into the directory and explore the casting pros who are ready to find the next big star—just like you!

Tag & Share: Got your result? Share it with **@asjailoucasting @CastingProstoKnow on Instagram** and tag **#WhatKindOfRealityTVStarAreYou**!

DIRECTORY OF REALITY TV CASTING PROS

Casting Pros to Know: Reality TV Edition - Directory

This directory key provides insight into the unique expertise, identities, and professional affiliations of the casting professionals featured in the *Casting Pros to Know: Reality TV Edition*. Each label highlights qualifications or lived experiences, ensuring you're connecting with individuals who bring cultural authenticity, industry expertise, and a commitment to representing real people authentically. These identifiers celebrate the diversity of professionals shaping reality TV.

Directory Key Descriptions

LGBTQI

- **What It Stands For:** Lesbian, Gay, Bisexual, Transgender, Queer (or Questioning), and Intersex.
- **What It Represents:** Professionals who identify within the LGBTQI community, bringing their lived experiences and cultural insight to casting.

CSA

- **What It Stands For:** Casting Society (formerly Casting Society of America).
- **What It Represents:** Membership in this prestigious organization, signifying a casting professional's credibility, expertise, and adherence to high industry standards.

AA (African American)

- **What It Stands For:** African American.
- **What It Represents:** Professionals who identify as African American, offering cultural authenticity and a deep understanding of the African American experience in their casting work.

BIPOC

- **What It Stands For:** Black, Indigenous, and People of Color.
- **What It Represents:** Professionals who identify within the BIPOC community, showcasing their ability to authentically represent and amplify the stories of diverse communities.

Why the Directory Key Matters

This key is a quick reference to help identify the unique qualifications and identities of casting professionals in the directory. Whether through lived experience or professional affiliations, these experts are dedicated to fostering inclusivity, cultural authenticity, and meaningful representation in reality TV. By working with these professionals, you're ensuring that real stories and real people are celebrated on screen.

NAME:	aaron nitido.	LGBTQI	LOCATION:	Los Angeles, California
TITLE:	Casting Associate			
CASTS FOR:	Unscripted			
CASTING HIGHLIGHTS:	The Bachelor, Beat Shazaam, Supermarket Sweep, Married at First Sight, Baking It Season 2, Password, The One That Got Away, Marriage Story (background casting)			
AWARDS:			CASTING COMPANY:	Kinetic Content
INSTAGRAM:	https://www.instagram.com/yourcastingfriend/?hl=en		IMDB:	https://www.imdb.com/name/nm11202750/
FACEBOOK:			FACEBOOK GROUP:	
EMAIL:	aanitido@gmail.com		LINKEDIN:	https://www.linkedin.com/in/aaron-nitido/
TIKTOK:			TWITTER:	
WEBSITE:			MAILING LIST LINK:	

NAME:	adrian wells.	LGBTQI	LOCATION:	New York, New York
TITLE:	Commercials and Unscripted			
CASTS FOR:				
CASTING HIGHLIGHTS:	Real Housewives Of Potomac Seasons 1-8, Summer House Martha's Vinyard Season 2, Real Housewives Of Atlanta Season 14& 15, Blood, Sweat, & Heels Season 1, 90 Day Fiance Season 2, and MTV True Life : I Am Genderqueer			
AWARDS:	GLAAD Award for MTV True Life 2016		CASTING COMPANY:	AdrianWellsCasting
INSTAGRAM:	https://www.instagram.com/ian.adrian/?hl=en		IMDB:	https://m.imdb.com/name/nm5187167/
FACEBOOK:	https://m.facebook.com/adrian.wellscastingpage		FACEBOOK GROUP:	
EMAIL:			LINKEDIN:	https://www.linkedin.com/in/adrian-wells-29978b5
TIKTOK:			TWITTER:	
WEBSITE:			MAILING LIST LINK:	

NAME:	alexa pellerin.	**LOCATION:**	Los Angeles, CA
TITLE:	Casting Producer, Casting Associate		
CASTS FOR:	Reality, TV		
CASTING HIGHLIGHTS:	VH1: Hall of Men, TLC: Untitled Dating Show, NBC: College Bowl, ABC: Untitled Prank Show, FOX: I Can See Your Voice		
AWARDS:		**CASTING COMPANY:**	
INSTAGRAM:	https://www.instagram.com/alexapellerin/?hl=en	**IMDB:**	https://m.imdb.com/name/nm6555672/
FACEBOOK:	https://www.facebook.com/alexa.pellerin/	**FACEBOOK GROUP:**	
EMAIL:	Alexapellerincasting@gmail.com	**LINKEDIN:**	https://www.linkedin.com/in/alexa-pellerin-588717132
TIKTOK:	https://www.tiktok.com/@alexapellerin	**TWITTER:**	https://twitter.com/alexapellerin
WEBSITE:	https://linktr.ee/alexapellerin	**MAILING LIST LINK:**	

NAME:	alexa zappia.	**LOCATION:**	Williamsville, New York
TITLE:	Casting Associate		
CASTS FOR:	Unscripted		
CASTING HIGHLIGHTS:	The Bachelor (ABC), Big Brother Canada (Global), Love is Blind (Netflix), Don't Forget the Lyrics (FOX), The Hustler (ABC), Worst Cooks in America (Food Network), The Julia Child Challenge (Food Network), Supermarket Sweep (ABC), Claim to Fame (ABC), Married at First Sight (Lifetime), Love for the Ages (NBC), The One That Got Away (Amazon Prime), Asking for a Friend (TVOne), Obsessed With My Mate (TLC), International Love (NBC).		
AWARDS:		**CASTING COMPANY:**	
INSTAGRAM:	https://instagram.com/zappiacasting/	**IMDB:**	https://m.imdb.com/name/nm11469705/
FACEBOOK:		**FACEBOOK GROUP:**	
EMAIL:	Zappiacasting@gmail.com	**LINKEDIN:**	
TIKTOK:	https://www.tiktok.com/@zappiacasting	**TWITTER:**	
WEBSITE:		**MAILING LIST LINK:**	

NAME:	alexander sharp.	LOCATION:	New York City, NY
TITLE:	Casting Producer		
CASTS FOR:	Reality		
CASTING HIGHLIGHTS:	Big Brother (CBS) Twentysomethings (Netflix)Chopped (Food Network) Big Shot with Bethenny (HBO Max)		
AWARDS:		CASTING COMPANY:	
INSTAGRAM:	https://www.instagram.com/sharp_casting/	IMDB:	https://www.imdb.com/name/nm11147482/?ref_=nv_sr_srsg_1
FACEBOOK:		FACEBOOK GROUP:	
EMAIL:	alexandersharpcasting@gmail.com	LINKEDIN:	https://www.linkedin.com/in/sharpalexander/
TIKTOK:		TWITTER:	
WEBSITE:	www.alexsharpcasting.com	MAILING LIST LINK:	

NAME:	alexandra schween.	LOCATION:	Sherman Oaks, California
TITLE:	Casting Associate, Casting Producer, and Casting Recruiter		
CASTS FOR:	Commercials, Film, Scripted, Theatre, and Unscripted		
CASTING HIGHLIGHTS:	20 Something Project-Netflix, Lego Masters-FOX, Prank Panel-ABC, Ellen's Game of Games-NBC, Beat Shazam-FOX, Dont Forget The Lyrics-FOX, 24 Hours to Hell and Back-FOX, The Chase-ABC, The Wheel-NBC		
AWARDS:		CASTING COMPANY:	S&S Casting
INSTAGRAM:	https://www.instagram.com/aschweener/	IMDB:	
FACEBOOK:		FACEBOOK GROUP:	
EMAIL:	castingschween@gmail.com	LINKEDIN:	
TIKTOK:		TWITTER:	
WEBSITE:		MAILING LIST LINK:	

NAME:	alexis best.		LOCATION:	Los Angeles, CA
TITLE:	Casting Manager			
CASTS FOR:	Unscripted			
CASTING HIGHLIGHTS:	The Challenge USA (CBS), The Challenge (MTV), Buddy Games (CBS), Real World (MTV/Facebook Watch), Watch Out for the Big Grrrls (Amazon Prime), Family or Fiancé (OWN), I Survived Bear Grylls (TBS)			
AWARDS:			CASTING COMPANY:	
INSTAGRAM:	https://www.instagram.com/alexisbcast/		IMDB:	
FACEBOOK:			FACEBOOK GROUP:	
EMAIL:			LINKEDIN:	
TIKTOK:	https://www.tiktok.com/@alexisbcast		TWITTER:	
WEBSITE:			MAILING LIST LINK:	

NAME:	alissa carlton.	CSA	LOCATION:	Los Angeles, California
TITLE:	Casting Director and Head of Casting			
CASTS FOR:	Unscripted			
CASTING HIGHLIGHTS:	Making the Cut, Project Runway, The Real World			
AWARDS:	2024 Nominee-Artios Award; Outstanding Achievement in Casting-Reality Series-Competition, Making the Cut, 2017 & 2018 Nominee-Primetime Emmy; Outstanding Casting for a Reality Program, Project Runway		CASTING COMPANY:	Vital Casting — VITALCASTING
INSTAGRAM:	instagram.com/vitalcasting		IMDB:	https://www.imdb.com/name/nm3798858/
FACEBOOK:			FACEBOOK GROUP:	
EMAIL:	alissa@vitalcasting.com		LINKEDIN:	
TIKTOK:			TWITTER:	
WEBSITE:	www.vitalcasting.com		MAILING LIST LINK:	

NAME:	allison kaz.		CSA	LOCATION:	Los Angeles
TITLE:	Casting Director				
CASTS FOR:	Reality				
CASTING HIGHLIGHTS:	LEGO MASTERS, TWENTY SOMETHINGS, MAKING IT, BAKING IT, MY KIND OF COUNTRY, FOODTASTIC, LOVE ISLAND, TEMPTATION ISLAND, MILLION DOLLAR ISLAND				
AWARDS:				CASTING COMPANY:	
INSTAGRAM:	https://www.instagram.com/castingkaz/			IMDB:	
FACEBOOK:	https://www.facebook.com/allison.kaz			FACEBOOK GROUP:	
EMAIL:	castingkaz@gmail.com			LINKEDIN:	
TIKTOK:	https://www.tiktok.com/@castingkaz			TWITTER:	
WEBSITE:	www.castingkaz.com			MAILING LIST LINK:	

NAME:	amanda ogen.			LOCATION:	Los Angeles, CA
TITLE:	Casting Associate				
CASTS FOR:	Unscripted				
CASTING HIGHLIGHTS:	Love is Blind, Big Brother, FBoy Island, Don't Forget the Lyrics, The Real Love Boat, Queen of the Universe				
AWARDS:				CASTING COMPANY:	
INSTAGRAM:	https://www.instagram.com/amandaogen/			IMDB:	https://www.imdb.com/name/nm10565951/
FACEBOOK:				FACEBOOK GROUP:	
EMAIL:	amandaogencasting@gmail.com			LINKEDIN:	
TIKTOK:	https://www.tiktok.com/@amandaogen			TWITTER:	
WEBSITE:				MAILING LIST LINK:	

NAME:	amberlee mucha.	LGBTQI	LOCATION:	Chicago, IL and LA, CA
TITLE:	Head of Casting			
CASTS FOR:	Film and Unscripted			
CASTING HIGHLIGHTS:	Help I Wrecked My House, Hometown Takeover, Revealed			
AWARDS:			CASTING COMPANY:	Verano Productions (Verano Productions)
INSTAGRAM:	https://www.instagram.com/p/Cz4m5LhC2Bc/		IMDB:	https://www.imdb.com/name/nm3301939/?ref_=nv_sr_srsg_2_tt_0_nm_3_q_amberlee%2520mucha
FACEBOOK:	https://www.facebook.com/amberleecasting/		FACEBOOK GROUP:	
EMAIL:	veranoproductions@gmail.com		LINKEDIN:	
TIKTOK:			TWITTER:	
WEBSITE:			MAILING LIST LINK:	

NAME:	amina mamaty.	AA	LOCATION:	New York, NY
TITLE:	Casting Producer			
CASTS FOR:	Reality, Commercial, TV			
CASTING HIGHLIGHTS:	Real Housewives of Potomac 5,6,7, Real Housewives of Atlanta 14,15, Are You The One, Finding Prince Charming			
AWARDS:			CASTING COMPANY:	
INSTAGRAM:	instagram.com/produceramina		IMDB:	
FACEBOOK:			FACEBOOK GROUP:	
EMAIL:			LINKEDIN:	www.linkedin.com/in/amina-mamaty-9a158640
TIKTOK:			TWITTER:	
WEBSITE:			MAILING LIST LINK:	

NAME:	anjelique williams.		LOCATION:	Houston, Texas
TITLE:	Casting Associate, Casting Producer, and Casting Recruiter			
CASTS FOR:	Unscripted			
CASTING HIGHLIGHTS:	Food Network's- Chopped OWN's-Family or Fiancé, MTV's The Challenge Hulu's-(NEW) Lisa Vanderpump Show (Untitled) airing Spring -Summer 2024, Surviving Bear Grylls w/ Bear Grylls WEtv- Love After Lock up OWN's Like Mother, Like Daughter			
AWARDS:			CASTING COMPANY:	Bunim Murray Productions
INSTAGRAM:	https://www.instagram.com/a.made.mois.elle/		IMDB:	
FACEBOOK:			FACEBOOK GROUP:	
EMAIL:	Msanjeliquewilliams@gmail.com		LINKEDIN:	www.linkedin.com/in/anjelique-williams-9b44b367
TIKTOK:			TWITTER:	
WEBSITE:			MAILING LIST LINK:	

NAME:	anna sturgeon.	CSA	LOCATION:	Covington, Kentucky
TITLE:	Casting Director and Casting Producer			
CASTS FOR:	Commercials and Unscripted			
CASTING HIGHLIGHTS:	Nailed It S1-S11, Nailed It Holidays S1-S3, Nailed It Big Baking Challenge, Too Hot to Handle S2-S4, Floor is Lava S2 & S3 (2021), Prisoner of Love (2021), Top Chef Amateurs S1 & S2 (2020-2021), The Ride That Got Away S2 (2020), Rebel Without A Crew (2017), Bar Rescue (Host/Celeb Casting) (2023), The Great American Baking Show S4 (2022), The Price of Glee: Docu-Series (2022), Fight to Survive (2022), Love Island S3 & S4 (2021-2022), Haute Dog S2 & S3 (2020), F-Boy Island (2020), American BBQ Showdown (2019), Sugar Rush S1-S5 (2017-2019), Project Runway S17 (2018), Cold Justice S5 (2017-2018) Shine On! (2017)			
AWARDS:			CASTING COMPANY:	
INSTAGRAM:	https://www.instagram.com/annacasting		IMDB:	https://www.imdb.com/name/nm5257349/
FACEBOOK:			FACEBOOK GROUP:	
EMAIL:	me@annasturgeon.com		LINKEDIN:	
TIKTOK:			TWITTER:	
WEBSITE:	www.annasturgeon.com		MAILING LIST LINK:	

NAME:	arian fay.	LOCATION:	Los Angeles, California
TITLE:	Casting Director, Casting Producer		
CASTS FOR:	Reality, TV, Film		
CASTING HIGHLIGHTS:	The Ultimatum on Netflix, Married at First Sight on Lifetime, Pop Goes the Vet on Animal Planet, Chasing the Cure on TBS, Ancient Aliens on History, Basketball Wives on VH1, True Life on MTV		
AWARDS:		CASTING COMPANY:	
INSTAGRAM:	https://www.instagram.com/a_isforappletini/	IMDB:	https://m.imdb.com/name/nm7744958/
FACEBOOK:	Facebook.com/Arian.m.Fay	FACEBOOK GROUP:	
EMAIL:	Arianfay89@gmail.com	LINKEDIN:	https://www.linkedin.com/in/arian-fay-76857811
TIKTOK:		TWITTER:	
WEBSITE:		MAILING LIST LINK:	

NAME:	ariel panzer.	LOCATION:	Los Angeles, California
TITLE:	Casting Director and Casting Producer		
CASTS FOR:	Unscripted		
CASTING HIGHLIGHTS:	American Idol, The Voice, I Can See Your Voice, World of Dance, AGT		
AWARDS:		CASTING COMPANY:	
INSTAGRAM:	https://instagram.com/arielpanzer?utm_source=qr	IMDB:	https://www.imdb.com/name/nm6297065/
FACEBOOK:		FACEBOOK GROUP:	
EMAIL:		LINKEDIN:	
TIKTOK:		TWITTER:	
WEBSITE:		MAILING LIST LINK:	

NAME:	ashanti strange.	AA	LOCATION:	Atlanta, GA
TITLE:	Casting Director, Casting Associate, Casting Assistant			
CASTS FOR:	Reality, TV, Film			
CASTING HIGHLIGHTS:	What happens in group chat			
AWARDS:			CASTING COMPANY:	
INSTAGRAM:	https://www.instagram.com/castingyourdreams/		IMDB:	https://www.imdb.com/name/nm9666590/
FACEBOOK:			FACEBOOK GROUP:	
EMAIL:	ashantistrangecasting@gmail.com		LINKEDIN:	www.linkedin.com/in/ashanti-strange-6b1190177
TIKTOK:			TWITTER:	
WEBSITE:			MAILING LIST LINK:	

NAME:	ashley goldson.	AA and BIPOC	LOCATION:	Hollywood, CA
TITLE:	Casting Assistant, Casting Associate, Casting Producer, and Casting Recruiter			
CASTS FOR:	Film and Unscripted			
CASTING HIGHLIGHTS:	Too Hot to Handle-w/ Fremantle, Love Island-City Media Ent., Love Language-Sharp Entertainment Temptation Island-Doron Ofir Casting, Too Hot to Handle-Doron Ofir Casting			
AWARDS:			CASTING COMPANY:	AGoldsun Casting
INSTAGRAM:	https://www.instagram.com/agoldsuncasting/		IMDB:	https://www.imdb.com/name/nm10897111/
FACEBOOK:			FACEBOOK GROUP:	
EMAIL:	Agoldsuncasting@gmail.com		LINKEDIN:	
TIKTOK:			TWITTER:	
WEBSITE:	Www.agoldsuntv.com		MAILING LIST LINK:	

NAME:	ashley wilson.		LOCATION:	Miami, FL
TITLE:	Casting Producer			
CASTS FOR:	Reality, New Media, TV			
CASTING HIGHLIGHTS:	Casting Producer, BRAVO "Real Housewives of Potomac" 2022, OWN "Ready to Love: Miami" 2022, TV One "For My Man" 2016, Casting Associate Producer, VH1 "My Celebrity Dream Wedding" 2021 Casting Associate, Snapchat "Phone Swap Miami" Snapchat 2020, VH1 "Love and Hip Hop New York" 2019-2020, Extras Casting Director, USA Network "Temptation Island" 2019, Casting Recruiter, ABC "The Bachelorette" 2016, Investigation Discovery "House of Horrors" 2016			
AWARDS:			CASTING COMPANY:	AWM
INSTAGRAM:	instagram.com/digitalinfluence.tv		IMDB:	
FACEBOOK:	Facebook.com/digitalinfluence.tv		FACEBOOK GROUP:	
EMAIL:	ashleyekwilson@icloud.com		LINKEDIN:	
TIKTOK:	TikTok.com/@thewilsonera		TWITTER:	
WEBSITE:	AshleyWilsonMedia.com		MAILING LIST LINK:	digitalinfluence.app

NAME:	asjai lou.	CSA AA , BIPOC and LGBTQI	LOCATION:	Los Angeles, CA
TITLE:	Casting Director, Casting Producer, Casting Associate			
CASTS FOR:	Reality, Commercial			
CASTING HIGHLIGHTS:	American Idol, Big Brother, Don't Forget The Lyrics, Real Housewives of Atlanta, The Great Christmas Light Fight, Put A Ring on It, The Cut, Married at First Sight: Honeymoon Island, Ready to Love			
AWARDS:	2024 and 2025 CSA Artios Award nominee		CASTING COMPANY:	
INSTAGRAM:	https://www.instagram.com/asjailoucasting/		IMDB:	https://www.imdb.com/name/nm11556777/
FACEBOOK:	https://www.facebook.com/asjailoucasting/		FACEBOOK GROUP:	
EMAIL:	assistant@asjailoucasting.com		LINKEDIN:	https://www.linkedin.com/in/asjailoucasting
TIKTOK:	https://www.tiktok.com/@asjailoucasting		TWITTER:	
WEBSITE:	https://asjailoucasting.com/		MAILING LIST LINK:	https://forms.gle/5zQUVhN58YwvbDbj8

NAME:	audra bryant.		AA and BIPOC	LOCATION:	Los Angeles, CA
TITLE:	Casting Associate and Casting Producer				
CASTS FOR:	Unscripted				
CASTING HIGHLIGHTS:	Jeopardy, America's Got Talent, Judge Steve Harvey, Ready to Love, Queen's Court, Buddy Games				
AWARDS:				CASTING COMPANY:	
INSTAGRAM:	https://www.instagram.com/abcasting1/			IMDB:	
FACEBOOK:				FACEBOOK GROUP:	
EMAIL:	AudraCasting@gmail.com			LINKEDIN:	https://www.linkedin.com/in/audrabryant
TIKTOK:				TWITTER:	
WEBSITE:				MAILING LIST LINK:	https://docs.google.com/forms/d/e/1FAIpQLSf1AKIW_VZ9BKIoLWsaIX-hdSLFnIRMUFD5_o8MoObMvIj91Hw/viewform?pli=1

NAME:	audrey annison.			LOCATION:	Los Angeles, CA
TITLE:	Casting Producer				
CASTS FOR:	Unscripted				
CASTING HIGHLIGHTS:	Queer Eye, Love Island, Alone, Hell's Kitchen, Pawn Stars				
AWARDS:				CASTING COMPANY:	ITV America
INSTAGRAM:	https://www.instagram.com/audrey.annison.casting/			IMDB:	https://www.imdb.com/name/nm6864417/
FACEBOOK:				FACEBOOK GROUP:	
EMAIL:	audrey.annison@itv.com			LINKEDIN:	
TIKTOK:				TWITTER:	
WEBSITE:				MAILING LIST LINK:	

NAME:	audrey pine wright.		LOCATION:	Studio City, California
TITLE:	Casting Associate, Casting Director, and Casting Producer			
CASTS FOR:	Unscripted			
CASTING HIGHLIGHTS:	American Idol Season 20, 21, 22			
AWARDS:			CASTING COMPANY:	APW
INSTAGRAM:	https://www.instagram.com/audreypinewright/?utm_source=qr		IMDB:	
FACEBOOK:	https://www.facebook.com/audpinewright		FACEBOOK GROUP:	
EMAIL:	audpinewright@icloud.com		LINKEDIN:	https://www.linkedin.com/in/audrey-pine-wright-apw-918a892/
TIKTOK:			TWITTER:	
WEBSITE:			MAILING LIST LINK:	

NAME:	avery richardson.	LGBTQI	LOCATION:	Los Angeles & Nashville
TITLE:	Casting Associate			
CASTS FOR:	Unscripted			
CASTING HIGHLIGHTS:	Naked and Afraid, Dance Moms: Reboot, Netflix's Outlast			
AWARDS:			CASTING COMPANY:	
INSTAGRAM:	https://www.instagram.com/lady_ave_/		IMDB:	
FACEBOOK:			FACEBOOK GROUP:	
EMAIL:	avrichardson24@gmail.com		LINKEDIN:	
TIKTOK:			TWITTER:	
WEBSITE:			MAILING LIST LINK:	

NAME:	bernette fondong. AA and BIPOC	**LOCATION:**	Washington, District of Columbia
TITLE:	Casting Assistant and Casting Associate		
CASTS FOR:	Unscripted		
CASTING HIGHLIGHTS:	The Ultimatum, 90 Day Fiancé, Twin Love, Buddy Games, Transfarmation		
AWARDS:	ITV won an emmy for Queer Eye as I worked there. Bunim-Murray won an emmy for Watch Out for the Big Grrrls while I worked there.	**CASTING COMPANY:**	Watt Pictures
INSTAGRAM:	https://www.instagram.com/bernetteisqueen/	**IMDB:**	
FACEBOOK:		**FACEBOOK GROUP:**	
EMAIL:	bernettefondong@gmail.com	**LINKEDIN:**	
TIKTOK:	https://www.tiktok.com/@bernetteisqueen	**TWITTER:**	
WEBSITE:		**MAILING LIST LINK:**	

NAME:	beverly tan.	**LOCATION:**	Los Angeles, CA
TITLE:	Casting Director		
CASTS FOR:	Reality, Commercial		
CASTING HIGHLIGHTS:	Love Off the Grid, Love in Paradise, Money Court, My Celebrity Dream Wedding, Heartbroke		
AWARDS:		**CASTING COMPANY:**	
INSTAGRAM:	https://www.instagram.com/beverlytanfilm/	**IMDB:**	https://www.imdb.com/name/nm6481849/
FACEBOOK:		**FACEBOOK GROUP:**	
EMAIL:	beverlytancasting@gmail.com	**LINKEDIN:**	https://www.linkedin.com/in/beverlytan/
TIKTOK:	https://www.tiktok.com/@beverlycasting	**TWITTER:**	
WEBSITE:	https://linktr.ee/beverlytan	**MAILING LIST LINK:**	

NAME:	bobby silva.	AA, BIPOC, and LGBTQI	LOCATION:	Kailua, Hawaii
TITLE:	Casting Producer			
CASTS FOR:	Unscripted			
CASTING HIGHLIGHTS:	Squid Game, The Challenge, Race to Survive S2 The Mole, Players, Mud Madness American Ninja Warrior 14, Race to Survive-Alaska Exposure S2, The Dog Games, The Mole, American Ninja Warrior 13 Dodgeball Thunderdome, Great American Baking Show Ultimate Surfer, Escaping History Married at First Sight, Million Dollar Mile, Love is Blind			
AWARDS:			CASTING COMPANY:	
INSTAGRAM:	https://www.instagram.com/suproducerhero/		IMDB:	https://www.imdb.com/name/nm1468523/
FACEBOOK:			FACEBOOK GROUP:	
EMAIL:			LINKEDIN:	
TIKTOK:			TWITTER:	
WEBSITE:	https://beardologist.com/		MAILING LIST LINK:	

NAME:	brandon powell.	LGBTQI	LOCATION:	Los Angeles,CA
TITLE:	Casting Producer			
CASTS FOR:	Unscripted			
CASTING HIGHLIGHTS:	The One-TvOne, Milf Manor-TLC, Rhythm & Flow-Netflix			
AWARDS:			CASTING COMPANY:	
INSTAGRAM:	https://www.instagram.com/mr.b33_/		IMDB:	
FACEBOOK:	https://www.facebook.com/brandon.b.powell.7		FACEBOOK GROUP:	
EMAIL:	Castedbybrando@gmail.com		LINKEDIN:	https://www.linkedin.com/in/brandon-powell-03b3621b3/
TIKTOK:			TWITTER:	
WEBSITE:			MAILING LIST LINK:	

NAME:	bryan ricke.	LOCATION:	Los Angeles, CA
TITLE:	Casting Editor		
CASTS FOR:	Unscripted		
CASTING HIGHLIGHTS:	Next in Fashion, Summer House, F-Boy Island, Lovers and Liar, The Great American Recipe, $100k Pyramid		
AWARDS:		CASTING COMPANY:	
INSTAGRAM:	https://www.instagram.com/bryanricke/	IMDB:	
FACEBOOK:		FACEBOOK GROUP:	
EMAIL:	bryan.j.ricke@gmail.com	LINKEDIN:	
TIKTOK:		TWITTER:	
WEBSITE:		MAILING LIST LINK:	

NAME:	cara weissman.	LOCATION:	New York, NY
TITLE:	Casting Director		
CASTS FOR:	Unscripted		
CASTING HIGHLIGHTS:	Pawn Stars, Wife Swap, House Hunters International, What Not to Wear, Pyramid Game Show, Match Me Abroad, Young and Pregnant, My True Crime Story, Psychic Kids, I Love a Mamas Boy, Hotel Intervention, My Super Sweet 16		
AWARDS:	Peabody Award (Half of Us); Emmy Nomination, (Cause/Effect) Outstanding Series: Special Class	CASTING COMPANY:	CW CARA WEISSMAN Casting Director
INSTAGRAM:	https://www.instagram.com/cara_castingdirector/	IMDB:	https://m.imdb.com/name/nm2185516/
FACEBOOK:		FACEBOOK GROUP:	
EMAIL:	GuestCasting@gmail.com	LINKEDIN:	https://www.linkedin.com/in/caraweissmancasting
TIKTOK:		TWITTER:	
WEBSITE:		MAILING LIST LINK:	

NAME:	christian estrada. BIPOC and LGBTQI	LOCATION:	Los Angeles, CA
TITLE:	Casting Producer		
CASTS FOR:	Unscripted		
CASTING HIGHLIGHTS:	Big Brother, American Idol, Love is Blind, The Great Food Truck Race, Making the Cut, Nailed It, The Real World, Bad Girls Club, Are You The One?, Born This Way, Survivor		
AWARDS:	2015-2016 Primetime Emmy Award-Born This Way-Contributions for Outstanding Unstructured Reality Program 2016-2017 Primetime Emmy Award-Born This Way-Contributions for Outstanding Casting For A Reality Program	CASTING COMPANY:	
INSTAGRAM:	https://www.instagram.com/chrisecasting/	IMDB:	
FACEBOOK:		FACEBOOK GROUP:	https://www.facebook.com/groups/realitytvcastings
EMAIL:	christianestradacasting@gmail.com	LINKEDIN:	https://www.linkedin.com/in/chrisecasting/
TIKTOK:	https://www.tiktok.com/@chrisecasting	TWITTER:	
WEBSITE:		MAILING LIST LINK:	

NAME:	christina calisi. CSA LGBTQI	LOCATION:	New York + Fire Island
TITLE:	Casting Director, Casting Editor, and Casting Recruiter		
CASTS FOR:	Commercials, Film, and Unscripted		
CASTING HIGHLIGHTS:	Ugliest House In America, House hunters, Alone, Martha gets down and dirty, Martha knows best, Big Brother, Kitchen Crash		
AWARDS:		CASTING COMPANY:	Christina Calisi Casting
INSTAGRAM:	https://instagram.com/ccalisicasting/	IMDB:	https://m.imdb.com/name/nm6645337/
FACEBOOK:		FACEBOOK GROUP:	
EMAIL:	cc@ccalisicasting.com	LINKEDIN:	https://www.linkedin.com/company/christina-calisi-casting/
TIKTOK:		TWITTER:	
WEBSITE:	Ccalisicasting.com	MAILING LIST LINK:	

NAME:	christine cavalieri.		LGBTQI	LOCATION:	Los Angeles, California
TITLE:	Casting Director and Casting Producer				
CASTS FOR:	Commercials and Unscripted				
CASTING HIGHLIGHTS:	Crime Nation- CW, Case Files- CBS, My Killer Body with K. Michelle- Lifetime, Pokemon- YouTube, Digital Addiction- A & E, To Tell the Truth- ABC, America's Funniest Home Videos- ABC, Kentucky Derby Doc.- Netflix				
AWARDS:				CASTING COMPANY:	Real2Reel Casting
INSTAGRAM:	https://www.instagram.com/real2reelcasting/?hl=en			IMDB:	https://www.imdb.com/name/nm2172999/
FACEBOOK:				FACEBOOK GROUP:	
EMAIL:	christine@real2reelcasting.com			LINKEDIN:	
TIKTOK:				TWITTER:	
WEBSITE:	https://www.real2reelcasting.com/			MAILING LIST LINK:	

	costas nicolas.		CSA LGBTQI	LOCATION:	Los Angeles, California
TITLE:	Casting Associate, Casting Director, Casting Producer, and Casting Recruiter				
CASTS FOR:	Commercials, Scripted, and Unscripted				
CASTING HIGHLIGHTS:	The Mole, Netflix | The Ultimatum, Netflix | Fast: Home Rescue, Weather Channel | Flip To A Million, HGTV | Building Off The Grid, Discovery | BULL, CBS (Scripted), An Unexpected Killer, Oxygen				
AWARDS:				CASTING COMPANY:	Costa Casting
INSTAGRAM:	https://www.instagram.com/costacasts/			IMDB:	https://www.imdb.com/name/nm3558519/
FACEBOOK:				FACEBOOK GROUP:	
EMAIL:	costa@tvcastingdirector.com			LINKEDIN:	
TIKTOK:				TWITTER:	
WEBSITE:	www.CostaCasting.com			MAILING LIST LINK:	

NAME:	cynthia simpson.	AA and BIPOC	LOCATION:	Brooklyn, New York
TITLE:	Casting Director			
CASTS FOR:	Unscripted			
CASTING HIGHLIGHTS:	Chopped, Married At First Sight, 60 days in			
AWARDS:	Emmy winning producer		CASTING COMPANY:	Cynthia-Knows.com
INSTAGRAM:	https://www.instagram.com/naturalcyn/?hl=en		IMDB:	
FACEBOOK:			FACEBOOK GROUP:	
EMAIL:			LINKEDIN:	
TIKTOK:			TWITTER:	
WEBSITE:	https://cynthia-knows.com		MAILING LIST LINK:	

NAME:	darren moore.	AA, BIPOC, and LGBTQI	LOCATION:	Hammonton, New Jersey
TITLE:	Casting Associate, Casting Director, Casting Editor, and Casting Producer			
CASTS FOR:	Commercials, Film, and Unscripted			
CASTING HIGHLIGHTS:	Finding Magic Mike, Relative Race, Iyanla Fix My Life, Nailed It			
AWARDS:			CASTING COMPANY:	Freelance
INSTAGRAM:	http://www.instagram.com/getmooredarren		IMDB:	
FACEBOOK:			FACEBOOK GROUP:	
EMAIL:	seemoorecasting@gmail.com		LINKEDIN:	
TIKTOK:			TWITTER:	
WEBSITE:			MAILING LIST LINK:	

NAME:	debbie pierre.	AA and BIPOC	**LOCATION:**	Roselle Park, New Jersey
TITLE:	Casting Associate and Casting Producer			
CASTS FOR:	Unscripted			
CASTING HIGHLIGHTS:	Love Island USA, Married At First Sight, Love Is Blind, The Circle, 90 Day Fiance			
AWARDS:			**CASTING COMPANY:**	DP
INSTAGRAM:	https://www.instagram.com/dpcastingtv/		**IMDB:**	
FACEBOOK:			**FACEBOOK GROUP:**	
EMAIL:	dpcasting01@gmail.com		**LINKEDIN:**	
TIKTOK:			**TWITTER:**	
WEBSITE:			**MAILING LIST LINK:**	

NAME:	dena holtz.		**LOCATION:**	Remote
TITLE:	Casting Associate and Casting Producer			
CASTS FOR:	Theatre and Unscripted			
CASTING HIGHLIGHTS:	MasterChef, Big Brother			
AWARDS:			**CASTING COMPANY:**	Reality Casting
INSTAGRAM:	https://www.instagram.com/producer_dena/		**IMDB:**	
FACEBOOK:	https://www.facebook.com/dena.holtz		**FACEBOOK GROUP:**	
EMAIL:	dmhcasting@gmail.com		**LINKEDIN:**	https://www.linkedin.com/in/denaholtz
TIKTOK:	https://www.tiktok.com/@producer_dena		**TWITTER:**	
WEBSITE:			**MAILING LIST LINK:**	

NAME:	desiree duckett.	AA and BIPOC	LOCATION:	Brooklyn, New York
TITLE:	Casting Producer			
CASTS FOR:	Commercials, Film, Scripted, and Unscripted			
CASTING HIGHLIGHTS:	The Bachelor, The Bachelorette, Ink Master, Queer Eye, Forged in Fire, Inmate to Roommate, How Far is Tattoo Far, Bakers Dozen, Find Love Live			
AWARDS:			CASTING COMPANY:	
INSTAGRAM:	https://www.instagram.com/desiduck23/		IMDB:	
FACEBOOK:			FACEBOOK GROUP:	
EMAIL:	Desiree.duckett@gmail.com		LINKEDIN:	
TIKTOK:			TWITTER:	
WEBSITE:			MAILING LIST LINK:	

NAME:	diona mankowitz.	CSA BIPOC, AA	LOCATION:	Los Angeles, CA
TITLE:	Founder/Owner			
CASTS FOR:	TV, Reality, Commercials			
CASTING HIGHLIGHTS:	Netflix's Love is Blind, HGTV's House Hunters, and Lifetime's Married at First Sight			
AWARDS:			CASTING COMPANY:	DIVERGENT CONTENT
INSTAGRAM:	https://www.instagram.com/divergent.content/		IMDB:	https://www.imdb.com/name/nm11384752/
FACEBOOK:			FACEBOOK GROUP:	
EMAIL:	diona@divergentcontent.com		LINKEDIN:	
TIKTOK:			TWITTER:	
WEBSITE:	https://www.divergentcontent.com/		MAILING LIST LINK:	

NAME:	doron ofir.	LGBTQI	LOCATION:	Los Angeles, California
TITLE:	Casting Director			
CASTS FOR:	Unscripted			
CASTING HIGHLIGHTS:	Jersey Shore, Rupauls Drag Race, American Idol, Legends of the Hidden Temple, Temptation Island, Rich Kids of Beverly Hills, Bridezillas			
AWARDS:	3 time-Reality Televison Awards-Outstanding Docu-Series, Outstanding Returning Cast, Outstanding Casting		CASTING COMPANY:	POPULAR PRODUCTIONS
INSTAGRAM:	https://www.instagram.com/doronofircast/		IMDB:	https://m.imdb.com/name/nm1416532/
FACEBOOK:			FACEBOOK GROUP:	
EMAIL:	Doronofircasting@gmail.com		LINKEDIN:	
TIKTOK:			TWITTER:	
WEBSITE:	Doronofircasting.com		MAILING LIST LINK:	

NAME:	easton edwin.	CSA	LOCATION:	New York
TITLE:	Casting Director			
CASTS FOR:	Unscripted			
CASTING HIGHLIGHTS:	Ugliest House in America, Swiping America, Haunted, Deadline: Crime with Tamron Hall, Dragnificent!			
AWARDS:			CASTING COMPANY:	Easton Maz Casting
INSTAGRAM:	https://www.instagram.com/eastonmaxcasting/		IMDB:	https://www.imdb.com/name/nm7085947/
FACEBOOK:			FACEBOOK GROUP:	
EMAIL:			LINKEDIN:	https://www.linkedin.com/in/eastonedwin/
TIKTOK:			TWITTER:	
WEBSITE:	http://Www.Eastonmaxcasting.com		MAILING LIST LINK:	

NAME:	emily eldridge.		LOCATION:	Los Angeles, CA
TITLE:	Casting Director, Casting Producer, and Head of Casting			
CASTS FOR:	Unscripted			
CASTING HIGHLIGHTS:	Shark Tank, Fox Snake Oil, CNBC Money Court, HGTV House Hunters Renovation, TLC Toddler's & Tiaras			
AWARDS:			CASTING COMPANY:	
INSTAGRAM:	https://www.instagram.com/eetvcasting/?hl=en		IMDB:	https://www.imdb.com/name/nm5828129/
FACEBOOK:	https://www.facebook.com/eetvcasting		FACEBOOK GROUP:	
EMAIL:	eetvcasting@gmail.com		LINKEDIN:	https://www.linkedin.com/in/emilyreldridge
TIKTOK:			TWITTER:	
WEBSITE:			MAILING LIST LINK:	

NAME:	emma green.	CSA	LOCATION:	Los Angeles, CA
TITLE:	Casting Director			
CASTS FOR:	Commercials, Film, Scripted, and Unscripted			
CASTING HIGHLIGHTS:	America's Got Talent, Jungle, Deep Water, Swimming For Gold, Lunatics			
AWARDS:			CASTING COMPANY:	FILM/ TV+ COMMERCIAL EMMA GREEN CASTING
INSTAGRAM:	https://www.instagram.com/emmagreencasting/		IMDB:	https://pro.imdb.com/name/nm2543084/
FACEBOOK:			FACEBOOK GROUP:	
EMAIL:	emmagreen.au@gmail.com		LINKEDIN:	https://www.linkedin.com/in/emmagreencasting/
TIKTOK:			TWITTER:	
WEBSITE:	www.emmagreencasting.com		MAILING LIST LINK:	https://cutt.ly/CastMe

NAME:	eric paul flores.	LGBTQI	LOCATION:	Chino, CA
TITLE:	Casting Associate and Casting Producer			
CASTS FOR:	Unscripted			
CASTING HIGHLIGHTS:	24 Hours To Hell and Back, Bar Rescue, Fear Factor, Multiple Game Show Network Shows Dr. Phil House Call			
AWARDS:			CASTING COMPANY:	
INSTAGRAM:	https://instagram.com/ef__cast-ing_?igshid=YTQwZjQoNmIoOA%3D%3D&utm_source=qr		IMDB:	https://www.imdb.com/name/nm9474719/?ref_=ext_shr_lnk
FACEBOOK:			FACEBOOK GROUP:	
EMAIL:	erikleazure@me.com		LINKEDIN:	https://www.linkedin.com/in/erik-leazure-a4743260
TIKTOK:			TWITTER:	
WEBSITE:			MAILING LIST LINK:	

NAME:	erik leazure.	LGBTQI	LOCATION:	Los Angeles, California
TITLE:	Casting Manager			
CASTS FOR:	Commercials and Unscripted			
CASTING HIGHLIGHTS:	The Bachelor, The Bachelorette, Bachelor In Paradise, Bachelor Summer Games, Bachelor Winter Games, Bachelor: Listen to your Heart, Catfish			
AWARDS:			CASTING COMPANY:	NZK Productions / ABC
INSTAGRAM:	https://www.instagram.com/guyinjeans/		IMDB:	https://m.imdb.com/name/nm6174881/
FACEBOOK:			FACEBOOK GROUP:	
EMAIL:	erikleazure@me.com		LINKEDIN:	https://www.linkedin.com/in/erik-leazure-a4743260
TIKTOK:			TWITTER:	
WEBSITE:			MAILING LIST LINK:	

NAME:	erin tomasello.	LOCATION:	Los Angeles, California
TITLE:	Casting Director		
CASTS FOR:	Unscripted		
CASTING HIGHLIGHTS:	Got to Get Out, Traitors season 1, All seasons of The Circle		
AWARDS:	Emmy winner	CASTING COMPANY:	Real and Diverse Casting
INSTAGRAM:	https://www.instagram.com/castingerin/?hl=en	IMDB:	https://www.imdb.com/name/nm3089002/
FACEBOOK:		FACEBOOK GROUP:	
EMAIL:	erikleazure@me.com	LINKEDIN:	https://www.linkedin.com/in/erik-leazure-a4743260
TIKTOK:		TWITTER:	
WEBSITE:	https://erin.live-website.com	MAILING LIST LINK:	

NAME:	francine dauw. LGBTQI	LOCATION:	Los Angeles, CA
TITLE:	Head of Casting		
CASTS FOR:	Commercials, Film, Scripted, Theatre, and Unscripted		
CASTING HIGHLIGHTS:	TLC's Dr. Pimple Popper, TLC's Too Large, TLC's 1000 Best Friends, TLC's Body Parts, TLC's Dr. Down Below, TLC's Bad Hair Day, Lifetime's Supernanny, Lifetime's This Time Next Year, Netflix's Dogs, Cat People, Queer Eye, WeTv's Commit or Quit, Discovery's The Bond, Amazon's Jury Duty, A&E's Cold Case Files, MTV's Catfish, Spike's Bar Rescue		
AWARDS:	Nominated for a 2022 Daytime Emmy for Outstanding Casting-Netflix's DOGS.	CASTING COMPANY:	Aberrant Creative (ABERRANT CREATIVE)
INSTAGRAM:	https://www.instagram.com/aberrant_creative/	IMDB:	https://www.imdb.com/name/nm3591008/?ref_=nv_sr_srsg_0_tt_0_nm_8_q_francine%2520dauw
FACEBOOK:		FACEBOOK GROUP:	
EMAIL:	casting@aberrantcreative.com	LINKEDIN:	
TIKTOK:		TWITTER:	
WEBSITE:	https://www.aberrantcreative.com	MAILING LIST LINK:	

NAME:	hayley weinstein.		LOCATION:	Los Angeles, California
TITLE:	Head of Casting			
CASTS FOR:	Unscripted			
CASTING HIGHLIGHTS:	The Price is Right, The Price is Right at Night, My Feet Are Killing Me, Chasing the Cure with Ann Curry, Finding Adventure, Date My City, Greed, Weakest Link. The Pack, Intervention-Philly, Extreme Makeover (PS season), Loe Connection with Pat Bullard			
AWARDS:	CSA Artios nominee for Intervention-Epidemic		CASTING COMPANY:	Hippodrum Casting
INSTAGRAM:	https://www.instagram.com/hippodrumcasting/		IMDB:	https://www.imdb.com/name/nm2542726/
FACEBOOK:			FACEBOOK GROUP:	
EMAIL:	hippodrumcasting@gmail.com		LINKEDIN:	
TIKTOK:			TWITTER:	
WEBSITE:			MAILING LIST LINK:	

NAME:	heather downie.	CSA	LOCATION:	Los Angeles, CA
TITLE:	Casting Director			
CASTS FOR:	Commercials and Unscripted			
CASTING HIGHLIGHTS:	Blowing LA, Undercover Billionaire, The Rev, Little Women: LA, Married at First Sight (Season 1), Little Women: NY, Hot and Heavy, Little Life on the Prairie			
AWARDS:	Member of the Television Academy		CASTING COMPANY:	Neon Pancake
INSTAGRAM:	https://www.instagram.com/neonpancakecasting/		IMDB:	https://www.imdb.com/name/nm4434333/
FACEBOOK:			FACEBOOK GROUP:	
EMAIL:	heather@neonpancake.com		LINKEDIN:	
TIKTOK:			TWITTER:	
WEBSITE:	neonpancake.com		MAILING LIST LINK:	

NAME:	heidi hill.	CSA / AA and BIPOC	LOCATION:	North Hollywood, California
TITLE:	Casting Director and Casting Producer			
CASTS FOR:	Scripted and Unscripted			
CASTING HIGHLIGHTS:	Queen's Court (NBCU/Peacock), Ready To Love (OWN), The American BBQ Showdown (Netflix), Project Runway (Bravo), Dated & Related (Netflix), Beat Shazam (FOX), The Cube (TBS), Ultimate TAG (FOX), Hell's Kitchen (FOX), Bar Rescue (Spike TV), Homestead Rescue (Discovery), Clipped! (HGTV), Craftopia (HBO Max), Kids Baking Championship (Food Network), Kids Say The Darndest Things (ABC)			
AWARDS:			CASTING COMPANY:	Heidi Hill Casting
INSTAGRAM:	https://www.instagram.com/heidihillcasting/		IMDB:	https://www.imdb.com/name/nm2311681/
FACEBOOK:	https://www.facebook.com/HeidiHillCasting/		FACEBOOK GROUP:	
EMAIL:	heidihillcasting@gmail.com		LINKEDIN:	https://www.linkedin.com/in/heidi-hill-csa-95a8a314/
TIKTOK:			TWITTER:	
WEBSITE:			MAILING LIST LINK:	

NAME:	ian connor.		LOCATION:	New York City / Los Angeles
TITLE:	Casting Producer			
CASTS FOR:	Reality, Scripted, and Theatre			
CASTING HIGHLIGHTS:	Squid Game: The Challenge (Netflix), Big Brother (CBS), Love Island USA (CBS / Peacock), The Circle (Netflix), The Bachelorette (ABC), Next Level Chef (Fox), Too Hot To Handle (Netflix), The Courtship (NBC), Floor Is Lava (Netflix), American Idol (ABC), Becoming A Pop Star (MTV), Digital Addiction (A&E), The Au Pairs (Dutch TV Series), Generation Gap (ABC)			
AWARDS:			CASTING COMPANY:	
INSTAGRAM:	https://instagram.com/iancasting		IMDB:	https://imdb.me/ianbconnor
FACEBOOK:	https://www.facebook.com/iancasting/		FACEBOOK GROUP:	
EMAIL:			LINKEDIN:	https://www.linkedin.com/in/ian-b-connor-9585b2b6
TIKTOK:	https://www.tiktok.com/@iancasting?_t=8VttUFjTVRW&_r=1		TWITTER:	
WEBSITE:	www.IanCasting.com		MAILING LIST LINK:	www.IanCasting.com

NAME:	jaimie beebe.	LOCATION:	Los Angeles, California
TITLE:	Casting Associate, Casting Director, Casting Producer, and Casting Recruiter		
CASTS FOR:	Commercials, Film, Scripted, and Unscripted		
CASTING HIGHLIGHTS:	Believers, Homestead Rescue, 90s House, Stranded with a Million Dollars, Big Brother		
AWARDS:		CASTING COMPANY:	Jaimie Casting
INSTAGRAM:	https://www.instagram.com/feathergirl77/	IMDB:	https://pro.imdb.com/name/nm2350551
FACEBOOK:		FACEBOOK GROUP:	
EMAIL:	jaimiecasting@gmail.com	LINKEDIN:	
TIKTOK:		TWITTER:	
WEBSITE:		MAILING LIST LINK:	

NAME:	jamie shaffer.	LOCATION:	Atlanta, GA
TITLE:	Casting Producer		
CASTS FOR:	Reality, TV		
CASTING HIGHLIGHTS:	My Killer Body, The Great Christmas Light Fight, Temptation Island		
AWARDS:		CASTING COMPANY:	
INSTAGRAM:	https://www.instagram.com/why_not_jamie/	IMDB:	
FACEBOOK:		FACEBOOK GROUP:	
EMAIL:		LINKEDIN:	
TIKTOK:		TWITTER:	
WEBSITE:		MAILING LIST LINK:	

NAME:	jasmine chavira.	LOCATION:	Atlanta, Georgia
TITLE:	Casting Associate		
CASTS FOR:	Unscripted		
CASTING HIGHLIGHTS:	VHI my dream celebrity wedding (ATL) Own Network My big fat family reunion		
AWARDS:		CASTING COMPANY:	Jasmine chavira casting
INSTAGRAM:	https://www.instagram.com/ferrarostarmusic1/	IMDB:	
FACEBOOK:		FACEBOOK GROUP:	
EMAIL:	Jasminechaviracasting@gmail.com	LINKEDIN:	
TIKTOK:		TWITTER:	
WEBSITE:		MAILING LIST LINK:	

NAME:	jason preston.	LOCATION:	Los Angeles, California
TITLE:	Casting Director		
CASTS FOR:	Commercials, Scripted, and Unscripted		
CASTING HIGHLIGHTS:	Nailed It, Hood Adjacent, Naked & Afraid, Bar Rescue, House Hunters, Addicted, True Life, the Profit, Backyard Stand-Up Show		
AWARDS:		CASTING COMPANY:	Freelance
INSTAGRAM:	https://www.instagram.com/goodbadunknown/	IMDB:	https://www.imdb.com/name/nm1063872/
FACEBOOK:		FACEBOOK GROUP:	
EMAIL:	jasonpaulpreston@gmail.com	LINKEDIN:	
TIKTOK:		TWITTER:	
WEBSITE:		MAILING LIST LINK:	

NAME:	jazzy collins.	CSA BIPOC, AA	LOCATION:	Los Angeles, CA
TITLE:	Casting Director			
CASTS FOR:	Reality, Commercial			
CASTING HIGHLIGHTS:	Lizzo's Watch Out For The Big Grrrls, The Circle, The Bachelor, The Bachelorette, LEGO, The Traitors			
AWARDS:	Emmy Winner for Outstanding Casting For a Reality Program 2023-The Traitors, Emmy Nomination for Outstanding Casting For a Reality Program 2022 -Lizzo's Watch Out For The Big Grrrls, CSA Artios Nomination 2021 & 2023-Reality Series-The Circle, CSA Artios Nomination 2023-Reality Series-Competition: The Traitors		CASTING COMPANY:	FORCED PERSPECTIVE
INSTAGRAM:	Instagram.com/jazzycasting		IMDB:	https://www.imdb.com/name/nm13154926/
FACEBOOK:			FACEBOOK GROUP:	
EMAIL:	jazzy@forcedperspective.tv		LINKEDIN:	https://www.linkedin.com/in/jazzy-collins-96889199/
TIKTOK:			TWITTER:	
WEBSITE:	http://www.forcedperspective.tv/		MAILING LIST LINK:	

NAME:	jeanette ochoa.	BIPOC	LOCATION:	Los Angeles, CA
TITLE:	Casting Director			
CASTS FOR:	Scripted and Unscripted			
CASTING HIGHLIGHTS:	Love Trip, Temptation Island, La Firma, Too Hot Too Handle, Patti Stanger dating show, Paradise Hotel, Hotel Hell, American Idol, The Voice, The Courtship, Double Shot at Love with Vinny & Pauly D, Florabama Shore, Bridezillas			
AWARDS:			CASTING COMPANY:	jo
INSTAGRAM:	https://www.instagram.com/jayy_jayy22/		IMDB:	https://m.imdb.com/name/nm6455280/
FACEBOOK:			FACEBOOK GROUP:	
EMAIL:	Jeanetteocasting@gmail.com		LINKEDIN:	https://www.linkedin.com/in/jeanette-ochoa-48a982a5/
TIKTOK:			TWITTER:	
WEBSITE:			MAILING LIST LINK:	

NAME:	jeff blair.	**LOCATION:**	Los Angeles
TITLE:	Casting Producer, Casting Associate		
CASTS FOR:	Reality		
CASTING HIGHLIGHTS:	The Circle, Love Island, Queen of the Universe, F-Boy Island, Married at first Sight		
AWARDS:		**CASTING COMPANY:**	
INSTAGRAM:	https://www.instagram.com/jeffblaircasting/	**IMDB:**	https://www.imdb.com/name/nm8008427/
FACEBOOK:		**FACEBOOK GROUP:**	
EMAIL:	jeffblaircasting@gmail.com	**LINKEDIN:**	https://www.linkedin.com/in/jeffmblair/
TIKTOK:		**TWITTER:**	
WEBSITE:		**MAILING LIST LINK:**	

NAME:	jeffrey marx. — CSA, LGBTQI	**LOCATION:**	Burbank, CA
TITLE:	Casting Associate, Casting Director, and Casting Producer		
CASTS FOR:	Commercials and Unscripted		
CASTING HIGHLIGHTS:	HBO's We're Here, MTV's The Real World and The Challenge, Project Runway, Nailed It, Iyanla Fix My Life, Generation Drag		
AWARDS:	2022 Emmy Award Winner for Outstanding Casting for Reality TV Program-Love On The Spectrum	**CASTING COMPANY:**	Freelance
INSTAGRAM:	https://www.instagram.com/jeffmarxthespot/	**IMDB:**	https://m.imdb.com/name/nm9324185/
FACEBOOK:	www.Facebook.com/Jeffrey.Marx	**FACEBOOK GROUP:**	
EMAIL:	jeffnowcasting@gmail.com	**LINKEDIN:**	https://www.linkedin.com/in/jeffrey-marx-a0717030/
TIKTOK:		**TWITTER:**	https://twitter.com/jeffmarxthespot
WEBSITE:		**MAILING LIST LINK:**	

NAME:	jerel wilhort. — AA and LGBTQI	**LOCATION:**	Los Angeles, CA
TITLE:	Casting Associate and Casting Producer		
CASTS FOR:	Commercials and Unscripted		
CASTING HIGHLIGHTS:	Love Island, House Hunters, To Tell the Truth		
AWARDS:		**CASTING COMPANY:**	
INSTAGRAM:	https://www.instagram.com/jerelwilhort/	**IMDB:**	https://www.imdb.com/name/nm5986095/
FACEBOOK:	https://www.facebook.com/jerelwilhort	**FACEBOOK GROUP:**	
EMAIL:	jerel.wilhort@gmail.com	**LINKEDIN:**	
TIKTOK:		**TWITTER:**	
WEBSITE:		**MAILING LIST LINK:**	

NAME:	jessica maillard.	**LOCATION:**	Sherman Oaks, California
TITLE:	Casting Producer		
CASTS FOR:	Unscripted		
CASTING HIGHLIGHTS:	Generation Gap, Encore!, The Great American Baking Show, The Big Brunch, Beyond Scared Straight, Bridezillas, Cupcake Wars, Hollywood Game Night, Wife Swap		
AWARDS:		**CASTING COMPANY:**	Casting Duo
INSTAGRAM:	https://www.instagram.com/crankykitten/?hl=en	**IMDB:**	
FACEBOOK:		**FACEBOOK GROUP:**	
EMAIL:		**LINKEDIN:**	
TIKTOK:		**TWITTER:**	https://twitter.com/JessicaKiernan
WEBSITE:		**MAILING LIST LINK:**	

NAME:	jessica pena.	**LOCATION:**	New York City, NY
TITLE:	Casting Producer		
CASTS FOR:	Reality		
CASTING HIGHLIGHTS:	Moonshiners, Master Distiller, Whiskey Business, Rattled, Lakefront Bargain Hunt, I Love A Mama's Boy, Smoke Ring, and Cars That Made the World		
AWARDS:		**CASTING COMPANY:**	
INSTAGRAM:	https://www.instagram.com/jp.tvcasting/	**IMDB:**	https://www.imdb.com/name/nm6922056/
FACEBOOK:	https://www.facebook.com/jessica.delpena	**FACEBOOK GROUP:**	
EMAIL:		**LINKEDIN:**	https://www.linkedin.com/in/jessicalpena/
TIKTOK:	https://www.tiktok.com/@magillacasting	**TWITTER:**	
WEBSITE:	https://linktr.ee/magillacasting	**MAILING LIST LINK:**	https://magilla.us13.list-manage.com/subscribe?u=aa634239e00e521e92077d216&id=ba8fe5420b

NAME:	jill hamburgo. — CSA, BIPOC	**LOCATION:**	New York
TITLE:	Casting Assistant, Casting Associate, Casting Director, Casting Producer, and Casting Recruiter		
CASTS FOR:	Commercials, Film, Scripted, and Unscripted		
CASTING HIGHLIGHTS:	Pawn Stars Do America S2, Apple TV's Little America S2, Love & Hip Hop from 2016-2019, 60s Days In S9, Nat Geo's Brain Games S5		
AWARDS:		**CASTING COMPANY:**	Freelancer
INSTAGRAM:	https://www.instagram.com/jilldoescasting/?hl=en	**IMDB:**	https://www.imdb.com/name/nm4131578/
FACEBOOK:	https://www.facebook.com/jilldoescasting	**FACEBOOK GROUP:**	
EMAIL:	Jilldoescasting@gmail.com	**LINKEDIN:**	https://www.linkedin.com/in/jill-hamburgo-csa-9800b84b/
TIKTOK:		**TWITTER:**	
WEBSITE:		**MAILING LIST LINK:**	

NAME:	jocelyn thomas.	AA and LGBTQI	LOCATION:	Los Angeles, California
TITLE:	Casting Producer			
CASTS FOR:	Unscripted			
CASTING HIGHLIGHTS:	Vanderpump Villa, Queens Court, Don't Forget The Lyrics, The Love Experiment, Prank Panel			
AWARDS:			CASTING COMPANY:	Jocelyn is Casting
INSTAGRAM:	https://instagram.com/limitlessjocelyn/		IMDB:	
FACEBOOK:			FACEBOOK GROUP:	
EMAIL:	JocelynIsCasting@gmail.com		LINKEDIN:	https://www.linkedin.com/in/jocelyn-thomas-24375851
TIKTOK:			TWITTER:	
WEBSITE:			MAILING LIST LINK:	

NAME:	josh randall.		LOCATION:	
TITLE:	Casting Producer			
CASTS FOR:	Unscripted			
CASTING HIGHLIGHTS:	American Idol, I Can See Your Voice on FOX, America's Got Talent, MTV's Are You The One, Living For The Dead on HULU, Barmageddon on USA, The Floor on FOX, We Are Family on FOX, My Kind of Country on Apple.			
AWARDS:			CASTING COMPANY:	
INSTAGRAM:	https://www.instagram.com/jrandofficial/		IMDB:	https://www.imdb.com/name/nm2712280/?ref_=nv_sr_srsg_3_tt_o_nm_8_q_Josh%2520randall
FACEBOOK:			FACEBOOK GROUP:	
EMAIL:	jrandallcasting@gmail.com		LINKEDIN:	
TIKTOK:	https://www.tiktok.com/@jrandofficial?lang=en		TWITTER:	
WEBSITE:			MAILING LIST LINK:	

NAME:	joy gordo.	CSA	LOCATION:	Los Angeles, CA
TITLE:	Casting Director, Casting Producer			
CASTS FOR:	Reality, Commercial			
CASTING HIGHLIGHTS:	The Amazing Race, The Circle, America's Got Talent, Love Is Blind, 12 Dates of Christmas, Dated & Related, Big Brother			
AWARDS:	Unscripted Casting Producer Spotlight Award		CASTING COMPANY:	CASTING WITH JOY
INSTAGRAM:	https://www.instagram.com/castingwithjoy		IMDB:	https://www.imdb.com/name/nm12193402/?ref_=fn_al_nm_1
FACEBOOK:	https://facebook.com/castingwithjoy		FACEBOOK GROUP:	
EMAIL:			LINKEDIN:	https://www.linkedin.com/in/joygordo/
TIKTOK:	https://www.tiktok.com/@castingwithjoy		TWITTER:	https://twitter.com/castingwithjoy
WEBSITE:	www.castingwithjoy.com		MAILING LIST LINK:	https://forms.gle/1w8DY628Y4qa1qwM7

NAME:	joy tenenberg.		LOCATION:	Los Angeles, California & New York City, NY
TITLE:	Casting Director, Casting Producer			
CASTS FOR:	Scripted, Theatre, and Unscripted			
CASTING HIGHLIGHTS:	Masterchef, Masterchef Junior, Gordon Ramsay's Food Stars, House Hunters, To Tell The Truth, Intervention, 100 Humans, Starry: A New Musical			
AWARDS:			CASTING COMPANY:	
INSTAGRAM:	https://www.instagram.com/thebroadwayunicorn/		IMDB:	https://m.imdb.com/name/nm1562538/
FACEBOOK:	https://www.facebook.com/joymichelle		FACEBOOK GROUP:	
EMAIL:	Castingjoy@gmail.com		LINKEDIN:	https://www.linkedin.com/in/joytenenberg/
TIKTOK:	https://www.tiktok.com/@thebroadwayunicorn		TWITTER:	https://twitter.com/joymichelle
WEBSITE:			MAILING LIST LINK:	

NAME:	joy barrett	CSA	LOCATION:	Los Angeles CA
TITLE:	Casting Producer			
CASTS FOR:	Unscripted			
CASTING HIGHLIGHTS:	Top Chef, Harry Potter: Wizards of Baking, Next in Fashion, Bake Squad, The Final Table, Buddy Games, The Big Nailed It Baking Challenge, Harry Potter: Hogwarts Tournament of Houses, Iron Chef, Chopped			
AWARDS:	2022 Emmy Nominee: Outstanding Casting for a Reality Program. 2024 Artios Award Nominee		CASTING COMPANY:	
INSTAGRAM:	https://www.instagram.com/joylb33/		IMDB:	https://www.imdb.com/name/nm3442346/?ref_=ra_sb_ln
FACEBOOK:	https://www.facebook.com/joy.barrett.39		FACEBOOK GROUP:	
EMAIL:			LINKEDIN:	https://www.linkedin.com/in/joy-barrett-140b5b27/
TIKTOK:			TWITTER:	
WEBSITE:			MAILING LIST LINK:	

NAME:	judy tsai.		LOCATION:	Brooklyn, NY
TITLE:	Casting Producer, Casting Associate			
CASTS FOR:	Reality			
CASTING HIGHLIGHTS:	Unexpected (TLC), Dr. Mercy (TLC)			
AWARDS:			CASTING COMPANY:	
INSTAGRAM:	https://www.instagram.com/easterntelevision/		IMDB:	
FACEBOOK:			FACEBOOK GROUP:	
EMAIL:			LINKEDIN:	
TIKTOK:			TWITTER:	
WEBSITE:			MAILING LIST LINK:	

NAME:	julianna guilianti.	LOCATION:	Philadelphia, Pennsylvania
TITLE:	Casting Associate		
CASTS FOR:	Film and Unscripted		
CASTING HIGHLIGHTS:	The Circle (Netflix), 12 Dates of Christmas (HBO Max), The Cube (TBS), Match Me In Miami (Roku)		
AWARDS:		CASTING COMPANY:	
INSTAGRAM:	Instagram.com/juliethunderfox	IMDB:	https://www.imdb.com/name/nm6557979/
FACEBOOK:		FACEBOOK GROUP:	
EMAIL:	Julianna.cossman@gmail.com	LINKEDIN:	https://www.linkedin.com/in/julianna-cossman
TIKTOK:		TWITTER:	
WEBSITE:		MAILING LIST LINK:	

NAME:	justin zagri.	LOCATION:	Burbank, California
TITLE:	Casting Editor		
CASTS FOR:	Unscripted		
CASTING HIGHLIGHTS:	Real Housewives NYC, SLC, Below Deck, Ultimatum Seasons 1 2 and 3, Lego Masters, Deal or No Deal, The Abbey, Botched		
AWARDS:		CASTING COMPANY:	Various
INSTAGRAM:	https://www.instagram.com/justinzdirector/	IMDB:	https://www.imdb.com/name/nm2808985/
FACEBOOK:		FACEBOOK GROUP:	
EMAIL:	jzagri@gmail.com	LINKEDIN:	https://www.linkedin.com/in/justinzagri
TIKTOK:		TWITTER:	
WEBSITE:		MAILING LIST LINK:	

NAME:	k'ia stone. — BIPOC, AA	LOCATION:	Los Angeles, CA
TITLE:	Casting Director, Casting Producer, Celebrity Booker & Talent Producer		
CASTS FOR:	Commercials, Film, Scripted, and Unscripted		
CASTING HIGHLIGHTS:	Black Pop, Unsung, Peace of Mind w/Taraji, PAUSE w/ Sam Jay		
AWARDS:	NAACP Image Awards, Unsung (2013, 2015, 2016, 2017, 2018)	CASTING COMPANY:	
INSTAGRAM:	instagram.com/mskiastone	IMDB:	https://www.imdb.com/name/nm6344805/?ref_=nv_sr_1
FACEBOOK:	https://www.facebook.com/kia.stone.771	FACEBOOK GROUP:	
EMAIL:	castingbykstone@gmail.com	LINKEDIN:	http://www.linkedin.com/in/kmstone
TIKTOK:		TWITTER:	https://twitter.com/mskiastone
WEBSITE:	www.blackgirlbucketlist.com	MAILING LIST LINK:	

NAME:	kate santos. — CSA, LGBTQI	LOCATION:	Los Angeles, CA
TITLE:	Casting Director, Casting Producer		
CASTS FOR:	Reality, Commercial, New Media, TV, Film		
CASTING HIGHLIGHTS:	Naked & Afraid, Undercover Boss, America's Next Top Model, Ultimate Tag, and Raid The Cage.		
AWARDS:		CASTING COMPANY:	KSG
INSTAGRAM:	https://www.instagram.com/KSGcasting/	IMDB:	https://www.imdb.com/name/nm7947837/
FACEBOOK:		FACEBOOK GROUP:	
EMAIL:	katecastingnow@gmail.com	LINKEDIN:	
TIKTOK:		TWITTER:	
WEBSITE:		MAILING LIST LINK:	Fill out the form on www.9to5content.com to be added to our database for upcoming castings!

NAME:	katie cieszynski.		LOCATION:	Los Angeles, California
TITLE:	Casting Associate and Casting Producer			
CASTS FOR:	Unscripted			
CASTING HIGHLIGHTS:	The Mole, My Feet Are Killing Me, Name That Tune, I Can See Your Voice, Summerhouse, The Bachelorette			
AWARDS:			CASTING COMPANY:	
INSTAGRAM:	http://www.instagram.com/castingwithkatie		IMDB:	
FACEBOOK:			FACEBOOK GROUP:	
EMAIL:	Castingwithkatie@gmail.com		LINKEDIN:	
TIKTOK:			TWITTER:	
WEBSITE:			MAILING LIST LINK:	

NAME:	katie griffin.	CSA	LOCATION:	New York
TITLE:	Casting Director, Casting Producer, and Head of Casting			
CASTS FOR:	Commercials, Film, Scripted, and Unscripted			
CASTING HIGHLIGHTS:	Whose Wedding Is It Anyway?, Cash Cab, What Not To Wear, Love at First Swipe-TLC, The Last Goodbye-LMN, The Best of Trading Spaces-OWN, Whose Wedding Is It Anyway?-Style Network, Married Away-Style Network, My Celebrity Wedding-Style Network, Cash Cab-Discovery, Can't Get a Date-VH1, Into Character-AMC			
AWARDS:			CASTING COMPANY:	Katie Griffin Casting KATIE GRIFFIN CASTING
INSTAGRAM:	https://www.instagram.com/katiegriffincasting/ https://www.threads.net/@katiegriffincasting		IMDB:	https://www.imdb.com/name/nm1653696/
FACEBOOK:	https://www.facebook.com/KatieGriffinCastingDirector		FACEBOOK GROUP:	https://www.facebook.com/groups/318680795502464
EMAIL:	info@katiegriffincasting.com		LINKEDIN:	
TIKTOK:	https://www.tiktok.com/@katiegriffincasting		TWITTER:	https://twitter.com/KGriffinCasting
WEBSITE:	https://www.katiegriffincasting.com		MAILING LIST LINK:	https://www.katiegriffincasting.com

NAME:	keicon cherry.	BIPOC	LOCATION:	Los Angeles, California
TITLE:	Casting Associate and Casting Producer			
CASTS FOR:	Unscripted			
CASTING HIGHLIGHTS:	Big Brother, Married at First Sight, MasterChef, MasterChef Jr, Love is Blind, Boomin love, Help I'm in a secret relationship, I want you back, BET Business show, Unmatchable, RWI, The Voice, The Cube, Don't Forget The Lyrics			
AWARDS:			CASTING COMPANY:	I work with a lot Kenitic, casting duo, Sharp entertainment
INSTAGRAM:	https://www.instagram.com/castingwithkeicon/		IMDB:	
FACEBOOK:			FACEBOOK GROUP:	
EMAIL:	keiconcherrycasting@gmail.com		LINKEDIN:	
TIKTOK:			TWITTER:	https://twitter.com/iam__Keicon
WEBSITE:			MAILING LIST LINK:	

NAME:	kelley allen.	CSA AA and BIPOC	LOCATION:	Los Angeles, CA
TITLE:	Casting Director and Head of Casting			
CASTS FOR:	Unscripted			
CASTING HIGHLIGHTS:	E! Network's hit show "Botched," Gordon Ramsay's: "24 Hours to Hell & Back," MTV's "Are You The One," OWN's "Ready to Love," Bravo's "Married to Medicine," TLC's "Extreme Sisters," HBO Max' "Sweet Life" and Netflix' #1 hit, "The Ultimatum" and the upcoming, highly anticipated-Netflix' "Rhythm & Flow" season two!			
AWARDS:			CASTING COMPANY:	
INSTAGRAM:	https://instagram.com/girlgangcasting?igshid=YTQwZjQoNmIoOA==		IMDB:	https://m.imdb.com/name/nm3811468/
FACEBOOK:			FACEBOOK GROUP:	
EMAIL:	iputyouontv@gmail.com		LINKEDIN:	
TIKTOK:			TWITTER:	
WEBSITE:	https://girlgangcastingcollective.com/		MAILING LIST LINK:	

NAME:	kelsey mccabe.		LOCATION:	New York
TITLE:	Casting Director and Casting Producer			
CASTS FOR:	Commercials, Theatre, and Unscripted			
CASTING HIGHLIGHTS:	Dating Around-Netflix, Beachfront Bargain Hunt-HGTV, Master Distiller-Discovery, Smoke Ring-Discovery+			
AWARDS:			CASTING COMPANY:	Casting by Kelsey
INSTAGRAM:	https://www.instagram.com/castingbykelsey/		IMDB:	
FACEBOOK:			FACEBOOK GROUP:	
EMAIL:			LINKEDIN:	
TIKTOK:			TWITTER:	
WEBSITE:			MAILING LIST LINK:	

NAME:	kimaya floyd.	AA and BIPOC	LOCATION:	Los Angeles, California
TITLE:	Casting Associate, Casting Director, and Casting Producer			
CASTS FOR:	Unscripted			
CASTING HIGHLIGHTS:	Ex on the Beach, After Happily Ever After, Let's Get Physical, Legit Tim, The Challenge			
AWARDS:			CASTING COMPANY:	Freelance
INSTAGRAM:	https://www.instagram.com/mayaiscasting/		IMDB:	
FACEBOOK:			FACEBOOK GROUP:	
EMAIL:	kimayafloyd@gmail.com		LINKEDIN:	https://www.linkedin.com/in/kimayafloyd/
TIKTOK:			TWITTER:	
WEBSITE:			MAILING LIST LINK:	

NAME:	kimberly driedger.	BIPOC, and LGBTQI	LOCATION:	Miami, Florida
TITLE:	Casting Producer			
CASTS FOR:	Unscripted			
CASTING HIGHLIGHTS:	Love Is Blind, Married At First Sight, The Ultimatum, The Real Housewives of Beverly Hills, Big Brother, Americas got Talent, Millionaire Matchmaker, Dating Naked, Are You The One?, Genius Junior, The Exhibit, Are You Smarter Than A 5th Grade?, The Taste, Fix My Choir, Million Dollar Listing, Tough Love, Making Mr. Right			
AWARDS:	Emmy nominations for Love Is Blind		CASTING COMPANY:	
INSTAGRAM:	http://instagram.com/kimberlydriedger		IMDB:	https://m.imdb.com/name/nm3401064/?ref_=ext_shr_lnk
FACEBOOK:			FACEBOOK GROUP:	
EMAIL:			LINKEDIN:	https://www.linkedin.com/in/kimberly-driedger-156a4043/
TIKTOK:			TWITTER:	twitter.com/kimdriedger
WEBSITE:			MAILING LIST LINK:	

NAME:	kira coplin.	CSA	LOCATION:	Los Angeles, CA
TITLE:	Casting Director, Casting Producer, and Head of Casting			
CASTS FOR:	Unscripted			
CASTING HIGHLIGHTS:	Real Housewives of Atlanta, Married to Medicine, Basketball Wives, The Mole, The Circle, Siesta Key, John Carpenter's Suburban Screams, Next in Fashion, My Feet Are Killing Me, Fboy Island, Winter House, Million Dollar Listing, After Happily Ever After, Naked and Afraid of Love			
AWARDS:			CASTING COMPANY:	9 to 5 Content
INSTAGRAM:	https://www.instagram.com/kira_casting/?hl=en		IMDB:	https://m.imdb.com/name/nm0178749/
FACEBOOK:			FACEBOOK GROUP:	
EMAIL:	Kira@9to5content.com		LINKEDIN:	https://www.linkedin.com/in/kiracoplin
TIKTOK:			TWITTER:	
WEBSITE:			MAILING LIST LINK:	

NAME:	kristen moss.		CSA	LOCATION:	Los Angeles, CA
TITLE:	Casting Director				
CASTS FOR:	Reality, Commercial, New Media, TV				
CASTING HIGHLIGHTS:	The Great Christmas Light Fight, MasterChef, To Tell The Truth, Let's Make A Deal, Fear Factor, The F Word, The Proposal, Master Minds, The Great Halloween Fright Fight				
AWARDS:	2024 Artios Nominee Creator of the American Reality TV Awards-3x 2023 Telly Award Winner			CASTING COMPANY:	KMoss Casting
INSTAGRAM:	https://instagram.com/reality_tv_castingcalls			IMDB:	IMDb.me/Kristen-Moss
FACEBOOK:	https://www.facebook.com/kmosscastingpage			FACEBOOK GROUP:	https://www.facebook.com/groups/realitycastingcalls
EMAIL:				LINKEDIN:	https://www.linkedin.com/in/kristen-moss-csa
TIKTOK:				TWITTER:	
WEBSITE:	KMossCasting.com			MAILING LIST LINK:	https://www.kmosscasting.com/contact

NAME:	kristen pate.		BIPOC	LOCATION:	Los Angeles, California
TITLE:	Casting Associate, Casting Director, Casting Manager, and Casting Producer				
CASTS FOR:	Commercials and Unscripted				
CASTING HIGHLIGHTS:	Password, Don't Forget The Lyrics, The Great Food Truck Race, 24 Hours To Hell and Back, Masterchef				
AWARDS:	2023 Clio Award Winner Campaign: Marvel's Black Panther: Wakanda Forever, Power in Partnership			CASTING COMPANY:	Cayenne Casting — CAYENNE CASTING
INSTAGRAM:	https://www.instagram.com/cayennecasting/?hl=en			IMDB:	
FACEBOOK:				FACEBOOK GROUP:	
EMAIL:				LINKEDIN:	
TIKTOK:				TWITTER:	
WEBSITE:	Cayennecasting.com			MAILING LIST LINK:	

NAME:	kristina hauser.	CSA	LOCATION:	Burbank, California
TITLE:	Casting Director and Casting Producer			
CASTS FOR:	Unscripted			
CASTING HIGHLIGHTS:	House Hunters Renovation, To Tell the Truth, Snake Oil, 25 Words or Less, Stephen Colbert's Tooning Out the News			
AWARDS:			CASTING COMPANY:	Tiki Casting
INSTAGRAM:	https://www.instagram.com/tikicasting/		IMDB:	https://m.imdb.com/name/nm1924326/
FACEBOOK:			FACEBOOK GROUP:	
EMAIL:	Casting@tikicasting.com		LINKEDIN:	
TIKTOK:			TWITTER:	
WEBSITE:			MAILING LIST LINK:	

NAME:	krystal cunningham.	CSA	LOCATION:	Los Angeles, California
TITLE:	Casting Director and Casting Producer			
CASTS FOR:	Unscripted			
CASTING HIGHLIGHTS:	America's Got Talent, American idol, Don't Forget the Lyrics			
AWARDS:			CASTING COMPANY:	
INSTAGRAM:	https://www.instagram.com/krystalamericanidolcasting/		IMDB:	https://m.imdb.com/name/nm6260784/
FACEBOOK:			FACEBOOK GROUP:	
EMAIL:	klc.casting@gmail.com		LINKEDIN:	
TIKTOK:			TWITTER:	
WEBSITE:			MAILING LIST LINK:	

NAME:	kyle khou.			LOCATION:	Las Vegas Nevada
TITLE:	Casting Producer				
CASTS FOR:	Reality				
CASTING HIGHLIGHTS:	American idol, Boyband for Universal				
AWARDS:	Emmy Winner			CASTING COMPANY:	
INSTAGRAM:	https://instagram.com/kylekhou?igshid=YmMyMTA2M2Y=			IMDB:	
FACEBOOK:				FACEBOOK GROUP:	
EMAIL:	Kylekhoucasting@gmail.com			LINKEDIN:	
TIKTOK:				TWITTER:	
WEBSITE:				MAILING LIST LINK:	

NAME:	laura clements.		CSA	LOCATION:	Tampa, Florida
TITLE:	Casting Director and Casting Producer				
CASTS FOR:	Commercials, Film, Scripted, and Unscripted				
CASTING HIGHLIGHTS:	Backyard Bar Wars, Girls Incarcerated, Chopped, Tiny House Nation, Alone, He Shed, She Shed, Holy & Hungry, Food Porn				
AWARDS:				CASTING COMPANY:	
INSTAGRAM:	https://www.instagram.com/laura_clements143/			IMDB:	
FACEBOOK:				FACEBOOK GROUP:	
EMAIL:	hello@laura-clements.com			LINKEDIN:	
TIKTOK:				TWITTER:	
WEBSITE:	https://www.laura-clements.com/			MAILING LIST LINK:	

NAME:	lauren kotlen.	LOCATION:	Denver, Colorado
TITLE:	Casting Director and Head of Casting		
CASTS FOR:	Unscripted		
CASTING HIGHLIGHTS:	Inmate to Roommate, 60 Days In, Tough Love, MTV Family Legacy, Betrayal, Rental Redo, My First Place, Dream House		
AWARDS:		CASTING COMPANY:	
INSTAGRAM:	Instagram.com/castingdirector13	IMDB:	https://m.imdb.com/name/nm2527500/
FACEBOOK:	https://www.facebook.com/castingdirector13?mibextid=LQQJ4d	FACEBOOK GROUP:	
EMAIL:	lauren.kotlen@gmail.com	LINKEDIN:	
TIKTOK:		TWITTER:	
WEBSITE:		MAILING LIST LINK:	

NAME:	lauren riccio-shearman.	LOCATION:	Bayside, New York
TITLE:	Casting Director and Casting Producer		
CASTS FOR:	Commercials, Film, and Unscripted		
CASTING HIGHLIGHTS:	The Deed & The Deed Chicago-S 1 & 2, You Bet Your Life-S 1 & 2, How Far Is Tattoo Far?, Regular Heroes on Amazon Prime, Beyond the Block-S 2 & 3, Hardcore Pawn, The Mel Robbins Show and Finding Magic Mike, TLC's The Next Great Baker, Tastemade's "A Scoop of Soul" for Ben & Jerry's, Tastemade's "Road Well Traveled" for Jeep Wagoneer, Tastemade's "Weekend Refresh", "Visit Myrtle Beach & DC"-branded spots, GSN's "Chain Reaction & Get A Clue.", A & E's "America's Top Dog"-S2.		
AWARDS:		CASTING COMPANY:	Speakeasy Casting
INSTAGRAM:	https://instagram.com/speakeasycastings/	IMDB:	https://m.imdb.com/name/nm4398729/
FACEBOOK:		FACEBOOK GROUP:	https://m.facebook.com/profile.php/?id=100063578770684
EMAIL:		LINKEDIN:	
TIKTOK:		TWITTER:	
WEBSITE:	www.speakeasycasting.com	MAILING LIST LINK:	

NAME:	lauren spears.	LOCATION:	Miami, Florida
TITLE:	Casting Associate		
CASTS FOR:	Unscripted		
CASTING HIGHLIGHTS:	Love Is Blind-Netflix, The Circle-Netflix, The Ultimatum-Netflix, Married At First Sight-Lifetime, Vanderpump Rules-Bravo, Claim To Fame-ABC, F Boy Island-HBO Max / CW, Love Island-CBS / Peacock		
AWARDS:		CASTING COMPANY:	Kinetic Content (currently)
INSTAGRAM:	https://www.instagram.com/thelaurenspears/	IMDB:	https://www.imdb.com/name/nm10796418/
FACEBOOK:		FACEBOOK GROUP:	
EMAIL:	lauren.n.spears@gmail.com	LINKEDIN:	https://www.linkedin.com/in/laurennicolespears/
TIKTOK:		TWITTER:	
WEBSITE:	Www.laurenspearscasting.com	MAILING LIST LINK:	

NAME:	lauren waters.	LOCATION:	Cape May, New Jersey
TITLE:	Casting Director and Casting Producer		
CASTS FOR:	Commercials and Unscripted		
CASTING HIGHLIGHTS:	Lifetimes Oops I had a baby, Magnolia Make Yourself at home, E! Cash at Your Door with Jason Biggs, ABC Disney, Singalong, NBC Graduate Together, ABC John Legend & Family: Father's Day Special, Vice News teens discuss abortion, Logo Transgender Town Hall, MTV Glam Slam, HGTV Married to Real Estate		
AWARDS:	News & Doc Emmy : Inside Rights: Teenagers Discuss Abortion	CASTING COMPANY:	Lauren Waters Casting
INSTAGRAM:	https://www.instagram.com/laurenwaterscasting/	IMDB:	https://www.imdb.com/name/nm1404940/
FACEBOOK:	https://www.facebook.com/LaurenWatersCasting/	FACEBOOK GROUP:	
EMAIL:		LINKEDIN:	
TIKTOK:	https://www.tiktok.com/@laurenwaterscasting	TWITTER:	https://x.com/waterscasting?s=21&t=uaVAkeFUcIaAB29NFC35jg
WEBSITE:	https://www.laurenwaterscasting.com/	MAILING LIST LINK:	

NAME:	lexie ramos.			LOCATION:	Rancho Cucamonga, California
TITLE:	Casting Manager				
CASTS FOR:	Unscripted				
CASTING HIGHLIGHTS:	AGT S15 (NBC), The Floor Is Lava S1 (Netflix), Come Dance With Me (CBS), Bachelorette 18 (ABC), Back in the Groove (Hulu), The Real Love Boat (CBS), FBoy Island S3 (CW), FGirl Island S1 (CW)				
AWARDS:				CASTING COMPANY:	
INSTAGRAM:	https://www.instagram.com/lexielynn95/			IMDB:	
FACEBOOK:				FACEBOOK GROUP:	
EMAIL:				LINKEDIN:	
TIKTOK:				TWITTER:	
WEBSITE:				MAILING LIST LINK:	

NAME:	lindsay liles.		CSA	LOCATION:	California
TITLE:	Casting Director				
CASTS FOR:	Unscripted				
CASTING HIGHLIGHTS:	The Bachelorette, Bachelor in Paradise, Listen to Your Heart, The Golden Bachelor (Lead)				
AWARDS:	Producing: Emmy Nomination 2010 for "Clean House." Critics Choice Nomination 2013 for "Marie."			CASTING COMPANY:	
INSTAGRAM:	https://www.instagram.com/lindsayliles/			IMDB:	https://m.imdb.com/name/nm2288253/
FACEBOOK:				FACEBOOK GROUP:	
EMAIL:	Lindsaylilescasting@gmail.com			LINKEDIN:	
TIKTOK:				TWITTER:	
WEBSITE:				MAILING LIST LINK:	

NAME:	lindsay rush.	**LOCATION:**	New Hope, Pennsylvania
TITLE:	Casting Associate, Casting Producer, and Casting Recruiter		
CASTS FOR:	Unscripted		
CASTING HIGHLIGHTS:	America's Got Talent, American Idol, Building The Band, Beast Games		
AWARDS:	Critics Choice Awards, MTV Movie & TV Awards, People's Choice Awards, Teen Choice Awards, Online Film & Television Association Awards, Gold Derby Awards, Hollywood Critics Association Television Awards, Kids Choice Awards	**CASTING COMPANY:**	Lindsay Rush/Gumshoe Entertainment
INSTAGRAM:	Instagram.com/lindsaymrush	**IMDB:**	https://www.imdb.com/name/nm8135402/?ref_=nv_sr_srsg_0_tt_0_nm_8_in_0_q_lindsay%2520rush
FACEBOOK:	Facebook.com/LindsayRush	**FACEBOOK GROUP:**	
EMAIL:	Lindsay@LindsayRush.com	**LINKEDIN:**	Linkedin.com/in/lindsaymrush
TIKTOK:		**TWITTER:**	
WEBSITE:		**MAILING LIST LINK:**	

NAME:	lisa leeking.	**LOCATION:**	Brooklyn, New York
TITLE:	Head of Casting		
CASTS FOR:	Unscripted		
CASTING HIGHLIGHTS:	Secret Chef (Hulu), Love and WWE: Bianca & Montez (2024), King of Collectibles (Netflix), Divided by Design (HGTV), Love & Hip Hop and the various spin-offs (Vh1), Grill It! with Bobby Flay (Food Nework)		
AWARDS:	Emmy for Cash Cab	**CASTING COMPANY:**	Wheelhouse, Spoke Studios and Butternut (in-house)
INSTAGRAM:	https://www.instagram.com/llkcasting/	**IMDB:**	https://www.imdb.com/name/nm4900221/
FACEBOOK:		**FACEBOOK GROUP:**	
EMAIL:	lisa@prontoproductions.tv	**LINKEDIN:**	https://www.linkedin.com/mwlite/profile/in/lisa-leeking-9973071
TIKTOK:		**TWITTER:**	
WEBSITE:	https://www.wheel-house.com/entertainment	**MAILING LIST LINK:**	

NAME:	lisa steinberg.	LOCATION:	New York
TITLE:	Casting Director and Casting Producer		
CASTS FOR:	Commercials and Unscripted		
CASTING HIGHLIGHTS:	Say Yes to the Dress, I Just Killed My Dad, Man, Woman, Dog, Secrets and Sisterhood: The Sozadahs, While You Were Out		
AWARDS:		CASTING COMPANY:	The Real Deal Casting
INSTAGRAM:	https://instagram.com/therealdealcasting/	IMDB:	
FACEBOOK:		FACEBOOK GROUP:	
EMAIL:	Lisa@therealdealcasting.com	LINKEDIN:	
TIKTOK:		TWITTER:	
WEBSITE:	Therealdealcasting.com	MAILING LIST LINK:	

NAME:	lydia solis. BIPOC	LOCATION:	Chicago, Illinois
TITLE:	Casting Associate and Casting Producer		
CASTS FOR:	Unscripted		
CASTING HIGHLIGHTS:	MTV help I'm in a secret relationship, History Secret Restoration, MTV Ghosted, MTV How far is Tattoo far		
AWARDS:		CASTING COMPANY:	Freelance
INSTAGRAM:	https://www.instagram.com/lydiacastingyou/	IMDB:	https://www.imdb.com/name/nm11117615/
FACEBOOK:		FACEBOOK GROUP:	
EMAIL:	Lydiacastingyou@gmail.com	LINKEDIN:	https://www.linkedin.com/in/lydia-solis-b2840a129/
TIKTOK:	https://www.tiktok.com/@lydiacastingyou?lang=en	TWITTER:	
WEBSITE:		MAILING LIST LINK:	

NAME:	lynly ehrlich.	**LOCATION:**	Atlanta Georgia
TITLE:	Casting Producer		
CASTS FOR:	Reality		
CASTING HIGHLIGHTS:	American Idol		
AWARDS:		**CASTING COMPANY:**	
INSTAGRAM:	https://www.instagram.com/carolinablueproductions/?hl=en	**IMDB:**	https://m.imdb.com/name/nm4190995/?ref_=nv_sr_srsg_0
FACEBOOK:		**FACEBOOK GROUP:**	
EMAIL:	Carolinablueproductions@gmail.com	**LINKEDIN:**	
TIKTOK:	https://www.tiktok.com/@lynlyismildlyfunny?lang=en	**TWITTER:**	
WEBSITE:		**MAILING LIST LINK:**	

NAME:	maddy sloan pesce.	**LOCATION:**	Tucson, AZ
TITLE:	Casting Producer		
CASTS FOR:	Reality		
CASTING HIGHLIGHTS:	The Apprentice, Family or Fiance, The Biggest Loser, Real World/ Road Rules, After Happily Ever After, My Fair Wedding, Beauty and the Geek, Laguna Beach, Blind Date, Miss Seventeen, Ex-Wives Club		
AWARDS:		**CASTING COMPANY:**	
INSTAGRAM:	https://www.instagram.com/maddysloancasting/	**IMDB:**	https://www.imdb.com/name/nm1311384/?ref_=nv_sr_srsg_0
FACEBOOK:	https://www.facebook.com/maddy.sloan.9/	**FACEBOOK GROUP:**	
EMAIL:	maddysloan@gmail.com	**LINKEDIN:**	https://www.linkedin.com/in/maddy-sloan-pesce-4313206a/details/experience/
TIKTOK:		**TWITTER:**	
WEBSITE:		**MAILING LIST LINK:**	maddysloan@gmail.com

NAME:	maria duke.		LGBTQI	LOCATION:	Brooklyn, New York
TITLE:	Casting Producer				
CASTS FOR:	Unscripted				
CASTING HIGHLIGHTS:	Real Housewives of Atlanta, Below Deck, Coming Out with Manny MUA, Design Star, Home Sweet Home, Christmas Cookie Showdown.				
AWARDS:				CASTING COMPANY:	
INSTAGRAM:	https://www.instagram.com/themariaduke/			IMDB:	https://staffmeup.com/profile/mariaduke
FACEBOOK:				FACEBOOK GROUP:	
EMAIL:	maria.c.duke@gmail.com			LINKEDIN:	
TIKTOK:				TWITTER:	
WEBSITE:	https://www.mariacduke.com/			MAILING LIST LINK:	

NAME:	matt solomon.			LOCATION:	Los Angeles, CA
TITLE:	Casting Director				
CASTS FOR:	Reality				
CASTING HIGHLIGHTS:	Real Housewives of Beverly Hills, Real Housewives of Orange County, Below Deck: Adventure				
AWARDS:				CASTING COMPANY:	
INSTAGRAM:	https://www.instagram.com/matthewgsolomon/			IMDB:	
FACEBOOK:				FACEBOOK GROUP:	
EMAIL:	MattCastingTV@gmail.com			LINKEDIN:	
TIKTOK:	@mattcastingtv			TWITTER:	
WEBSITE:	https://aintthatsomethingentertainment.com/			MAILING LIST LINK:	

NAME:	melissa kellner. CSA	LOCATION:	Los Angeles, CA
TITLE:	Casting Producer		
CASTS FOR:	Commercials and Unscripted		
CASTING HIGHLIGHTS:	House of Villains-E!, Pressure Cooker-Netflix, True Story with Ed Helms & Randall Park-Peacock, Supermarket Sweep-ABC, Gordon Ramsay's Next Level Chef-FOX		
AWARDS:		CASTING COMPANY:	Mel Kel Casting
INSTAGRAM:	https://instagram.com/melkel_melissakellner	IMDB:	https://pro.imdb.com/name/nm4251411
FACEBOOK:		FACEBOOK GROUP:	
EMAIL:	melkelcasting@gmail.com	LINKEDIN:	Linkedin.com/in/melkel
TIKTOK:		TWITTER:	
WEBSITE:		MAILING LIST LINK:	

NAME:	michael warwick. LGBTQI	LOCATION:	Los Angeles, CA
TITLE:	Casting Director, Casting Producer, and Head of Casting		
CASTS FOR:	Film and Unscripted		
CASTING HIGHLIGHTS:	Gentle Art of Swedish Death Cleaning, Baking It, On the Road		
AWARDS:		CASTING COMPANY:	MW TALENT
INSTAGRAM:	https://www.instagram.com/mwtalentbiz/?hl=en	IMDB:	https://m.imdb.com/name/nm0913258/
FACEBOOK:		FACEBOOK GROUP:	
EMAIL:		LINKEDIN:	https://www.linkedin.com/in/michael-warwick-mw?utm_source=share&utm_campaign=share_via&utm_content=profile&utm_medium=ios_app
TIKTOK:		TWITTER:	
WEBSITE:		MAILING LIST LINK:	

NAME:	mike rose.		LGBTQI	LOCATION:	Los Angeles, California
TITLE:	Casting Associate				
CASTS FOR:	Unscripted				
CASTING HIGHLIGHTS:	Are You The One-MTV and Paramount+, Season 8 + 9, Too Hot To Handle-Netflix, Season 4 + 5, Love Island-CBS, Season 1 + 2, Vanderpump Villa-Hulu, The One That Got Away-Amazon Prime, Snake Oil-FOX				
AWARDS:	(GLAAD Award)			CASTING COMPANY:	Freelance
INSTAGRAM:	http://instagram.com/MikeRoseLA			IMDB:	
FACEBOOK:				FACEBOOK GROUP:	
EMAIL:	MikeRoseCasting@gmail.com			LINKEDIN:	
TIKTOK:				TWITTER:	
WEBSITE:				MAILING LIST LINK:	

NAME:	molly cohen.		LGBTQI	LOCATION:	Los Angeles, CA
TITLE:	Casting Producer				
CASTS FOR:	Unscripted				
CASTING HIGHLIGHTS:	The Bachelorette, Squid Game: The Challenge, Are You The One?, Married At First Sight, Guy's Grocery Games, Wipeout				
AWARDS:				CASTING COMPANY:	
INSTAGRAM:	Instagram.com/ohhcohen			IMDB:	https://www.imdb.com/name/nm6847978/?ref_=ext_shr_lnk
FACEBOOK:				FACEBOOK GROUP:	
EMAIL:	casting.mollycohen@gmail.com			LINKEDIN:	
TIKTOK:				TWITTER:	
WEBSITE:				MAILING LIST LINK:	

NAME:	moriah pulido.	AA, BIPOC, and LGBTQI	LOCATION:	Winston Salem, North Carolina
TITLE:	Casting Producer, Casting Associate			
CASTS FOR:	Commercials and Unscripted			
CASTING HIGHLIGHTS:	Treasure Trails (S1), The Mole (S2), Don't Forget The Lyrics (S2), Survive The Raft (S1), The Great Christmas Light Fight (S10), The One That Got Away (S1), The Bake Squad (S1), Iyanla: Fix my Life (S10), To Tell The Truth (S5)			
AWARDS:			CASTING COMPANY:	
INSTAGRAM:	https://www.instagram.com/castingbymoriah/		IMDB:	https://www.imdb.com/name/nm8078042/?ref_=fn_al_nm_1
FACEBOOK:			FACEBOOK GROUP:	
EMAIL:	moriahhallcasting@gmail.com		LINKEDIN:	https://www.linkedin.com/in/moriah-hall-casting
TIKTOK:			TWITTER:	
WEBSITE:			MAILING LIST LINK:	

NAME:	nancy yearing.	LGBTQI	LOCATION:	Los Angeles, CA
TITLE:	Casting Producer			
CASTS FOR:	Unscripted			
CASTING HIGHLIGHTS:	America's Got Talent, American Idol			
AWARDS:			CASTING COMPANY:	
INSTAGRAM:	https://www.instagram.com/nancyyearing/?hl=en		IMDB:	
FACEBOOK:			FACEBOOK GROUP:	
EMAIL:			LINKEDIN:	https://www.linkedin.com/in/nyearing/
TIKTOK:			TWITTER:	
WEBSITE:			MAILING LIST LINK:	

NAME:	olivia titus.	LGBTQI	LOCATION:	Brooklyn, New York
TITLE:	Casting Associate			
CASTS FOR:	Unscripted			
CASTING HIGHLIGHTS:	Maury, Beat Bobby Flay, Hot Ones the Game Show, Cash Cab on Bravo, Lingo!, Awake Surgery on TLC, Love After Lockup			
AWARDS:			CASTING COMPANY:	Freelance
INSTAGRAM:	https://www.instagram.com/oliviamakestv/		IMDB:	
FACEBOOK:			FACEBOOK GROUP:	
EMAIL:	olivia.titus324@gmail.com		LINKEDIN:	https://www.linkedin.com/in/olivia-titus-65153b11b/
TIKTOK:			TWITTER:	
WEBSITE:			MAILING LIST LINK:	

NAME:	paisley baker.	CSA	LOCATION:	Sherman Oaks, California
TITLE:	Casting Director and Casting Producer			
CASTS FOR:	Commercials, Film, Scripted, and Unscripted			
CASTING HIGHLIGHTS:	House Hunters, HGTV, Holiday Gingerbread Showdown, Food, 100 Humans, Netflix, Cognition Builders (working title), Lifetime, Hotel Impossible, Travel, Millionaire Matchmaker, Season 5, Bravo, Casting Director:, Surprising Santa Clause, HGTV, Epic Win, MTV, Executive in Charge Casting:, Jersey Shore, MTV, Ru Paul's Drag Race, Logo, A Shot At Love with Tila Tequila, MTV, Design Star, HGTV			
AWARDS:			CASTING COMPANY:	Coat Check Creative (COAT CHECK CREATIVE)
INSTAGRAM:	https://www.instagram.com/coatcheck3/		IMDB:	https://www.imdb.com/name/nm0048810/
FACEBOOK:	https://www.facebook.com/CoatCheckCreative/		FACEBOOK GROUP:	https://www.facebook.com/groups/472794410108214/
EMAIL:	CoatCheckCreative@gmail.com		LINKEDIN:	https://www.linkedin.com/in/paisleybaker3/
TIKTOK:	https://www.tiktok.com/@coatcheckcreative?lang=en		TWITTER:	
WEBSITE:	https://coatcheckcreative.com		MAILING LIST LINK:	

NAME:	pedro gomez jr.		BIPOC and LGBTQI	LOCATION:	Orange County, California
TITLE:	Casting Director and Casting Producer				
CASTS FOR:	Unscripted				
CASTING HIGHLIGHTS:	Love Is Blind, The Amazing Race, The Ultimatum, Married At First Sight, MasterChef, MasterChef Junior, Guys Grocery Games, Idiotest				
AWARDS:	Emmy Nominated Casting Producer Love Is Blind			CASTING COMPANY:	PG @Pedrowillcastu
INSTAGRAM:	Instagram.com/pedrowillcastu			IMDB:	https://m.imdb.com/name/nm5939437/
FACEBOOK:				FACEBOOK GROUP:	
EMAIL:	Pedrojgomezcasting@gmail.com			LINKEDIN:	https://www.linkedin.com/in/pedro-gomez-jr-25998157/
TIKTOK:				TWITTER:	
WEBSITE:				MAILING LIST LINK:	

NAME:	pollyanna jacobs.			LOCATION:	Santa Monica, California
TITLE:	Casting Director				
CASTS FOR:	Unscripted				
CASTING HIGHLIGHTS:	Married at First Sight, Love is Blind, The Ultimatum: Marry or Move On, The Ultimatum: Queer Love, Claim to Fame, The Amazing Race, Sexy Beasts, Kids Baking Championship, Buying it Blind, Love Without Borders				
AWARDS:	Casting team nominated for an Emmy for Love is Blind for seasons 4 & 5			CASTING COMPANY:	
INSTAGRAM:	https://www.instagram.com/pollyannacasting/?hl=en			IMDB:	https://www.imdb.com/name/nm0414588/
FACEBOOK:				FACEBOOK GROUP:	
EMAIL:	pollyannacasting@gmail.com			LINKEDIN:	
TIKTOK:				TWITTER:	
WEBSITE:				MAILING LIST LINK:	

NAME:	rachel natoli.	CSA	LOCATION:	Los Angeles, California
TITLE:	Casting associate			
CASTS FOR:	Unscripted			
CASTING HIGHLIGHTS:	Bar Rescue, Vanderpump Rules, Dated & Related, Married at First Sight, Love is Blind, The Ultimatum, Sexy Beasts, Flip to a Million, Flirty Dancing, 24 Hours to Hell and Back			
AWARDS:			CASTING COMPANY:	Rachel Natoli Casting
INSTAGRAM:	https://www.instagram.com/rachelnatolicasting/		IMDB:	https://www.imdb.com/name/nm13912515/
FACEBOOK:			FACEBOOK GROUP:	
EMAIL:	rachelnatolitv@gmail.com		LINKEDIN:	https://www.linkedin.com/in/rachelnatoli/
TIKTOK:			TWITTER:	
WEBSITE:			MAILING LIST LINK:	https://www.jotform.com/form/231097019032145

NAME:	rachel reilly.		LOCATION:	Birmingham, Alabama
TITLE:	Casting Assistant, Casting Associate, Casting Manager, Casting Producer, and Casting Recruiter			
CASTS FOR:	Commercials, Scripted, and Unscripted			
CASTING HIGHLIGHTS:	The Golden Bachelor, My Dream Quiencenira, Big Brother Canada, Love Island			
AWARDS:			CASTING COMPANY:	
INSTAGRAM:	Instagram.com/rachelereillyvillegas		IMDB:	https://www.imdb.com/name/nm2990141
FACEBOOK:			FACEBOOK GROUP:	
EMAIL:	RachelEReillyVillegas@gmail.com		LINKEDIN:	
TIKTOK:			TWITTER:	Twitter.com/rachelereilly
WEBSITE:	Na		MAILING LIST LINK:	

NAME:	randi godshaw dinh.	LOCATION:	New York
TITLE:	Casting Director and Casting Producer		
CASTS FOR:	Unscripted		
CASTING HIGHLIGHTS:	Tiny House Nation, Alone, 90 Day Fiancé, 90 Day: The Single Life, Ghosted, Pawn Stars, The Four, How Far is Tattoo Far, The Book of John Grey		
AWARDS:		CASTING COMPANY:	
INSTAGRAM:	https://www.instagram.com/randicastingtv/	IMDB:	
FACEBOOK:		FACEBOOK GROUP:	
EMAIL:		LINKEDIN:	https://www.linkedin.com/in/randigodshawdinh/
TIKTOK:		TWITTER:	
WEBSITE:		MAILING LIST LINK:	

NAME:	rebecca bingham.	LOCATION:	Los Angeles / Virginia
TITLE:	Casting Producer, Casting Associate, Casting Assistant, Casting Editor		
CASTS FOR:	Reality, Commercial, New Media		
CASTING HIGHLIGHTS:	sMothered (TLC) , A Haunting (Travel), Blood Money (Hulu)		
AWARDS:		CASTING COMPANY:	
INSTAGRAM:	https://www.instagram.com/beccacastsunscripted/	IMDB:	https://www.imdb.com/name/nm5352740/
FACEBOOK:		FACEBOOK GROUP:	
EMAIL:	Beccacastsunscripted@gmail.com	LINKEDIN:	
TIKTOK:	https://www.tiktok.com/@beccacastsunscripted	TWITTER:	
WEBSITE:	https://linktr.ee/Beccacastsunscripted	MAILING LIST LINK:	

NAME:	rebecca ringley.	CSA	LOCATION:	Los Angeles, CA
TITLE:	Casting Director			
CASTS FOR:	Commercials, Scripted, and Unscripted			
CASTING HIGHLIGHTS:	Real Housewives of Beverly Hills (BRAVO), Real Housewives of Orange County (BRAVO), The Chase (ABC), A Wilderness of Error (FX & HULU), Marrying Millions (LIFETIME), Match Me Abroad (TLC), 90 Day Fiance: Love In Paradise (TLC), The Exhibit (Smithsonian & MTV), How Close Can I Beach? (HGTV), Vacation Rental Potential (A&E)			
AWARDS:	Member, Television Academy		CASTING COMPANY:	Rebecca Ringley Casting (REBECCA RINGLEY)
INSTAGRAM:	https://www.instagram.com/rebeccaringleycasting/		IMDB:	https://www.imdb.com/name/nm6238399/
FACEBOOK:			FACEBOOK GROUP:	
EMAIL:			LINKEDIN:	https://www.linkedin.com/in/rebecca-ringley-21867120/
TIKTOK:			TWITTER:	
WEBSITE:	rebeccaringleycasting.com		MAILING LIST LINK:	https://forms.gle/ETmuFg1Y5FYhz6Xu9

NAME:	rebecca snavely.	AA, BIPOC, and LGBTQI	LOCATION:	Los Angeles, CA
TITLE:	Casting Director, Casting Producer, and Head of Casting			
CASTS FOR:	Unscripted			
CASTING HIGHLIGHTS:	Making the Cut, Project Runway, Like Mother Like Daughter, Born This Way, Best Ink			
AWARDS:	Emmy nomination-Project Runway		CASTING COMPANY:	Vital Casting (VITALCASTING)
INSTAGRAM:	https://www.instagram.com/vitalcasting/		IMDB:	https://www.imdb.com/name/nm0810906/?ref_=fn_al_nm_1
FACEBOOK:			FACEBOOK GROUP:	
EMAIL:	rebecca@vitalcasting.com		LINKEDIN:	
TIKTOK:			TWITTER:	
WEBSITE:	https://www.vitalcasting.com/		MAILING LIST LINK:	

NAME:	renee egan.		LOCATION:	Los Angeles, California
TITLE:	Casting Director and Casting Producer			
CASTS FOR:	Unscripted			
CASTING HIGHLIGHTS:	Farmer Wants a Wife, Vanderpump Villa, Farmer Wants a Wife, Travel Ensemble Show, F'n Fit, Power Games, Untitled Relationship Show, Surviving Family, After Happily Ever After, Secret Resort Show, Being Trans (Podcast), Joe Millionaire, Match Me Abroad, FBoy Island, Going Fur Gold, The Holzer Files, Hot Properties, The Profit, Million Dollar Matchmaker, Famously Single, Love at First Kiss, Say It In Song 2.0, The Face of Torrid 2017, The, Startup Bus, Money Pit, Adventure Capitalists, Sober Coaches, 10 Things, First Impressions, Survive My Wilderness			
AWARDS:			CASTING COMPANY:	RTE Casting
INSTAGRAM:	instagram.com/reneethea		IMDB:	https://www.imdb.com/name/nm3247301/
FACEBOOK:			FACEBOOK GROUP:	
EMAIL:	renee@rtecasting.com		LINKEDIN:	
TIKTOK:			TWITTER:	
WEBSITE:			MAILING LIST LINK:	

NAME:	renee massie.		LOCATION:	Long Beach, California
TITLE:	Casting Director, Casting Producer, and Casting Recruiter			
CASTS FOR:	Commercials, Film, Scripted, Theatre, and Unscripted			
CASTING HIGHLIGHTS:	America's Got Talent, American Ninja Warrior, Game of Talents, Go Big Show, To Tell the Truth			
AWARDS:			CASTING COMPANY:	Renee Massie Casting
INSTAGRAM:	https://www.instagram.com/reneecasting/?hl=en		IMDB:	https://www.imdb.com/name/nm4499248/
FACEBOOK:	https://www.facebook.com/ReneeMassieCasting/		FACEBOOK GROUP:	
EMAIL:	reneecasting@gmail.com		LINKEDIN:	https://www.linkedin.com/in/renee-massie2022/
TIKTOK:	https://www.tiktok.com/@reneecasting		TWITTER:	
WEBSITE:	https://reneemassiecasting.squarespace.com/		MAILING LIST LINK:	

NAME:	richard ralivasquez.			LOCATION:	Los Angeles
TITLE:	Casting Producer				
CASTS FOR:	Reality				
CASTING HIGHLIGHTS:	America's Got Talent, I Can See Your Voice, Queen of the Universe, Making it, Extreme Home Makeover				
AWARDS:				CASTING COMPANY:	
INSTAGRAM:	https://www.instagram.com/richardreal/?hl=en			IMDB:	https://www.imdb.com/name/nm6026914/?ref_=nv_sr_srsg_0
FACEBOOK:				FACEBOOK GROUP:	
EMAIL:	richardreal10@gmail.com			LINKEDIN:	
TIKTOK:				TWITTER:	
WEBSITE:				MAILING LIST LINK:	

NAME:	rita koutsoulis.		CSA	LOCATION:	Stockton, California
TITLE:	Head of Casting				
CASTS FOR:	Unscripted				
CASTING HIGHLIGHTS:	Are You the One? Global Edition (Paramount+), Are You the One? Fluid (MTV), Snake Oil (FOX), Deal or No Deal (CNBC), People Puzzler (GSN), America Says (GSN), Common Knowledge (GSN), Switch (GSN)				
AWARDS:				CASTING COMPANY:	Kastopolis Inc — KASTOPOLIS
INSTAGRAM:	https://www.instagram.com/kastopolisinc/			IMDB:	https://www.imdb.com/name/nm3616412/
FACEBOOK:				FACEBOOK GROUP:	https://www.facebook.com/groups/kastopolisinc
EMAIL:	rita.koutsoulis@gmail.com			LINKEDIN:	
TIKTOK:				TWITTER:	
WEBSITE:	https://kastopolisinc.com/			MAILING LIST LINK:	

NAME:	robert allen.	LGBTQI	LOCATION:	Los Angeles, CA
TITLE:	Casting Assistant, Casting Associate, and Casting Producer			
CASTS FOR:	Commercials and Unscripted			
CASTING HIGHLIGHTS:	Dr. 90210 (Re-boot Season 7), MasterChef (Season 13 & 14), Windy City Rehab (Season 5), Barmageddon (Season 1), Judge Steve Harvey (Season 1), Foodtastic (Season 1), Dr. 90210 (Re-boot Season 7), MasterMinds (Season 1), Homestead Rescue (Season 7, 8 & 9), Resturant Impossible (Season 14), Backyard Bar Wars (Season 1), Love is Blind (Season 1), Married at First Sight (Season 12), Spy Games (Season 1)			
AWARDS:			CASTING COMPANY:	Endemol Shine North American
INSTAGRAM:	https://www.instagram.com/rchristianallen/		IMDB:	
FACEBOOK:	https://www.facebook.com/christian.allen.9212/		FACEBOOK GROUP:	
EMAIL:	rchristianallen@gmail.com		LINKEDIN:	
TIKTOK:			TWITTER:	
WEBSITE:			MAILING LIST LINK:	

NAME:	robyn kass.	CSA	LOCATION:	Los Angeles, CA
TITLE:	Casting Director			
CASTS FOR:	Unscripted			
CASTING HIGHLIGHTS:	Big Brother US and Big Brother Canada- 30+ seasons, Bachelor / Bachelorette, Survivor, Love Island, Squid Game: The Challenge, The Mole			
AWARDS:			CASTING COMPANY:	Kassting Inc — KASSTING inc
INSTAGRAM:	https://www.instagram.com/kassting/		IMDB:	
FACEBOOK:			FACEBOOK GROUP:	
EMAIL:	Robyn@kasstinginc.com		LINKEDIN:	
TIKTOK:			TWITTER:	
WEBSITE:	kasstinginc.com/kassting.php		MAILING LIST LINK:	

NAME:	rose rosen.	CSA / BIPOC	LOCATION:	Tampa, Florida
TITLE:	Casting Director			
CASTS FOR:	Commercials, Film, Scripted, Theatre, and Unscripted			
CASTING HIGHLIGHTS:	Cowboy U, Bridezillas, Highway To Sell, Santa Sent Me To The ER			
AWARDS:	Legend Award SCFF		CASTING COMPANY:	
INSTAGRAM:	https://www.instagram.com/roserosencsa/		IMDB:	IMDb.me/roserosen
FACEBOOK:	https://www.facebook.com/castingbyroserosen		FACEBOOK GROUP:	
EMAIL:			LINKEDIN:	https://www.linkedin.com/in/rose-rosen-csa-4a81bb6/
TIKTOK:	https://tiktok.com/@rosecasting		TWITTER:	https://x.com/roserosen
WEBSITE:	http://castingbyroserosen.com/		MAILING LIST LINK:	

NAME:	sally harrison.		LOCATION:	Los Angeles, California
TITLE:	Casting Associate and Casting Producer			
CASTS FOR:	Unscripted			
CASTING HIGHLIGHTS:	Ready to Love, MTV's Catfish, Netflix's The Ultimatum Marry or Quit, WE's Love After Lockup			
AWARDS:			CASTING COMPANY:	
INSTAGRAM:	https://www.instagram.com/trubeauty__		IMDB:	https://www.imdb.com/name/nm15449870/?ref_=ext_shr_lnk
FACEBOOK:			FACEBOOK GROUP:	
EMAIL:			LINKEDIN:	https://www.linkedin.com/in/sally-harrison-bob0639a?utm_source=share&utm_campaign=share_via&utm_content=profile&utm_medium=ios_app
TIKTOK:			TWITTER:	
WEBSITE:			MAILING LIST LINK:	

NAME:	shae wilbur.		LOCATION:	Florida
TITLE:	Casting Producer			
CASTS FOR:	Reality, Commercial, TV			
CASTING HIGHLIGHTS:	American Idol, AGT, Next Big Thing (BET)			
AWARDS:			CASTING COMPANY:	
INSTAGRAM:	https://www.instagram.com/shaewilbur/		IMDB:	
FACEBOOK:			FACEBOOK GROUP:	
EMAIL:	Shaecasting@gmail.com		LINKEDIN:	
TIKTOK:			TWITTER:	
WEBSITE:	https://linktr.ee/shaewilbur		MAILING LIST LINK:	

NAME:	sharon carcamo.	BIPOC	LOCATION:	Philadelphia, Pennsylvania
TITLE:	Casting Assistant, Casting Associate, and Casting Recruiter			
CASTS FOR:	Commercials, Film, Scripted, and Unscripted			
CASTING HIGHLIGHTS:	Spanish language projects for Asi Studios TelevisaUnivision			
AWARDS:	Casting Society of America BIPOC Alliance Mentee Fall 2020, NALIP Emerging content creators scholarship 2021 Latino Media Fes		CASTING COMPANY:	
INSTAGRAM:	https://www.instagram.com/sharoncasts/		IMDB:	https://www.imdb.com/name/nm5673388/
FACEBOOK:			FACEBOOK GROUP:	
EMAIL:	sharoncasts@gmail.com		LINKEDIN:	https://www.linkedin.com/in/phantomlibertyfilms/
TIKTOK:			TWITTER:	
WEBSITE:			MAILING LIST LINK:	

NAME:	shawn furar.		LGBTQI	LOCATION:	Los Angeles, CA
TITLE:	Casting Associate				
CASTS FOR:	Unscripted				
CASTING HIGHLIGHTS:	Ellen's Game of Games, Netflix's The twenty something project, Beat Shazam, Prank Tank, Cheathab (couples dating show that was in development on bravo), Family Game Fight				
AWARDS:				CASTING COMPANY:	S&S
INSTAGRAM:	https://www.instagram.com/sfurar10/			IMDB:	
FACEBOOK:				FACEBOOK GROUP:	
EMAIL:	Castingwithshawn@gmail.com			LINKEDIN:	
TIKTOK:				TWITTER:	
WEBSITE:				MAILING LIST LINK:	

NAME:	stacy conner.			LOCATION:	Los Angeles, CA
TITLE:	Casting Associate, Casting Editor				
CASTS FOR:	Reality				
CASTING HIGHLIGHTS:	Temptation Island, Claim to Fame, The Challenge 38, The Cube, Don't Forget The Lyrics				
AWARDS:				CASTING COMPANY:	
INSTAGRAM:	https://www.instagram.com/realstacyconner/			IMDB:	
FACEBOOK:	https://www.facebook.com/realstacycasting/			FACEBOOK GROUP:	
EMAIL:	realstacycasting@gmail.com			LINKEDIN:	https://www.linkedin.com/in/sconner/
TIKTOK:	https://www.tiktok.com/@realstacyconner			TWITTER:	
WEBSITE:				MAILING LIST LINK:	

NAME:	steph baca.	BIPOC	LOCATION:	New York, New York
TITLE:	Casting Director and Casting Producer			
CASTS FOR:	Commercials, Unscripted, and Development			
CASTING HIGHLIGHTS:	MPower on Disney+ with Marvel Studios, Indian Matchmaking on Netflix, Cash Cab on Bravo, Hot Ones: The Game Show on TruTv, Love After Lockup on WeTv, 90 Day: The Single Life on TLC			
AWARDS:			CASTING COMPANY:	Freelance
INSTAGRAM:	https://www.instagram.com/steph.baca.casting/		IMDB:	https://www.imdb.com/name/nm2838896/
FACEBOOK:			FACEBOOK GROUP:	
EMAIL:	steph.baca.casting@gmail.com		LINKEDIN:	https://www.linkedin.com/in/steph-baca-05b1408/
TIKTOK:	https://www.tiktok.com/@sb_casting?lang=en		TWITTER:	
WEBSITE:			MAILING LIST LINK:	

NAME:	stevie goldstein.	LGBTQI	LOCATION:	Los Angeles, California
TITLE:	Casting Director and Casting Producer			
CASTS FOR:	Commercials, Film, and Unscripted			
CASTING HIGHLIGHTS:	The Mole, Undercover Boss, Next In Fashion, Bake Squad, Married At First Sight, Temptation Island, Homestead Rescue, Guy's Grocery Games			
AWARDS:			CASTING COMPANY:	Stevie Casting — STEVIE CASTING
INSTAGRAM:	https://www.instagram.com/steviecasting		IMDB:	https://www.imdb.com/name/nm8535750/
FACEBOOK:			FACEBOOK GROUP:	
EMAIL:	steviecasting@gmail.com		LINKEDIN:	
TIKTOK:			TWITTER:	
WEBSITE:	https://www.steviecasting.com/		MAILING LIST LINK:	

NAME:	susan salgado.	LOCATION:	Las Vegas, Nevada
TITLE:	Casting Director, Casting Producer, and Head of Casting		
CASTS FOR:	Commercials and Unscripted		
CASTING HIGHLIGHTS:	Help! I Wrecked My House 3 & 4 (2022 & 2023), Becoming A Pop Star, Finding Magic Mike, Queer Eye (Season 9)		
AWARDS:		CASTING COMPANY:	Salgado Entertainment, LLC aka Triple Threat Casting — SALGADO ENTERTAINMENT
INSTAGRAM:	https://www.instagram.com/tripletcasting/	IMDB:	https://www.imdb.com/name/nm0758205/?ref_=fn_al_nm_1#casting_director
FACEBOOK:	https://www.facebook.com/susan.salgado.33	FACEBOOK GROUP:	https://www.facebook.com/groups/562097563998336
EMAIL:	tripletcasting@yahoo.com	LINKEDIN:	
TIKTOK:		TWITTER:	
WEBSITE:		MAILING LIST LINK:	

NAME:	tamara brandel.	LOCATION:	Los Angeles, California
TITLE:	Casting Director and Casting Producer		
CASTS FOR:	Commercials and Unscripted		
CASTING HIGHLIGHTS:	Seven seasons of American Idol, Real Housewives of Beverly Hills, Real Housewives of New Jersey, Real Housewives of Orange County, Real Housewives of Miami, Summer House, Southern Charm, Married to Medicine LA and Atlanta		
AWARDS:		CASTING COMPANY:	TamiBCasting INC
INSTAGRAM:	https://www.instagram.com/tamibcasting/	IMDB:	https://www.imdb.com/name/nm2285230/
FACEBOOK:		FACEBOOK GROUP:	https://www.facebook.com/groups/48198368959
EMAIL:	tamibcastingtv@gmail.com	LINKEDIN:	https://www.linkedin.com/in/tami-brandel-6447006/
TIKTOK:	https://www.tiktok.com/@tamibcasting	TWITTER:	
WEBSITE:	www.tamibcasting.com	MAILING LIST LINK:	

NAME:	telon weathington.	CSA / AA and BIPOC	LOCATION:	Los Angeles, California
TITLE:	Casting Associate and Casting Producer			
CASTS FOR:	Scripted and Unscripted			
CASTING HIGHLIGHTS:	The Great Christmas Light Fight, The Great Halloween Fright Fight, Ready to Love, All the Single Ladies, Big Brother, Put a Ring On It, F Boy Island, Married at First Sight, Bride & Prejudice, Holiday Baking Championship, Halloween Baking Championship, Celebrity Name Game			
AWARDS:			CASTING COMPANY:	
INSTAGRAM:	www.instagram.com/layditee		IMDB:	
FACEBOOK:			FACEBOOK GROUP:	
EMAIL:	castingtelon@gmail.com		LINKEDIN:	
TIKTOK:			TWITTER:	
WEBSITE:			MAILING LIST LINK:	

NAME:	tessa stefanello.	BIPOC	LOCATION:	New York, New York
TITLE:	Casting Director			
CASTS FOR:	Scripted and Unscripted			
CASTING HIGHLIGHTS:	Say Yes To The Dress, The Bachelorette, The Bachelor, House Hunters, The Nate and Jeremiah Home Project, Swiping America, Ugliest House In America, Critter Fixer			
AWARDS:			CASTING COMPANY:	
INSTAGRAM:	https://www.instagram.com/tessaoriginal/		IMDB:	
FACEBOOK:	https://www.facebook.com/tessa.julieta		FACEBOOK GROUP:	
EMAIL:	tessastef@gmail.com		LINKEDIN:	https://www.linkedin.com/in/tessa-stefanello/
TIKTOK:			TWITTER:	
WEBSITE:			MAILING LIST LINK:	

NAME:	thea washington.	CSA / AA, BIPOC, and LGBTQI	LOCATION:	Severna Park, Maryland
TITLE:	Casting Director, Casting Producer, and Casting Recruiter			
CASTS FOR:	Commercials, Film, Scripted, and Unscripted			
CASTING HIGHLIGHTS:	Ready to Love, Queens Court. Great Christmas Light Fight			
AWARDS:			CASTING COMPANY:	
INSTAGRAM:	https://www.instagram.com/theawashingtoncasting/ | @TheaWashingtonCasting		IMDB:	https://www.imdb.com/name/nm7995063/
FACEBOOK:	https://www.facebook.com/theawashingtoncasting/		FACEBOOK GROUP:	
EMAIL:			LINKEDIN:	
TIKTOK:			TWITTER:	
WEBSITE:			MAILING LIST LINK:	

NAME:	theresa green.	AA and BIPOC	LOCATION:	Atlanta, Georgia
TITLE:	Casting Editor			
CASTS FOR:	Unscripted			
CASTING HIGHLIGHTS:	Real Housewives of Atlanta, Real Housewives of Potomac, Basketball Wives, Unexpected Summer House, Winter House			
AWARDS:			CASTING COMPANY:	
INSTAGRAM:	https://www.instagram.com/_greentee/?hl=en		IMDB:	
FACEBOOK:			FACEBOOK GROUP:	
EMAIL:			LINKEDIN:	
TIKTOK:			TWITTER:	
WEBSITE:			MAILING LIST LINK:	

NAME:	tiffany wilson.	**LOCATION:**	Marietta, Georgia
TITLE:	Casting Associate, Casting Producer, and Casting Recruiter		
CASTS FOR:	Scripted and Unscripted		
CASTING HIGHLIGHTS:	Divorce Court, Cutlers Court, Judge Steve Harvey, Relatively Wild, Boomin Love		
AWARDS:		**CASTING COMPANY:**	
INSTAGRAM:	https://www.instagram.com/tiffwilsocasting/	**IMDB:**	
FACEBOOK:		**FACEBOOK GROUP:**	
EMAIL:	tiffwilsocasting@gmail.com	**LINKEDIN:**	
TIKTOK:	https://www.tiktok.com/@tiffwilsocasting	**TWITTER:**	
WEBSITE:		**MAILING LIST LINK:**	

NAME:	tina seiler.	**LOCATION:**	Delray Beach, Florida
TITLE:	Casting Producer		
CASTS FOR:	Unscripted		
CASTING HIGHLIGHTS:	Fixer Upper on HGTV (All 5 seasons), Restored by the Fords on HGTV, Trip Flip on Travel Channel		
AWARDS:		**CASTING COMPANY:**	Tina Seiler Casting
INSTAGRAM:	https://www.instagram.com/tvtinas/	**IMDB:**	https://www.imdb.com/name/nm0782612/
FACEBOOK:		**FACEBOOK GROUP:**	
EMAIL:	castingbytina@gmail.com	**LINKEDIN:**	https://www.linkedin.com/in/tina-seiler-13a27b5/
TIKTOK:		**TWITTER:**	
WEBSITE:		**MAILING LIST LINK:**	

NAME:	tony miros.	CSA / LGBTQI	LOCATION:	Hollywood, CA
TITLE:	Casting Director, Casting Producer, and Head of Casting			
CASTS FOR:	Scripted and Unscripted			
CASTING HIGHLIGHTS:	Squid Game: The Challenge, Love For The Ages, The Great Christmas Light Fight, Claim to Fame, Business Hunters, My Kind of Country, We're Here			
AWARDS:	2018 Nominee Artios Award Outstanding Achievement in Casting-Reality Series-MTV's "True Life" Episode 29 "We Are Transitioning (2016)"		CASTING COMPANY:	Tony Miros Casting TONY MIROS CASTING
INSTAGRAM:	https://www.instagram.com/tonymiroscasting		IMDB:	https://www.imdb.com/name/nm2428427/
FACEBOOK:			FACEBOOK GROUP:	https://www.facebook.com/groups/143310769022899
EMAIL:	tonymiroscasting@gmail.com		LINKEDIN:	
TIKTOK:			TWITTER:	
WEBSITE:			MAILING LIST LINK:	

NAME:	torriel simon.	AA and BIPOC	LOCATION:	Van Nuys, CA
TITLE:	Casting Director			
CASTS FOR:	Unscripted			
CASTING HIGHLIGHTS:	Ellen Game of Games, Celebrity Name Game, Dating Naked, Are you the One, Rhythm and Flow, Signed, Love Connection, Home Sweet Home and many more			
AWARDS:	NAACP award- Rhythm and Flow		CASTING COMPANY:	Bunim and Murray TCS PRODUCTIONS
INSTAGRAM:	https://www.instagram.com/torricasting/		IMDB:	https://www.imdb.com/name/nm5890279/
FACEBOOK:			FACEBOOK GROUP:	
EMAIL:	torricasting@gmail.com		LINKEDIN:	https://www.linkedin.com/in/torriel-simon-a5718727
TIKTOK:			TWITTER:	
WEBSITE:			MAILING LIST LINK:	

NAME:	valerie penso-cuculich.	LOCATION:	Hollywood, California
TITLE:	Casting Director, and Casting Producer		
CASTS FOR:	Commercials and Unscripted, Docuseries & Game Shows		
CASTING HIGHLIGHTS:	Love Island, Too Hot To Handle, Real Housewives of Dubai, Below Deck, I'm Having Their Baby, The Millionaire Matchmaker, Supermarket Sweep, Baggage, Chef Wanted		
AWARDS:		CASTING COMPANY:	No Alibi Media
INSTAGRAM:	https://www.instagram.com/valeriesworld/ www.instagram.com/noalibimedia_	IMDB:	https://www.imdb.com/name/nm0672335/
FACEBOOK:		FACEBOOK GROUP:	
EMAIL:	noalibimedia@gmail.com	LINKEDIN:	www.linkedin.com/in/valerie-penso-cuculich-70b5ab2/
TIKTOK:	https://www.tiktok.com/@castingvalerie	TWITTER:	https://twitter.com/valeriepenso?lang=en
WEBSITE:	www.noalibimedia.com	MAILING LIST LINK:	

NAME:	vanessa garcia.	LOCATION:	Los Angeles, California
TITLE:	Casting Producer		
CASTS FOR:	Reality, TV		
CASTING HIGHLIGHTS:	Undercover Boss, Love is Blind, The Love Boat		
AWARDS:	Nominated twice for Emmy: Undercover Boss Nominated for Emmy: Love is Blind	CASTING COMPANY:	
INSTAGRAM:	https://www.instagram.com/vanessa_kingstonbach/?hl=en	IMDB:	
FACEBOOK:		FACEBOOK GROUP:	
EMAIL:		LINKEDIN:	
TIKTOK:		TWITTER:	
WEBSITE:		MAILING LIST LINK:	

NAME:	vinnie potestivo.	LOCATION:	New York , NY
TITLE:	Casting Director		
CASTS FOR:	Reality, New Media, TV, Film		
CASTING HIGHLIGHTS:	Punk'd, Wild 'n Out, The Challenge, Laguna Beach, The Hills, House of Style, 8th & Ocean, Making Da Band, Say What? Karaoke, The Tom Green Show, The Ashlee Simpson Show, Direct Effect, Headbanger's Ball, All Things Rock, Real Housewives of NJ, Millionaire Matchmaker, A Question of Love		
AWARDS:	2008 Winner Prism Award, Substance Abuse in Documentary TV Program, I Won't Love You to Death: The Story of Mario and His Mom 2021 Winner Davey Award, I Have A Podcast 2021 Winner Emmy, Best Human Interest Series (News), Red Flags	CASTING COMPANY:	
INSTAGRAM:	Instagram.com/vinniepotestivo	IMDB:	https://m.imdb.com/name/nm2003375/
FACEBOOK:	Facebook.com/yoitsvinnie	FACEBOOK GROUP:	Facebook.com/vinniepotestivo
EMAIL:	HELLO@vpetalent.com	LINKEDIN:	LinkedIn.com/in/vinniepotestivo
TIKTOK:	tiktok.com/@vinniepotestivo	TWITTER:	Twitter.com/vinniepotestivo
WEBSITE:	vpetalent.com	MAILING LIST LINK:	

CASTING PROS TO KNOW: FEATURED STORY

Asjai Lou's Casting Journey: The People, Places & Experiences That Shaped Me

Every edition of this book will feature a casting professional and their unique story—but I'm opening this tradition by sharing mine. This chapter isn't just a highlight reel. It's a reflection of the journey that shaped my creative eye and the life experiences that make me who I am—both in and outside of casting. From growing up immersed in culture, to finding my place behind the scenes, to discovering the power of seeing real people and giving them space to shine—every step has led me here. You'll get a glimpse into the mentors who poured into me, the environments that inspired me, and the lessons that helped me find my voice as a casting professional. These are the moments that built my foundation—not overnight success, but a journey of learning, listening, and trusting my instincts. Casting, to me, has always been about more than filling roles. It's about recognizing the beauty in real people's stories and helping the world see them too. So here's where it begins—with my story. And in every edition that follows, you'll meet more casting pros who continue to shape this industry with their own journeys, voices, and impact

Welcome to the first Featured Story—a space where I share the defining moments of my life and career, giving you a deeper look at who I am beyond casting. This section is about more than just my professional journey; it's about the experiences, challenges, and personal milestones that have shaped me into the person I am today.

To start this tradition, I'm opening up about the pivotal moments that influenced my path—the mentors who guided me, the lessons learned along the way, and the unexpected turns that led to my biggest breakthroughs.

But this isn't just about me. Each edition of this book will highlight a different casting professional, showcasing their insights, experiences, and contributions to the industry. Together, we're building a platform where casting pros can share their journeys, connect, and inspire others.

In this chapter, I'll take you behind the scenes to explore how I found my purpose in casting, what this industry has taught me, and why casting is about so much more than just filling roles. It's about storytelling, authenticity, and making a lasting impact—both on-screen and in the lives of real people.

Let's dive in—this journey starts here, and I'm excited to take it with you.

My Casting Journey: From Headshots to Casting Pro

If you'd told nine-year-old me that flipping through a stack of headshots and playing a game of "who belongs in the scene" would spark a career shaping the stars of tomorrow, I'd have laughed. But now, looking back, I see that moment for what it truly was—the spark that started it all.

It began in the casting office of *New York Undercover*, where my mom's friend, Tracy Moore, was managing casting duties while keeping an eye on me and her daughter, Radiance. To keep us occupied, Tracy handed over a stack of headshots and said, "Pick people who look like they belong in a jail scene."

Radiance wasn't interested, but I was hooked. I carefully studied each photo, imagining backstories, analyzing expressions, and deciding who radiated "gritty jail vibes." It felt like solving a puzzle, and I was determined to get it right. When Tracy checked my picks, she smiled and said, "You nailed it."

That small, seemingly ordinary moment planted a seed. At the time, I didn't know it would grow into a career, but it was my first glimpse into the art of casting. It showed me the magic of finding the right faces, the right stories, and the right energy to bring a scene to life—and I was captivated.

Lesson for Casting: *Every great casting decision starts with curiosity and a willingness to imagine the unseen. Trust your instincts, and don't be afraid to dive deep into the details.*

Early Lessons in Casting and Filmmaking

Growing up, filmmaking wasn't just something I watched—it was something I lived. My mom, Sharron Cannon, work in production gave me a front-row seat to the behind-the-scenes magic that brings stories to life.

One of my most unforgettable experiences was on the set of *I Like It Like That*, a groundbreaking film that still holds a special place in my heart. The legendary Darnell Martin, the first Black woman to direct a studio film with Columbia Pictures, handed me a chance to peer through the camera lens and taught me how to frame a shot. Watching her orchestrate the rhythm and flow of filmmaking opened my eyes to the meticulous artistry of storytelling—crafted one frame at a time.

Casting director Yolande Geralds added her own brilliance, filling the screen with unforgettable faces that made every scene come alive. She cast me, my brother Kenny Allen, my cousin Jasmine, and our friends as part of the summertime hangout-on-the-block scenes. For a group of kids, it was nothing short of stardom. Those moments were defining for the film—and for us.

The production office of *I Like It Like That* was where I learned that magic on-screen starts with quick thinking and preparation off-screen. One day, producer Lane Janger burst into the office and—bam!—smashed a bottle over my head. My mom's reaction was immediate and furious, convinced it was real glass. Thankfully, it wasn't. It was a breakaway bottle, carefully crafted for fight scenes. That moment taught me about the precision and trust that make movie magic possible.

And if I'm being honest, Lane might've been getting back at me for my "swear jar" hustle. I charged a quarter for every curse word I heard in the busy production office—and let's just say it was a lucrative venture. By the end of the day, I'd leave with bags of quarters and a grin that stretched ear to ear.

Lesson for Casting: *Quick thinking, creativity, and preparation are the building blocks of magic—both on-screen and behind the scenes.*

From High School Spark to Music Video Dreams

By the time I reached high school, my love for storytelling had transformed into a full-blown passion. Attending the Professional Performing Arts School (P.P.A.S.) was like stepping into the TV show *Fame*. It was a place where creativity and talent spilled into every corner.

Dancers pirouetted down the hallways, singers belted out high notes that echoed through the stairwells, and musicians turned lunchroom tables into beat-making studios. Meanwhile, the musical theatre and acting kids—myself included—were always bringing the drama, both on and off the stage.

My peers weren't just dreaming big—they were living it. Broadway prodigies, Disney stars, and even Grammy-winning artists like Alicia Keys walked the same halls. My late friend Lee Young was a constant source of light, filling every room with his energy, humor, and undeniable talent.

While many of my classmates were chasing the spotlight, I found myself captivated by what happened behind the scenes. With the encouragement of incredible principals like Mindy Chermack and Kim Bruno, I began to carve out my own path, one that leaned into my love for storytelling and the art of creating moments that connect.

That path led me to a life-changing opportunity during my senior year. My mom introduced me to Mellicent Dyane, a powerhouse in music video casting. Mellicent needed an intern, and I jumped at the chance. One day I was organizing files, and the next, I was helping cast for icons like Kanye West and The White Stripes.

This wasn't just any internship—it was during the golden age of hip-hop and music videos, a time of unparalleled creativity and cultural influence. Budgets were massive, directors were visionaries, and sets were bursting with energy and innovation. Mellicent became my mentor, trusting me to dive headfirst into this fast-paced, culture-shaping world.

Working on projects that defined an era wasn't just thrilling—it was transformative. The experience deepened my love for casting and gave me a front-row seat to the magic of bringing creative visions to life. Those music video dreams became the foundation for everything I've built since.

Lesson for Casting: *Behind every great production is a team of dreamers and doers who see beyond the surface. Collaboration is the key to success.*

From Music Videos to Commercials—and Finding Love

After college, I made the leap to Los Angeles—not just to advance my career, but to be with my late partner, Amanjah Anthony. A fellow P.P.A.S. alum and my high school crush, Amanjah wasn't just my partner; he was my anchor, my muse, and my biggest cheerleader. He had a way of seeing the best in me, even when I doubted myself. His encouragement reminded me to take risks, trust my instincts, and unapologetically chase my dreams.

Once in LA, fate continued to align. A college friend, Gino, introduced me to Melissa Feliciano, who was working with Paul Hunter—a legend in music videos transitioning into commercials. Melissa welcomed me into her world with open arms, and it didn't take long for me to fall in love with the detail-driven, high-stakes craft of commercial casting.

At 1020 Studios in Hollywood, Alyson Horn became another transformative figure in my journey. Alyson was tough as nails and uncompromising—there were no shortcuts or easy answers with her. She pushed me to rise to every challenge, teaching me to break down scripts with precision, master comedic timing, and, most importantly, trust my instincts.

Her tough love didn't just sharpen my skills; it strengthened my resilience. In an industry as competitive as casting, those lessons became invaluable. Alyson didn't just make me a better casting professional—she instilled in me the confidence and tenacity to thrive no matter what challenges came my way.

Lesson for Casting: *Resilience is your greatest asset in casting. Learn to trust your instincts, embrace challenges, and grow through every experience.*

Meeting Cindy and Lyle: Building Good People Casting

It was at Alyson Horn's studio that I met Cindy Estrada, Alyson's studio manager and the person who would become one of my biggest allies. As Alysons associate, I faced countless challenges that pushed me to grow, and Cindy became my lifeline, saving me from Alyson's wrath more times than I can count.

We didn't just work together—we became more like sisters. To this day, Cindy and I share an unshakable bond. She and her husband, Felix, have stood by me through some of the darkest moments in my life, offering unwavering kindness and wisdom. I'm endlessly grateful for their support, which has meant more to me than words can express.

When Cindy and Lyle Dohl founded Good People Casting, it marked a transformative moment in my career. Their innovative approach to real people casting for commercials broke new ground in the industry. Unlike traditional casting, which relied on platforms like Casting Networks and Breakdown Services to source actors and models, real people casting was an entirely different challenge.

At the time, there were no established platforms for finding real people. It required street casting, tapping into word-of-mouth networks, and scouring social media for fresh, everyday faces with no entertainment experience. Cindy and Lyle took me under their wing and taught me the ropes. Once I got a taste for it, I was hooked.

Real people casting was tougher, but it was also deeply rewarding. I had the chance to change lives, giving people who never thought they were "enough" an opportunity to see their own potential. That's what drives my initiative #iCu today—encouraging everyday people to take a chance on themselves and step into a world they might never have considered.

Real people casting is about so much more than finding talent; it's about opening doors for those who didn't even know they could walk through them. It's about showing people that their stories, their personalities, and their authentic selves are more than enough. Cindy, Lyle, and Good People Casting didn't just teach me a skill—they reinforced a mission that I carry with me every day.

Lesson for Casting: *Real people casting isn't just about finding faces; it's about finding stories. Always look beyond the surface to uncover the unexpected.*

The Reality TV Chapter

My journey into reality TV began with a pivotal nudge from Zac Dixon, who steered me in the right direction. Zac introduced me to Bonnie Clark, who then connected me with Donna Driscoll at Kinetic Content. Donna brought me onto my very first reality TV project, *Married at First Sight: Honeymoon Island*, and everything instantly clicked.

Reality TV became the perfect space for me to combine my love of storytelling with my talent for finding bold, unforgettable personalities. It was a natural fit, and from that point on, my career soared. I've since worked with major networks like OWN, CBS, Bravo, ABC, MTV, and VH1, contributing to iconic shows and groundbreaking projects that have left a mark on the genre.

Some career highlights include casting *Making the Cut* season 3 winner Yannik Zamboni, fan favorites from *Big Brother* like Jasmine Davis, Britini D'Angelo, and Claire Rehfuss (who later won *The Amazing Race*), and powerhouse singers like Jay Copeland, Nutsa, and Gabby Samone on *American Idol*. I've also cast for reality staples like *Real Housewives of Atlanta*, *Ready to Love*, and *The Great Christmas Light Fight*.

Beyond reality TV, I've lent my expertise to major campaigns for Fortune 500 brands like McDonald's, Volkswagen, Walmart, T-Mobile, and Nike, with commercials that aired during the Super Bowl and the Olympics. I've also been fortunate to cast for projects featuring legendary artists like Beyoncé, Andre 3000, Mariah Carey, Dipset, Mary J. Blige, Common, Kelis, Fabolous, and Lil' Kim, collaborating across commercials, music videos, and other creative ventures.

Reality TV opened the door to a world where I could bring authentic stories and compelling personalities to life. Whether it's helping networks find their next star or shaping the cast of a groundbreaking series, this chapter of my career has been about more than just casting—it's been about amplifying voices, building connections, and creating unforgettable moments.

Lesson for Casting: *In reality TV, authenticity is everything. Look for bold personalities and genuine stories that resonate deeply with audiences.*

Experiences That Defined Me

Growing Up on the Universal Studios Lot

Some of the most defining moments of my life didn't happen in a classroom or on a set—they happened on the Universal Studios lot. Growing up alongside my mom, Sharron Cannon, and my godfather, Jim Brubaker, the former president of Universal Pictures, felt like living inside a blockbuster. These two worked on legendary films like Angelina Jolie's breakout movie *GIA, Above the Rim. Nutty Professor,* and *Life,* to name a few.

For my cousin Jasmine, my brother Kenny, and me, the lot was our ultimate playground. We'd steal golf carts, zoom over to the Jurassic Park ride, hop the fence, and ride it over and over as if it were our personal attraction. The *Jurassic Park* and *E.T.* rides were our absolute favorites—though Kenny hated *E.T.* Jasmine and I couldn't get enough, and one day, after we begged for just one more ride (and then another), Kenny had enough and wandered off. When we realized he was gone, panic set in as we searched frantically to find him. Thankfully, he didn't get far, but it's a story we laugh about to this day.

Another favorite pastime was driving golf carts alongside the Universal tram ride as it passed by the studio lots. Jasmine and I would wave enthusiastically at the tourists, convinced they thought we were the next big Hollywood stars. And to be honest, we believed it too—we were sure we were destined to take over the industry someday.

Kenny had his own big moment on the lot when he learned how to ride a bike. Beast, a towering family friend who was working with Wyclef Jean on the *Life* soundtrack, decided to teach him. With his larger-than-life personality and height, Beast picked Kenny up, held him high in the air, and told him to pedal as fast as he could. Then he let him go. Kenny flew forward, crashed, and somehow came out of it knowing how to ride—all in one fearless attempt.

The Universal Studios lot wasn't just a workplace for my mom or a backdrop for iconic films—it was where we learned to dream, to take risks, and to believe anything was possible. For me, these experiences didn't just shape my childhood; they laid the foundation for everything I've built since.

Lesson for Casting: *Creativity flourishes in unexpected places. Keep your eyes open for inspiration—it can come from the most surprising moments and people.*

My First Music Video: Lionel Martin and Classic Concepts

I vividly remember being cast in my very first music video, directed by the legendary Lionel Martin and cast by Tracy Moore. This was before *I Like It Like That* and during the golden age of Classic Concepts, the ultimate hub for music video magic. Classic Concepts wasn't just another office I visited as a kid—it was *the* place to be. My mom and Tracy often freelanced there, and I tagged along, soaking up the energy of a space responsible for some of the greatest music videos of all time.

Classic Concepts was also where my mom's lifelong friendship with Beast began. His brother, Handsome, worked there as a producer, and I had the biggest schoolgirl crush on him. Handsome and his wife, Leslie Ann, were effortlessly cool—just being in their presence felt like stepping into a world of magic and possibility.

This was the same creative playground where Lionel Martin thrived and where Hype Williams got his start as a creative director. To this day, I wonder if Hype's iconic use of blue light was inspired by Lionel's work. If you've ever watched a Lionel Martin video, you know his signature style—wet streets and that unforgettable blue glow that became staples of '90s music videos.

Another pivotal figure at Classic Concepts was Teisha Albert Pankey, the office manager and a legend in her own right. Teisha later joined my mom at Viacom and became a staple in my life. She always had the best stories—insider tales about how some of the most iconic music videos came to life. Sitting with her and hearing those stories gave me a deep appreciation for the artistry, hustle, and sheer magic happening behind the scenes.

I'll never forget how much I idolized Josie, one of the top-rated dancers of that era. I even had jumbo braids just like hers. So, imagine my excitement when the hairstylist on set looked at me and said, "I'm going to do your hair just like Josie!" She had no idea how much I admired her, but that small moment made my entire day—and it's a memory I'll treasure forever.

Classic Concepts wasn't just a production house; it was a creative sanctuary that laid the foundation for my passion.

Lesson for Casting: *Great casting is about understanding style and storytelling. Pay attention to the creative forces shaping the industry—they'll teach you how to see beyond the obvious.*

A Gift from Tupac

One of the most unforgettable moments of my childhood came when my mom was working on *Above the Rim*. As the director of product placement, she had access to just about everything—and when I say we were decked out in Reebok clothes and shoes for years, I mean it! But the real highlight of that job was her working with Tupac.

I used to beg my mom to take me to hang out with Tupac, but it never happened. Looking back, I'm pretty sure she was trying to shield me from some of his "extracurricular activities." Instead, she found a way to let me feel connected. She'd call me on her massive cell phone—the kind that was about as big as my arm—and sneak it into her purse while she was with him. I'd sit on the other end, quietly listening to Tupac's voice, imagining I was right there in the room with them.

One day, my mom brought home a gift that felt like pure magic. The stylist had given her a shirt Tupac had worn, and she passed it on to me. To say I treasured it would be an understatement. I slept with that shirt on my pillow every night, convinced it carried his "special smell." To me, it wasn't just a shirt—it was a connection to someone larger than life, and I treated it like the most valuable thing I owned.

But then disaster struck. One morning, I woke up to find the shirt no longer smelled like Tupac. Instead, it had the unmistakable scent of fabric softener. My mom had washed it! As a child, I was devastated, feeling like she'd washed away all the magic. In a fit of dramatic rage, I threw the shirt in the trash.

Looking back, I can't believe I did that. That shirt wasn't just a piece of fabric—it was a piece of history, a connection to one of the most iconic figures of our time. Even if it smelled like Tide, it was still Tupac's shirt.

Lesson for Casting: *Cherish the connections you make in this industry. They're not just memories—they're reminders of the people and moments that shape your journey.*

A Moment with Michael Jackson and Rodney Jerkins

It all started with the late, great LaShawn Daniels, who believed in my girl group and brought us to Rodney Jerkins, eager to sign us. We met Rodney at Sony Studios in downtown NYC, which had been transformed into a Disney wonderland. Disney characters hung from the ceiling, and the entire space radiated creativity and magic—it was the coolest setup I'd ever seen.

Sony Studios had been cleared out for Rodney and the King of Pop himself, Michael Jackson, as they worked on the *Invincible* album. The energy in the building was electrifying, and stepping into that space felt like entering a dream.

As we prepared to meet Rodney, our nerves were high. We'd recently undergone a significant transformation in our group's image. Gone were the TLC-inspired baggy clothes—we'd embraced a more mature, form-fitting look. On top of that, our original lead singer had decided to go solo, and we'd replaced her with someone new. We knew Rodney's expectations were high, and we were eager to show him our growth.

But as soon as Rodney saw us, his reaction was immediate and unfiltered. "No! Where are my little girls?" he shouted, his tone a mix of aggression and disappointment. His disapproval was palpable, and we could feel the weight of it in the room.

We nervously tried to explain, saying, "We grew up," but it wasn't enough to calm him down. Rodney was visibly upset, and the tension was amplified by the presence of Michael Jackson, who quietly observed the entire exchange. Michael stood there, larger than life yet radiating a gentle, calming presence that somehow softened the blow of Rodney's outburst.

The room itself was intimate—just us, LaShawn, Rodney, Michael, and Michael's son, Prince. As Rodney's frustration simmered, I turned my attention to Prince, who was jumping on bare mattresses scattered across the floor. It didn't take long for me to join him—we laughed, jumped, and played, creating our own little world amidst the tension. For a moment, it was as if the weight of the situation hadn't even registered.

Seeing Michael up close was both exhilarating and surreal. I had no idea he could grow a beard, but there he was, sporting a patchy one that caught me completely off guard. Despite the drama, I managed to hug him and tell him I loved him—a moment that still feels unreal and will forever hold a special place in my heart.

At the time, Rodney's outburst felt like a crushing blow. We'd walked into the room with dreams of securing a record deal, only to watch the opportunity slip away in real time. But looking back now, it's a story I tell with pride.

How many people can say they were in an intimate room with Michael Jackson, no security, no barriers, just us? I'll never forget jumping on mattresses with Prince, hugging Michael, and witnessing Rodney's raw, unfiltered passion. Even though it didn't lead to a deal, the experience was magical and unforgettable. Rodney's generosity allowed us to share in that moment, and while it wasn't the outcome we'd hoped for, it was still a dream come true.

Lesson for Casting: *The biggest opportunities don't always lead to success,* *but they leave you with invaluable lessons and unforgettable experiences. Embrace the journey.*

Meeting Devante Swing: A Full-Circle Moment

As a child, I was obsessed with Devante Swing—he was my ultimate schoolgirl crush. When my mom worked on a Jodeci music video with Classic Concepts, I begged her to let me tag along to meet him. But nope, Mom wasn't having it. She shut it down, and I was devastated. My dream of meeting him didn't happen then, but little did I know, life had something special in store.

Years later, while I was in a girl group, fate stepped in. Devante rented the studio next to ours for his Basement Crew. I still remember the first time I saw him there. He came down the stairs, bottle of Hennessy in hand, celebrating like he was on top of the world—and honestly, he was. He'd just signed on to produce Michael Jackson's *Invincible* album, the very same project we'd been around Michael recording.

Soon, Devante started watching our rehearsals, and to my surprise, he loved us. He'd offer pointers to help improve our stage presence, and we soaked up every piece of advice like sponges. He saw potential in us and made us feel like we were on the brink of greatness.

Of course, there was that one time he got on my nerves. During his celebratory mood, he accidentally spilled Hennessy on me—not once, not twice, but three times. By the third spill, I'd had enough and let him know it. After that, every time he saw me, he'd give me those puppy eyes and say, "You don't like me much, do you?"

The truth is, I adored him. He had no idea how much I'd admired him since I was a young girl. Years later, as an adult, I visited my longtime friend LB in California, who happened to be at Devante's house. When LB reminded him I was in the girl group from back in the day, Devante looked at me and said, "Oh yeah, I remember you—you don't like me too much."

Although it stung a little that this was his lasting memory of me, I was also happy he remembered me at all. That visit turned into an unforgettable experience. I stayed and recorded my first solo record, *Let Me Be the One,* which was a smash, if I do say so myself. LB had a way with R&B, and together, we created magic that night.

But the real magic happened later. After we finished recording, we heard a commotion coming from Devante's living room. Curious, we walked in and found Devante at the piano, playing Jodeci's hit *Cry for You.* To our surprise, Mike Tyson was singing lead, with the lead singer of the Mary Jane Girls, Devante, and now us singing background vocals.

It turned into an impromptu Jodeci night, starring Devante Swing and Mike Tyson. Who would've thought Iron Mike had that kind of humor and charisma? At the time, the world didn't really see that side of him, but in that moment, he was the life of the party.

The night was filled with music, laughter, and an energy that could only be described as magical. It was a full-circle moment I'll never forget—one that reminded me how life has a funny way of bringing your dreams back to you when you least expect it.

Lesson for Casting: *Full-circle moments happen when you least expect them. Always be open to reconnecting with people and places from your past—they often bring new opportunities.*

A Magical Time with Imajin

My time with the boy band Imajin wasn't just a fond memory—it was a masterclass in talent, resilience, and creativity. These guys were incredibly gifted, and watching them rehearse, land their record deal, go on tour, achieve gold status, and shoot music videos was nothing short of inspiring. We were like the sister group to their brotherhood. While our vibe wasn't as polished as theirs, we had heart and determination. If I'm being honest, we were probably doing the absolute most! But those moments were pure magic, filled with creative energy, camaraderie, and the undeniable spirit of winning.

In high school, I signed a production deal with Planet Sound, led by John Grossberg and Bert Price of Dbl Phatt Productions. This was the epicenter of talent—so many greats walked through those doors and recorded in those studios. Imajin, made up of Olamide, John, Talib, and Jamal, was the boy band signed to Dbl Phatt, and they were already on fire. Their achievements inspired everyone around them, including us. The hope was that our girl group would be next.

What most people didn't see, though, was the reality behind the music. We saw Imajin rehearse all day, live in a small studio with limited resources, and record all night. They were homeschooled to fit their demanding schedules. While the world saw pop star perfection, the reality was far from glamorous. None of us were living in luxury—we were all just scraping by, driven by passion and belief in our dreams.

The energy and creativity in that building were electrifying. Our studio was tucked away in the basement, isolating us from the outside world, but inside, magic was happening. The roster was stacked with talent: LB, Rell, Miz, Johnny (aka Cupac), Bert Price, Sonya, Lena, and our girl group—originally me, Ariel, and Lindsay, and later me, Lindsay, and Sunni. We practiced every day after school, driven by dreams of success and the belief that we were destined for greatness.

Imajin didn't realize it, but we were their biggest fans. Watching them thrive and grow as artists inspired us to push even harder. Their energy was infectious, and their success lit a fire in all of us. At the same time, being around them sharpened my eye for recognizing talent. I was surrounded by artists, producers, songwriters, musicians, and engineers—a big family of creatives who pushed us to be our best. Back then, it was all about the vibe. Creativity was abundant, but none of us fully grasped the business side of things. This was a lesson in balancing creativity with professionalism, something I'd carry into my casting career.

Looking back, this was the time when I truly began to understand the depth of my creativity. At the time, I didn't fully grasp the lessons I was learning, but those years—filled with highs and lows—were shaping me into the person I am today. They taught me the importance of resilience, the value of hard work, and the ability to adapt to challenges.

Lesson for Casting: *Every team you work with teaches you something valuable. Collaboration fuels creativity, and being inspired by others will always elevate your work. But most importantly, don't judge success by what you see on the surface. True greatness often comes from struggles and sacrifices that happen behind closed doors.*

Backstage with Broadway Legends

Backstage at *Ain't Misbehavin'* with Nell Carter was one of the most formative chapters of my life. I was around 5 or 6 years old, and it was my first real introduction to entertainment and the bright lights. At the time, I had no idea how legendary my self-appointed God Momma, Nell Carter, truly was. To me, she wasn't a Broadway icon—she was my magical God Momma, and I adored her. She made me feel like I was living a Cinderella life, complete with glamorous adventures and none of the struggle.

Whenever my parents had something to do, Nell would eagerly offer to watch me. Those were some of the most fun and unforgettable moments of my childhood. Whether we were riding in luxurious limousines or having designers measure me for custom outfits, Nell made me feel like a star. To my young mind, it was all a magical adventure.

The cast of *Ain't Misbehavin'* was stacked with talent: André De Shields, Charlaine Woodard, Ken Page, Armelia McQueen, Luther Henderson, and my dad, Kenneth Crutchfield, who played drums onstage, keeping the rhythm alive. If you search "Ain't Misbehavin' 1978 Broadway Musical" on YouTube, you'll see my dad performing—a piece of history I hold close to my heart.

Charlaine Woodard also played a significant role during that time. I spent personal moments with her backstage, mesmerized by her talent and warmth. I'd watch videotapes of her performances, memorizing every step and dreaming of one day stepping into her role.

Years later, my brother Kenny joined the picture, but his Broadway experience came during *Jelly's Last Jam*, where my dad was once again playing in the band. Sitting onstage during *Jelly's Last Jam* was a completely different kind of magic. Kenny and I sat next to conductor Linda Twine in the pit, watching her baton gracefully guide the rhythm of the show over our heads. How cool is that?

During the day, while my dad rested, Kenny and I recreated the show in our own way. I memorized the songs and dance moves, assigning Kenny the role of Jelly. He always played along, even though I'm sure he got tired of it. That's just who Kenny is—my biggest supporter and the sweetest person, always putting my happiness first.

Another influential figure during those years was Billie Allen, Luther Henderson's wife and a talented director. Billie and I shared a special bond, and I was fortunate enough to travel to Japan with her during a tour. Her creativity, grace, and warmth left a deep impression on me, showing me how art and connection can transcend boundaries.

Those early experiences—first with *Ain't Misbehavin'* and later with *Jelly's Last Jam*—weren't just my introduction to entertainment; they were life lessons in creativity, resilience, and love. The bright lights, the extraordinary talent, and the bonds I formed planted seeds of inspiration that continue to grow in my life and career.

Lesson for Casting: *Every project you work on is an opportunity to learn from others. Take the time to observe, connect, and grow—it will shape the stories you bring to life.*

Growing Up in Brooklyn

Brooklyn: Where Life and Dreams Began

I'm Cali born, Brooklyn raised, and Harlem living, but Fort Greene/Clinton Hill, Brooklyn, is where so much of my identity was shaped. It was exactly like Spike Lee captured in his films—vibrant, alive, and brimming with culture. The streets were our playground, with kids jumping double Dutch, chalking hopscotch grids on the sidewalks, and blasting '90s hits from radios perched in windows. The stoop wasn't just a place to sit; it was where stories were told, jokes were shared, and life unfolded.

For elementary school, I attended PS 11 from kindergarten all the way through 6th grade. My favorite teacher, Ms. Davenport, still lives in my head today—she made such an impact on my life. Her encouragement and care planted seeds of confidence in me that I carry to this day.

Brooklyn also represents family in my mind. It was the place where my parents were still married, and we lived in the absolute most beautiful brownstone on the block. That home wasn't just a place; it was a symbol of stability and love. Later, it became the first brownstone on the block to sell for 1.5 million dollars—a bittersweet milestone in a neighborhood so rich with memories. But when my parents divorced, everything changed. The departure from Brooklyn followed shortly after, and my heart broke. I had dreams of joining the 113 Marching Band, but those plans were cut short when my mom decided to move us to Harlem.

I'll always remember those Brooklyn days with a mix of joy and nostalgia. Across the street was the Institutional Church of God in Christ, a cornerstone of the community and *the* place to be in the '90s. I sang in the children's choir there, and it became more than just a church—it was a second home. It nurtured my love for music and forged lifelong friendships with Tiffany Nolley and Janelle Lesley. The church wasn't just a hub; it was a beacon of soul, culture, and community. I'll never forget witnessing Hezekiah and Monique Walker's wedding. It was pure magic—like my Cinderella fantasies come to life. You had to be there to feel the energy. At that moment, it was everything. The church's music ministry was unmatched, inspiring my love for soulful expression and showing me the power of collective harmony.

Our block felt like something out of a movie—a tight-knit community of Black families that operated like one big extended family. Our house was the central hub. When the Brooklyn heat kicked in, it was where all the kids would come to grab their Super Soakers for epic, block-wide water fights. Those battles were legendary—filled with laughter, joy, and the kind of moments that live in your heart forever.

Even though life eventually took me to Harlem, where I attended P.P.A.S. (the Professional Performing Arts School), Brooklyn will always be my foundation. From the gospel harmonies that filled the church to the rhythm of life on the stoop, Brooklyn grounded me in culture, love, and unfiltered joy. It gave me dreams, lessons, and memories that still shape who I am today.

Shout out to Rickey Brown, Jennifer Doss, Terell Travis.

Lesson for Casting: *Authenticity connects people. The real stories and vibrant communities you've lived in or experienced are your greatest assets when building connections and telling stories that resonate.*

Summers in Port Tampa: A City Girl Meets Country Life

As a child, my summers were spent in Port Tampa, Florida, where my mom's side of the family lived. It was a world apart from New York and California—a slower pace, no sidewalks, and the bay surrounding us. My family owned several properties in the area, which gave my cousin Jasmine and me endless places to explore and countless ways to get into mischief.

While I was a city girl through and through, my cousin Jasmine was the epitome of a country girl, and she made sure I got a full dose of her world. She had me catching tadpoles in ditches, sucking honey from flowers, and even catching snakes—yes, snakes! Jasmine tackled every adventure with fearless enthusiasm, while I cautiously followed along, constantly swatting at swarming insects I'd never even seen in NYC. The Florida sun was relentless, making every moment feel like we were on an intense outdoor expedition, and I was often ready to call it quits long before Jasmine.

The one thing I absolutely refused to do—and my brother Kenny shared this trait—was walk barefoot in the grass. To Jasmine, it was second nature, but to us city kids, it was downright terrifying. We'd cringe at the thought of stepping on something slimy or sharp, much to Jasmine's amusement. She teased us endlessly, laughing at how soft we were compared to her fearless country ways.

Jasmine's love for country life extended to her favorite activity: pea-picking trips with our Aunt Clara. She'd light up at the chance to spend hours in the fields, carefully picking peas and then prepping them at home. I, on the other hand, had zero interest. The scorching sun, the buzzing insects, and the thought of bending over a plant for hours was too much for me. My protests were legendary—I'd throw full-on tantrums until Aunt Clara finally gave in and let me sit in the car, where I'd wait (grumpily) for them to finish. It just wasn't my thing.

One of my favorite memories, though, was sneaking over to my grandfather's house after he left for his graveyard shifts. Jasmine and I would stay up all night, calling the local radio stations during their Lovers Groove segment. We'd put on what we thought were "grown-up" voices and give shoutouts to our at-home boyfriends—never mind that we were only in the 4th grade. The VJs were completely over us, clearly frustrated by our endless calls. What made it even more ridiculous was Jasmine's voice—it sounded just like Mickey Mouse, and we could barely keep it together as we listened to her high-pitched "grown-up" voice trying to sound sultry. We thought we were unstoppable and absolutely hilarious.

Port Tampa wasn't just about mischief; it was also where I gained a cultural edge. Every summer, I came back to NYC armed with the latest music, dances, and styles I'd picked up in Florida. Tampa was where the swag truly lived, and I loved being ahead of the curve, turning heads with moves no one in the city had seen yet.

And the food—don't even get me started. Tampa's fusion of Italian, Hispanic, Cuban, and soul food was unlike anything else. Every bite was bursting with flavor, and to this day, no place has matched the culinary magic of Tampa. Just thinking about it brings back the tastes, smells, and joy of those carefree days.

Those summers were magical, even with the blazing sun and swarming bugs. They were filled with family, laughter, and memories that taught me to embrace different experiences and find joy in unexpected places. Though I never fully embraced the barefoot-in-the-grass life—or the pea-picking trips—I treasure those summers in Port Tampa. They were a collision of city and country that left a mark on me forever.

Lesson for Casting: *Stay curious and explore different cultures, communities, and perspectives. The more you understand the richness of human experience, the better you can bring those stories to life.*

Surrounded by Greatness

As I reflect on my journey, one thing becomes clear: I've been surrounded by greatness my entire life. From the love and creativity of my parents to the legendary figures who crossed my path, I've been immersed in an environment where winning energy, passion, and artistry thrived. These experiences didn't just shape who I am—they instilled in me the belief that we all have the potential to create something extraordinary.

Greatness came in many forms: my dad's rhythm driving Broadway hits, my mom's work on iconic films, and my godfather's leadership at Universal Studios. It was in the magic of summers in Port Tampa, where life slowed down, but love and laughter were abundant. It was in the streets of Brooklyn, where vibrant culture and community shaped my resilience and creativity. It was in the electric energy of Planet Sound studios, where dreams were born, and in the soulful melodies backstage at *Ain't Misbehavin'*.

Every step of my journey has been a masterclass in creativity and perseverance. I've learned to appreciate the beauty in all stories, whether they're filled with triumphs or challenges. Those moments—working with icons, experiencing the unexpected, and finding magic in the mundane—taught me that greatness isn't just about talent. It's about courage, connection, and the willingness to tell your story, no matter how small or big it may seem.

Here's the truth: we all have a story. It may not look like mine, but that doesn't make it any less valuable. Your voice, your perspective, and your journey matter. Never be ashamed of what you've gone through, because it's those very experiences that make your story uniquely yours.

I've fallen in love with helping everyday people find and tell their stories. I've seen how lives change when someone realizes their voice is worth hearing. It's why I'm committed to sharing my knowledge, creating resources, and building a community that celebrates authenticity and individuality.

Because the reality is, we need your story just as much as you need to tell it. Your experiences can inspire, teach, and connect with others in ways you may not even realize. So, take the leap. Trust that your story matters. Together, we can create something unforgettable—something that uplifts, inspires, and leaves a mark.

The energy of greatness I've been fortunate to experience isn't just something I carry; it's something I want to share. Let's build something extraordinary, together.

Lesson for Casting: *The power of storytelling is universal. It's not just about finding the right person—it's about honoring their story and giving it a platform to inspire others.*

Giving Back: Internships, Courses, and What's Next

My journey has been shaped by incredible mentors and life-changing experiences, and I'm committed to paying it forward. The casting industry has given me so much, and I believe it's my responsibility to open doors for others who are eager to learn and grow.

Each year, I host an **internship program** to guide aspiring casting pros into the world of real people casting. This hands-on experience allows participants to dive into the intricacies of the craft—from creating pitch sheets to discovering talent in unexpected places. Interns leave with valuable skills, insider knowledge, and the confidence to navigate this exciting and fast-paced industry.

For those not quite ready to commit to an internship, I'm developing **comprehensive courses** to demystify the casting process. These courses are tailored for everyday people and aspiring casting professionals alike. Whether you dream of being cast yourself or want to break into casting, these resources will provide the tools and insights to succeed. From audition preparation to crafting a compelling personal narrative, these courses are all about empowerment and preparation.

But that's not all—I'm also creating an **innovative app** that will connect casting professionals with fresh, everyday faces who have little to no entertainment experience. The app will serve as a resource for real people to learn about the casting process while showcasing how they can become part of it. It's a new way to open doors and uncover stories waiting to be told.

Want to stay updated on the app, courses, and upcoming opportunities? **https://www.asjailoucasting.com/join-the-mailing-list** to be the first to know when these resources launch and how you can get involved.

This is my way of giving back—to the industry, to aspiring professionals, and to everyday people who deserve to have their stories told. Let's shape the future of casting together.

Lesson for Casting: *Mentorship and knowledge-sharing strengthen the industry. By lifting others up, you create a network of talent and support that benefits everyone.*

A Story Still Being Written

Every step of my journey—whether flipping through headshots as a curious child, walking the Universal Studios lot, casting for reality TV, or working with global brands—has taught me this: everyone has a story worth telling. Each experience, no matter how big or small, adds to the rich tapestry of who we are.

Your story matters. It might not look like mine, but that's the beauty of it. Our unique experiences, struggles, and triumphs shape us in ways no one else can replicate. I've come to love discovering the stories of everyday people, helping them see the extraordinary in the ordinary, and giving them the tools to share it with the world.

That's why I'm creating resources like this book, developing courses, and hosting internships. It's not just about casting; it's about empowering others to see the value in their own narratives. Through these efforts, I want to ensure that no voice goes unheard and no story remains untold.

This journey isn't just about me—it's about everyone who has been part of my story and those who will join it in the future. It's about celebrating the casting pros who shape the industry, honoring the real people who step into the spotlight, and building a movement that connects us all. My experiences have shown me that when we embrace our stories and share them boldly, we inspire others to do the same.

Together, we're creating something bigger than ourselves—a movement that uplifts, connects, and celebrates the power of storytelling. This story is still being written, and the best part? You're a part of it too. Let's make it unforgettable.

Lesson for Casting: *The work we do goes beyond filling roles—it's about changing lives and connecting people to something greater.*

YOUR STORY IS POWERFUL.
DON'T LET IT GO UNTOLD.

ACKNOWLEDGING MY SUPPORTERS

TO ALL THOSE WHO BELIEVED IN ME:

Sharron Cannon Kenny Allen

Andre Savage **TO MY TEAM THANK YOU** Theresa Green

Thea Washington Emmelyn Carta

Khrissy Telon Weathington

Mellicent Dyane
Alyson Horn
LaGrande Powe
LISA FIELDS
Melissa Feliciano
PETER COHEN
Jocelyn Fillman
Diona Vaughan Mankowitz
Zac Dixon
Charisse Simonian
CINDY ESTADA
THANK YOU
Lyle Dohl
Allison Kaz
Josh Randall
Jesse Tannenbaum
MICHAEL SANFORD
Kelly Allen
Jen DeMartino
KRISTEN MOSS
Damon Furberg
Liz Lewis
Rebecca Snavely
Donna Driscoll
ALISSA HAIGHT CARLTON
Rayna Apploff
TRACEY MOORE
amazon
Uber
BIG BROTHER
Google
TLC
bravo
IHOP
SHOUT OUT TO ALL CSA MEMBERS! #ICU
Isaam Sharef
isaamsharef@icloud.com
@isaamsharef on IG

ACKNOWLEDGMENTS

Wow, what a journey this has been! Creating *Casting Pros To Know: Reality TV Edition* has been an absolute labor of love, and it wouldn't have been possible without the incredible casting professionals who poured their wisdom, experience, and time into making this book a reality. You are the heart and soul of this project, and I am forever grateful for your contributions.

This book is more than a directory; it's a celebration of our vibrant casting community and the invaluable work we do together. To every casting pro who generously shared their insights and allowed me to feature their contact information—thank you for opening doors for aspiring reality TV stars and giving them a chance to shine. Your dedication to discovering and elevating real people's stories is what keeps this industry thriving. You are the unsung heroes behind the magic, and this book is a tribute to your hard work, passion, and impact.

As casting pros, we bring the sparkle to reality TV by finding personalities that captivate audiences worldwide. You're not just creating entertainment—you're changing lives and giving people the opportunity to tell their stories. Yet, I know there are times when we feel underappreciated, when no one is celebrating our wins or acknowledging the countless hours and effort we put into this craft. To each of you, I say: #iCu. I see your contributions, your sacrifices, and your passion. Your work matters. You are important. You have changed lives, and you are the reason so many networks, streamers, and production companies thrive today. Never doubt that what you do is vital and irreplaceable.

Like every industry, we have challenges to address. It's time for us to set aside our differences, come together, have the uncomfortable conversations, and move forward with unity and purpose. We need more care, consideration, and stronger communication amongst ourselves. Let's build bridges and foster an environment where every casting pro feels valued, supported, and heard. Together, we can rise above the challenges and create an even more impactful future.

I envision a future where we continue to uplift one another, share knowledge, and create even more opportunities. Together, we can build a stronger, more united industry that celebrates the art of casting and the joy it brings to millions of viewers. By leveraging our combined knowledge and expertise, we can generate new opportunities and ensure a more equitable future for all of us.

To all the casting professionals featured in this book, you are rockstars. Thank you for inspiring me and countless others with your talent and generosity. To anyone I may have missed, this is just the beginning! This is the first edition, but it won't be the last. I would love to feature even more casting pros in the future, give you the chance to tell your story, and become an author with me. My goal is to help us create additional income streams and opportunities to thrive. I'm an open book and not hard to find. Reach out to me, and I'll be more than happy to include you in this journey. You can DM me @AsjaiLouCasting on Instagram—I would love to have you on board.

And to every aspiring reality TV stars out there, know that these pros see you, believe in you, and are ready to help you take your shot. Let's keep making magic together!

With gratitude and excitement for what's next,

Asjai Lou
Casting Director, Casting Producer
www.asjailoucasting.com

www.ingramcontent.com/pod-product-compliance
Lightning Source LLC
Chambersburg PA
CBHW041041050426
42335CB00056B/3192

* 9 7 8 1 9 5 9 8 1 1 6 4 0 *